a Gift for my Sister

Ann Pearlman

First published by Simon & Schuster UK Ltd, 2011
A CBS COMPANY

1 3 5 7 9 10 8 6 4 2

Simon & Schuster UK Ltd
1st Floor
222 Gray's Inn Road
London WC1X 8HB

www.simonandschuster.co.uk

Simon & Schuster Australia, Sydney
Simon & Schuster India, New Delhi

A CIP catalogue record for this book
is available from the British Library

ISBN 978-1-84739-840-6

Printed and bound by CPI Group (UK) Ltd, Croydon, CR0 4YY

Dedication to come

On the Verge

Sky

Every day we walk a razor-thin line between the ordinary and the tragic.

That thought bolts me awake.

3:42. The green numbers on my clock blare. The rest of the room is dark. The numbers are a beacon in the black. Why do I wake at the same exact time every morning? 3:42. As though Mia's death had implanted an internal alarm.

Troy is curled around his folded hands.

No sounds come from Rachel's room.

The air-conditioning snaps on.

Some of us tiptoe, anxious about chasms on either side of the path we walk, and some of us skip along, ignoring them. And me? I thought if I walked a direct line with a firm destination in view, fulfilling each goal along the way, I'd be safe. Having a safety net was my plan to thwart lurking misfortune.

I felt as though it were my father's fault for dying. What else does a child think when parents seem all-powerful?

My father's death came at me from out of the blue like a peculiar and deadly snap of the fingers. One day he pulled me high on the swing, his arms stretched so I was above his head, singing "Fly, Sky. Fly," and pushed hard so I could reach for a cloud with my toes. I saw the glint of the sun on his hair, the flash of red and yellow leaves in trees blurred by my speed. Or have I nourished the image so much, this last memory of my still-healthy father, that I added the trees I know so well from the park when all there was, really, was the sight of the sky and the feel of the wind licking me as I soared?

The next day, he entered the hospital.

A week later, he was dead.

I was seven.

He was thirty-four.

Mom tried to explain that he was still around me, and loving me. I watched her tongue tap her teeth and her lips move, but it didn't make sense then.

It still doesn't.

I was the only child in my class whose father was dead. The other kids ignored me as though it were contagious.

I was the only kid I knew with a dead father until my freshman year of high school. Then, a kid's dad died from a heart attack. He was absent from my algebra class for a week, which had the other kids whispering, and when he returned, he laughed at a joke as though things were ordinary. I knew that game, because even as a seven-year-old I had played it. If you pretend things are ordinary, maybe for a few minutes they will be. And sometimes, sometimes—and this is both scary and exhilarating—it works.

And for a few minutes you forget you have a dead father.

3:45.

Anyway, I digress. I don't know why I think about him every morning. I guess because his death was a startling change that twirled my life so fast it skipped to another path. Some things happen suddenly, and some you know are coming. Like death from cancer after a long battle. But I didn't even get to prepare myself, I didn't have the time to be scared. It just happened.

Bang.

I wonder how my life would have been different if my father had lived.

Number-one way: Tara wouldn't be my sister.

I'd probably have a different sister. Or a brother.

Tara was an embarrassing kid and then a rebellious teenager. She was so different from me. I guess that partly comes from having different fathers.

But what I really wonder about is Troy. I met Troy in eighth grade and we've been inseparable ever since. I read somewhere that girls without fathers are often sexual early and are promiscuous to fill a yearning for a man in their lives. I guess I was sexual early, but I've only been with one man. Troy. My best friend, soul mate, husband, and finally, at last, father of my baby.

I say "at last" because Troy and I, so perfect for each other, are actually even genetic matches. As a result, each conception has a fifty percent chance of a deadly genetic disease, which led to three miscarriages and a stillbirth. A lot of deaths. I would have traded everything for a healthy baby. Just please, God, give me a healthy baby. Please. I begged as if you could make bargains with the future. I imagined parts of me I'd exchange, aspects of my life I'd cast away.

My pleas were answered. And I hadn't lost anything. Because then, finally, there was Rachel in spite of it all. Rachel with my father's gray eyes, as though a piece of him were a part of her. I look in her eyes and see him loving and watching me. Just like Mom promised. His eyes and the rasp of his beard are my most vivid memories, and sometimes, just sometimes, Troy's face feels almost the same, but more gentle.

4:15.

Count your blessings. Troy turns toward me, pulling me to him, spooning me. I turn to him and, in the vague light from the window, I see his eyes shift and know he's dreaming. Soon, I'll hear the creak of Rachel's crib springs as she stands up, holds on to the rails, and begins bouncing and calling, "Mommymommymommymommy. Daddydaddydaddydaddy."

Since Mia died, I wake up early and try to make sense of it. The digital green lights flash on the clock. The house is quiet, as though I can figure out the answer to some question I haven't asked in Troy and Rachel's systematic breathing.

I'm okay. Troy's okay. Rachel's okay. I'm sad. That's all. Life is unfair. So unfair.

But everyone knows that.

Lawyers especially. That's what we try to counter, that's our mission. To make life fair. To even the playing field. To redress grievances.

This is what happened: Mia was my closest girl friend, my BFF. We met in a tort study group at law school. She tried to get pregnant and I tried not to have dead babies. We struggled over case law and fertility and trained for a breast cancer marathon together. Troy and I and she and Marc, her husband, went camping in the Rocky Mountains and gambling in Las Vegas. We talked about opening up a law firm together. Then she took drugs to stimulate ovulation and developed a cyst. While they were removing the cyst, she had a reaction to the anesthetic and went into a coma. She was brain dead. We watched appliances force air into her lungs, and drip fluids and nutrients into her arms.

Four days later, Marc unplugged her equipment. We held each other's hands and cried.

There was an eerie silence when the machines stopped their breathing.

A lazy echo in the room. Then Mia was no more.

Twenty-six and dead.

That's worse than thirty-four.

That was two and a half weeks ago.

Since then, I wake up with a bolt and try to figure it all out.

4:30.

Why does my life revolve around tragedy when I have so many blessings? Rachel. Troy. A job that I love. A boss who allows me to work part time until Rachel is in preschool full time.

When genetic testing results on Rachel were okay, I asked Mia, "You're not going to be so sad about this for yourself that we won't be friends anymore, are you?"

We had just finished running five miles on the beach. I was already slow from the extra weight of the pregnancy, and we were both breathless. She said, "I wish it were me, but if not me, I'm glad it's you." It was California winter. Not quite so many flowers. The impatiens sparse and pale. We had run along the beach, the breeze keeping us cool, and now we were walking through a marina that reflected the cloudless sky and a few palm trees.

"We can share her. You can come over anytime for a baby fix."

"I'll catch up to you. In a few months, these new drugs will work and we'll be pushing strollers while we run." I thought, *Tara's baby is six months older than Rachel, Mia's might be six months younger.* I like symmetry. That was more than two years ago.

It didn't work out that way.

A week ago, Rachel jumped in a swimming pool for the first time and I reached for the phone to call Mia.

Then I remembered she was dead, and my arm fell limply to my side. I saw a woman in Nordstrom with hair streaked like hers and I called, "Mia!" And then blushed, embarrassed.

I miss her selfishly. I miss that she's not here for me.

But, mostly, I just miss her. It's as though I'm *her* missing her life. I try to explain it, but even Troy looks at me blankly. I feel sad the way I know Mia would feel at not getting to live the rest of her own life. But she doesn't know. She doesn't even know she died. I mourn Mia as though I'm Mia mourning her own life. There. Does that say it? I mourn the loss of her years with Marc, the unborn babies, the fascinating cases she'll never try, the great books she never read, the glorious food she didn't get to eat, the places she never visited, the love not made. All of it.

My thoughts ramble and always come back to this point.

How unfair it is for her.

4:45.

And then I fall asleep.

"Mommymommymommymommy," Rachel calls.

6:01.

Rachel's arms are stretched for me to pick her up. She jumps up and down in her crib, her mouth open, laughing at the sight of me. I feel the sweetness of baby warmth as I inhale her aroma. Her hair, so silky and fine, tickles my cheek.

I hug her tight to me, so tight, as though I can squeeze extra life into her and protect her from all harm.

"I love you, Mommy," she says. "Eat granola?"

"Sure. With cherries and walnuts in it."

"Yipppeeee."

I stand her on her changing table and unbutton the crotch of her PJs. "Think you're old enough for big-girl panties? Like Mommy wears? Want to try them?

"Like Mommy?"

"Just like Mommy." We've been preparing for this day, and she's gone in her potty a few times.

"Yeah." Her eyes widen and I reach down to the shelf and grab the pull-ups that have been waiting for her. I put them on her and lift her from the changing table.

"Okay. Let's see you pull them down." I know she can do this and she does.

"See, Mommy, no problem."

"Okay, so when you have to go, tell Mommy and I'll help you. Or just go on your own."

"Eat now?"

She always wakes up starved. I carry her potty to the dining room with us. She walks down the stairs one foot at a time, holding on to the railing. Rachel thinks about each step before she makes it. Jumping into the swimming pool into my waiting arms was uncharacteristic of her, as she is usually so cautious.

"You're my little mermaid," I'd said, laughing.

I make my own granola, roasting oatmeal with flax seed, wheat germ, sunflower seeds drizzled with honey or maple syrup, and cinnamon, mixed with water. Sometimes I add almond extract. Sometimes I add vanilla. I stir it every ten minutes for forty minutes while it roasts at 300 degrees. Before I eat it, I toss in fruits and nuts. I add chopped walnuts and cherries to Rachel's bowl and then milk. On mine, I sprinkle slivered crystallized ginger and almonds.

I'm almost out of cherries and almonds. I add them to the grocery list in my iPhone notes. The note says: *dish detergent, eggs, coffee, fabric softener, olive oil, cherries, almonds.*

I hear Troy taking a shower.

Rachel delicately picks out the cherries and walnuts, one at a time. She places one in her mouth, concentrating as she consumes the flavor.

I take the opportunity to run upstairs and steal a few minutes with Troy. He's just out of the shower, drying off. He looks up, surprised to see me.

I grab another towel from the rack and begin dabbing his back, slicked with water coursing around the bumps in his spine. When his back is dry, I stand on my tiptoes to kiss his shoulder.

He turns me around and holds me close, his body warm and moist against me. The steamed mirror exposes a foggy image of us pressed together. Me in blue shorts and a yellow T-shirt, and his pinkish-beige length, the brown of his hair, like Rachel's, fragments of colors blurred by condensation. He's all one beautiful length and I fill with warmth every time I see him.

He gives me a kiss, slow and serious, enjoying the texture of my tongue and my lips. "I'll be home early tonight," he promises.

"I'll be here," I laugh.

I pull back to look at him, his face as dear and familiar as my own, as though he's my mirror, another version of me. I kiss his nose. One of his ears misses a piece at the tip, and his other ear has it. As though each ear is a puzzle of pieces that have been split. Rachel has that, too. I touch his ears and circle the shell of each of them, like a nautilus. I shake my head slowly, aware that having him in my life has been a miracle.

"Ah, darling," he says, and his eyes close. "Maybe tonight you could get a babysitter and we can just check into a motel. We can have the whole evening together."

"On this short notice?" I laugh.

"You've been so sad and preoccupied since Mia's death." He wraps his arms tightly around me.

"Still can't sleep." And then I notice a pimple, swollen and red, on his shoulder. "Hey. That looks painful." I point at it with my index finger.

He turns his head to see it. "It is. Been putting cortisone on it, but . . ." He shakes his head and shrugs.

"Might be turning into a boil. You want me to lance it?"

"Done that twice. I've had it for about two weeks." He turns his head toward the shoulder and glances at it in the mirror.

I lean closer. It's red with a pale yellowish top. Smaller bumps cluster around the edges, and the flesh around it is almost purple. "Since Mia's death?" I guess I haven't been paying attention. "Looks like a rash. Is it itchy?"

He shakes his head. "It used to look like a spider bite before I lanced it."

"How 'bout some antibiotic cream and a Band-Aid?"

"Tried that. And hydrogen peroxide, and iodine and Mercurochrome."

I pull out a tube of triple antibiotic cream, twist off the lid. I wonder why he didn't say anything. I guess he hasn't wanted to bother me.

"I don't think it's a big deal. Just a pimple or insect bite." He shrugs. "When's everyone coming?"

"Next week. Mom and Allie arrive on Wednesday." I wash my hands.

"And when's the concert?"

"Saturday. Aaron's mom, Sissy, is coming Friday. Don't

know when exactly Aaron and Tara and the rest of the band arrive."

"Crew. Rap bands are crews." He shakes his head, watching as I peel the paper protecting the Band-Aid. "Imagine skinny, hyper Tara a rap star."

"You still think of her as five. You're not fourteen anymore, either. But they're not stars. This is just their first national tour." I smooth down the adhesive strips and rub the Band-Aid flat.

He winces.

"At least the pimple–boil–insect bite is covered," I say.

"Larry says they're on their way." Larry is the entertainment attorney Troy and I introduced to Aaron. "That number-seven single makes them practically stars. It's amazing that Tara and Aaron have pulled this off. Who'd have thought they'd still be together?"

The tenderness in his voice and his thrill at her success bothers me. "She used to have a crush on you."

"She helped me woo you." He rubs the mist from the mirror and combs his hair.

"Woo me? She wouldn't get off your lap whenever you came over. You were the only thing that distracted her from her obsession with music."

He pats the top of his head to get the few strands of his cowlick to lie flat. "That was because she wanted everything her older sister had. Besides, I didn't have the guts to ask *you* to sit on my lap. I hoped you might follow her lead. And eventually you did." He laughs.

Troy has forgotten what a difficult teenager Tara was, or maybe he's simply forgiven her. Troy and I were just starting law school when Mom called late one night. It was 3 a.m. in Ann Arbor. "I don't know where your sister is," she said, without even saying hello or asking how I was. "I've been frantic. I've called her cell a hundred times and it goes to voice mail. Texted over and over and over. I'm standing by the front door, looking out the window at every car that passes, hoping it'll stop and she'll get out."

"She's probably just at a party, hanging out with her friends."

"Probably getting high or drunk." Mom finished my thought. "I tell myself that but I can't stop thinking about all the terrible things that could happen: She could have run away, or be in a car accident, in some hospital. Or worse. Dead. She could be drunk at a fraternity party. What if she gets gang raped?"

"You know Tara. This is just Tara being Tara." I heard Mom's quick intake of air.

"She does what she wants with no concern for anyone but herself. Just like her father. Like he's come back to haunt me."

I didn't know what to say. But part of me was smugly pleased when Mom criticized Tara or her father.

"She's never been out this late without calling, even if it's with some lame excuse."

"Mom. She's probably just partying."

But Mom couldn't stop. "I tell her, 'Call and let me know where you are, that you're okay. You have a cell phone,' but she doesn't even do that."

And then Tara walked in the door. "Mom. What are you doing up?" I heard her ask.

"Where the hell were you?"

"With *friends*!"

"I was worried." Mom stretched out the word worried so that Tara could sense her anxiety.

"I was fine." I could almost see Tara shrug.

"Why didn't you call?"

"I'm out of minutes, Mom. Why didn't you pay attention to my bill?"

Tara's voice was crisp. She wasn't screaming or angry. She was indifferent. That was it. A chilling cold indifference.

"I'm tired. Think I'll go to bed," Tara's voice got softer as she walked away from Mom.

"Well, she's home," Mom said to me.

"I heard."

"I'll talk to you tomorrow."

"She's just being a kid," Troy said that night, leaning against the headboard reading a syllabus. "Tara works hard on her music. A nerd with a wild streak. She'll be okay. You watch."

By the time Tara was seventeen, she was pregnant. Piled on top of that was her boyfriend's prison time, for dealing drugs, their crazy dreams of rap stardom, and her refusal to get married. Now, four and a half years later, Aaron, Levy, and Sissy are part of our family. Mom and Sissy are friends. And in an ironic twist of fate, my wayward sister is on the road to being famous.

"Your T-shirt seam may be irritating that pimple. The Band-Aid should help."

"Hey. You want to play doctor with me?" Troy jokes, his cowlick stuck down for now.

"Mooooommmyyyyyyy," Rachel yells. "All gone!"

"Tonight." I wink and then take off down the stairs, to find Rachel's cereal bowl tipped over on the tray and the milk dribbling to the floor.

"Okay. Help me mop this up." I pull her from the high chair and hand her a paper towel. She squeezes milk and bits of granola on the floor and tries to make finger paintings in the glop. I quickly wipe away the mess and hand her some spray cleaner, which she spritzes joyfully. Everything is fun to her.

Troy comes down soon after. "There's some granola," I offer.

"No time." He pours coffee and milk in a commuter cup and smears peanut butter and jelly on bread. "Gotta hit the traffic." He checks his watch, grabs his laptop, and kisses Rachel and me. At the door he turns, points a finger at me, and says, "Tonight." Then turns to Rachel and says, "I'll see both of my beautiful ladies tonight."

The door kisses the jamb as it swings shut.

The sun slants in through a window and throws a rectangle on Rachel's hair, turning it into blazing spun gold.

I pick her up and swing her around. "The floor is clean and it's a beautiful day made just for us."

I can get through each day. It's the nights and early mornings that are hard. Maybe I've turned a corner. Maybe I've figured something out, but I don't know exactly what. The answers I look for each morning at 3:42 flicker in my head as if I know them, but can't recognize them.

"Hey. You wanna go to the potty?" I carry Rachel to her potty, and watch while she pulls down her pants and sits down.

I hand her a book and turn on the faucet. I don't know why, but Mom always did that and it seemed to encourage me to go.

Rachel's eyes get big. "I did it. I pee-peed in the potty!"

She laughs, her little white teeth shining like pearls.

She stands up and points, her pull-ups sliding to her ankles. "I did it."

"You sure did," I say with disbelief. I take out the container to pour the urine down the toilet.

"You're going to throw it away? Throw my pee-pee away?" Rachel's eyes are wide, her mouth open in bald horror. How could I throw her amazing achievement away when just a moment ago we'd been so happy with it?

"We'll save it and show Daddy. Then you can put it in the toilet—how's that?"

Her smile returns.

Later that afternoon, before Troy gets home, before we have a chance to eat dinner and talk about our day over a glass of wine, or sit on our balcony and watch the sea lap the sand, or finish the flirting that we started that morning, the telephone rings. It's Stuart, my mentor and one of the partners at my firm.

"Hey, I went over that case law for the Hanson case. Got decisions that'll buoy up our arguments," I tell him before he even says hello.

"Sky." His patient voice carries that tinge of bad news. My mind skitters to what it could be. We're being sued for malpractice? On one of the cases I worked on? Another member of the firm died?

"Sky, I have some, ah, unfortunate news."

"What?" I start pacing with the phone pressed to my ear. *Sesame Street* is on the TV and Rachel sits on the floor, teaching a line of stuffed animals.

"As you know, our billable hours have decreased and, really, I guess, we were able to let you work part time because we didn't have much work, and now, well, we have even less. So we have to let you go." He pauses.

I know that they—the partners—are billing those hours for themselves, even though my fees are lower than theirs.

"Please be reassured . . ."

I resent his formality, selfishly creating distance so that firing me is less painful for him.

"When things change we'll contact you, and if you're still available we would love to have you back. I'll help you find a position with another firm, though I wouldn't relish you being our competition." He forces a chuckle. "We're going to miss you." And then his voice warms as he adds, "*I* will miss you."

His words seem to echo. I replay them in my mind as soon as he says them. *We have to let you go. Please be reassured. Another position.* I'm trying to integrate them. "I loved the work. And I love working with you." I shouldn't have said that.

He sighs. "This is difficult for me, for all of us."

For a minute there's silence on the phone while I consider my options. Maybe I should start my own firm. If Mia were still alive, I would. Maybe Troy and I could start a firm, but we need the consistent paycheck and benefits that come with his job.

"When do you think you could clear out your desk? We'd all like to take you out to lunch, too."

I don't know if that would feel nice or like rubbing salt in my wound. "I don't know. I'll have to get back to you." Maybe I'll go get my things tonight, while everyone is asleep. I know they will have already changed the passwords on my computer and made sure their client list is unavailable to me.

If I can't trust Stuart, who can I trust?

"Well. Let me know. And I'll help you any way I can, Sky. You've been invaluable to the firm."

Not so invaluable, I think. Even if you do a great job, and work weekends and evenings to meet deadlines, you're expendable. Even though Stuart gave me wonderful ratings on work evaluations. *And* accompanied that A+ rating with maximum merit salary increases. But I guess at the end of the day, I wasn't all that important.

Now what? Another thing in my life just ended, out of the blue.

I'm walking along an abyss that threatens tragedy every day.

CHAPTER ONE

On the Verge

Tara

I watch Aaron as he stands before the stove. He's not wearing a shirt and the muscles of his chest are outlined, his six-pack moving as he twists slightly and reaches for the tarragon and garlic powder, sprinkles them over the eggs, and then picks up a spatula. He lifts the cooked eggs and tilts the pan so raw egg flows under them. He does this gently, this movement at the edge, and it reminds me how he kisses the rim of my bra and panties, respecting the margins of my modesty.

Even though I'm in no way modest with him. He can do whatever he can imagine with me. I'm his. Every ounce, every speck of skin, every dollop of breath and fluid. I've even given him my music. But this scares me, and I hide from him, even from myself sometimes.

I wish it were simple for me, and uncomplicated. I wish I could give myself to him with complete trust and security, and wrap myself in the love that he offers me, but I feel my billowing love for him and get scared. How do I know he'll stay loyal when temptation hits?

Aaron has the same expression on his face now as when he writes lyrics. He raps under the name of Special Intent. When he is Special Intent, writing, rapping, performing, he's focused, no, *enveloped* in concentration. As though nothing exists but this word, this line, this moment.

He takes my breath away standing there, just being him. And he's not even aware I'm here. How can I completely trust him when we're each separated by our own skin and unaware of what's in the other's mind? What if as soon as I give myself to him completely, he leaves? I have to keep a piece of me hidden. I feel safe that way. He wants me because he can't completely have me. I dangle myself before him so I don't get hurt. Emotionally, I keep my distance, and he knows it.

Levy is on my hip, snuggling into my shoulder, warm and close. He reaches out his arm. "Daaaaddddy."

Aaron puts down the spatula, turns off the burner, and wraps his arms around both of us, kissing each of our foreheads. "Breakfast almost done," he says as he pulls Levy from me, slides him in his high chair—"Here you go, Smidgen—" and then proceeds to sprinkle parmesan on top of the omelet while I pour orange juice in Levy's sucky cup.

Ah, such sweet domesticity. These moments are like the space between notes when the hum of one still hangs in the air before the next perfect sound develops. And he has no idea what's going on in my mind.

And here it is. The bubbling-brook sound of Levy laughing at a silly face his father makes.

"We gotta finish packing our clothes today," Aaron says as he sits. "Get that done early. Rehearsal today at five. And then we pack the instruments. And we gone again."

"Don't know if you're reminding yourself or me," I say. He laughs.

"Are we gonna take my truck?" Levy asks.

"Sure," Aaron says, "but just one."

"We'll pack your toys, some books, your blankee, don't worry."

"Hiawatha." Levy puts down his cup and quotes, "*By the shores of Gitchi Gumee, by the shining Big-Sea-Water—* gotta have him."

"Should put him on stage and we'll do *his* backup," Aaron jokes.

I've read that poem to Levy every night for the last year. Now we recite it together and turn the pages to see the pictures. "Sissy's coming at, like, four to pick him up," I say. Sissy is the best mother-in-law in the world. She's not just my mother-in-law. She's my friend.

"She book her air for the L.A. concert?"

"Yep. Everyone will be there." It will be the first time my family has seen us perform. "Sky, Troy, and Rachel, my mom, Sissy. Oh, and Mom's bringing her friend, Allie."

He frowns.

"Yeah, Allie's visiting a friend and then they're going to a spa or something. I'm glad we have a few extra days in L.A. before Vegas." I have the dates and the map for our tour firmly in my mind. We'll be home two months after L.A., in time for Mom's cookie party, Christmas, and Levy's third birthday. Levy, born on Christmas day, was a gift to the world. But every baby is a gift.

I look around the apartment where we've lived for the last three and a half years. The Indian bedspread over the couch, the silk flowers Mom gave me after my first recital when I was six, the prism hanging in the window that I used as a focus point during labor. I haven't even had a chance to redecorate; since Levy was born, we've been so busy.

"Can we go to the Grand Canyon? I've always wanted to see it and we'll be so close in Vegas."

"The dudes want to go, too. Our dream's almost here, babe," Aaron says. "We're on the verge." He places Levy's plastic plate on his tray and divides up the omelet.

"You and Levy are my dreams come true." As soon as I voice the words, I want to snatch them out of the air.

He laughs the bass version of Levy's gurgle. "And

you're my angel. None of this means nothing without you. We're a team. A team on the verge of a dream."

We don't have mushy conversations much, but we tell each other *I love you* whenever we leave each other instead of saying goodbye. A lot of people must do that, but to us, it's a reminder of our special connection.

"You think this will change us?" I know his answer, but I need to hear it.

"Don't want it to. Just think, we won't have to worry about money anymore. We can buy a house when we get back. We'll have some time."

"We'll worry about money differently." I pick up my fork and begin eating. Buying a house together feels like a big commitment.

"Have more fun." He dots his eggs with Red Hot sauce.

"Be able to help people."

"Shit. We doin' that already. Supporting the whole crew. My homies. Right now it's mostly expenses and promises." His eggs are on his fork. "Before we were in that comfortable place of struggle and hope, wondering when it was going to happen. 'Member when we was writing lyrics and music without any expectation, just for the way it made us feel?" He eats the eggs on his fork. "Now we'll be creating with certainty instead of hope, because our hard work will be paying off." He nods. "Babe, it's happening. We should enjoy the hell out of the blessing."

Sometimes he says what I think, before I even know

I'm thinking it. I wondered about our luck since our demo CD started getting attention, and "Prohibitions of Prison" made it to number seven on the rap charts, and then this tour was booked. At first I was thrilled, but then there was that question of why me, why are we so lucky? There are others as talented, maybe even as hard-working, so how come we get to hit it big?

Destiny?

Karma?

Blind luck?

His cell phone rings. "Hey, Red, you there already?"

Levy smashes his eggs with his fork and then picks up the bits with his fingers.

"Use your fork, Levy."

Levy squints at me. I wipe his hands and then he picks up his fork. He hates to have his hands or mouth wiped.

"The crew there?"

"You're pretty good with that fork." I try to encourage Levy.

"Give me about thirty," Aaron says into the phone.

And so our day begins.

Our last day before the whirlwind. Or maybe we're already in it. Maybe I've been in it since I met him.

That was five and a half years ago. Seems like forever. Seems like just yesterday. Even though I fought against it, I sense that our lives have been bound since before we were born.

*

I was fifteen when I met Aaron, and he was seventeen. He was singing. Well, not singing, but making weird noises that accompanied the sticky swish of his roller against the wall as he painted. The wet kiss of the white paint, the slight sucking noise on the smooth wall. He was scat singing, and then I was ushered into the room.

"You do the woodwork and edges," the Habitat from Humanity staffer told me. "Oh, this is Aaron. Aaron, this is Tara."

He nodded at me.

"Hey," I said. That was it.

I was handed a pail of white paint, a brush, and a small foam roller. He stopped singing and we worked silently. Him on one wall and me on window molding. All I could hear was the sticky paint, the whirl of his roller, the slurpy slap of the brush, the sweep of our clothes against our skin as we worked. The house was empty and each sound was exaggerated.

It seemed as if we stood like that, each in our own corner of the room doing our own thing, for hours. I wanted to say something, but I'm not too good with small talk.

So, I started humming a melody and he went back to making his louder, more bass sounds, and we made a weird music together. Music is always easier than talking.

Then we started being silly, and I started making up lyrics.

He added the exaggerated sound of his roller, *dupwa*

dupwa. The tune rolled like the words that came to me from the brush slap-dashing paint on the wood. Then he started freestyling instead of doing the percussion.

He put his roller down, turned me around, and said, "Who are you?"

I shrugged and said, "Tara."

His eyes were so intensely black that they ricocheted from heaven to hell and pinned me against the wall I was painting.

And then we started talking. Him, the black dude from Detroit on some special work-release program from kiddie jail, and me, the white nerdy girl from bougieville. But we were way beyond all that from the beginning.

Luck. See what good luck I have?

Sometimes it feels I have all the bad luck in the world, too.

But I don't care about what a lot of people care about. I don't care much about clothes, for example. Or popularity. Or scads of money. I don't even care about being careful, or if I fit in. My family is all divorced and my sister is only my half sister, and when I was growing up, all the other families seemed so perfect and intact. I knew from third grade there was no way I could fit in. Sky, my way-too-straight-edged sister, always tried to fit in and somehow managed to accomplish that. But me, I was weird and geeky and angry at all the stupid rules from the beginning. I was always thinking about sounds and music. Always in my own head thinking my thoughts.

I almost didn't volunteer for Habitat for Humanity that day. I would have preferred to lounge in bed under my warm covers, daydreaming about finding some black nail polish to go with my freshly dyed black hair. Then I thought, shit, I'm late. So I grabbed the bus.

Why not.

Just like that. Just like on a warm day in the middle of winter, I met Aaron, completely out of the blue.

So he says, "You tryin' to be some Goth babe?"

I shrug. "I just did it last week. Called Black Pearl. Think I'll get some more hoops in my ears and my nose pierced. Whaddya think?"

He tilts his head. "If you want. But you beautiful without all that. You probably beautiful with your real-color hair. What color was it?"

"Red."

He frowns then. "You dyed away red hair? Red hair is hot."

Maybe I got tired of being hot. I didn't tell him why I dyed my hair, not then. I told him long after that, just before I dyed it back to my natural color.

Here's the reason. My dad and my mom are divorced because he fooled around on her. He betrayed and humiliated her.

My first memory is Mom screaming her throat raw at him for being with another woman. A door slammed. She cried. I was alone in my crib, holding on to the top bar and wailing, and no one came. I used to think there was something *she* did that couldn't keep him faithful. Like she wasn't pretty enough. Or good enough in bed. Or nice enough. He was gone by the time I have any other memories and then, by the time I was eleven or twelve, he started living with another woman, Joanne. Joanne had blond air and blue eyes. Skinny. Always made-up and dressed like she was in an advertisement. She tried hard to be good to me, buying me presents, taking me to concerts and shopping. I liked her, and sometimes she even felt like family.

Then, one day, I was walking down Main Street, anticipating buying a bunch of tiny plastic snakes to sew onto my jean jacket, and there was my dad. He was holding hands with a woman who had long black hair. Long black hair almost down to her waist. You know, that beautiful hair that so many Asian women have. Long, straight, and heavy with the essence of hairness. Hair to coil or to let blow free in the wind. Black like the night, and the keys on a keyboard.

My father met my eyes. And looked right through me as if I weren't there.

He didn't drop her hand, that woman with the beautiful black hair.

He didn't stop and introduce me.

He didn't smile at me.

He didn't say hello to me.

He saw me.

Ignored me.

As though I didn't exist.

My smile froze for a second as they walked past me.

I crossed the street and bought black dye.

Men want something different.

And then I did the worst thing I've ever done. I've never told anyone before and no one ever caught me, although I think I wanted to be caught. Sometimes I don't know what I'm going to do until I do it. This time I did know. A couple of years before I saw him with the other woman, my father showed me the bank statement with both our names and over ten thousand dollars. "It's for your college education," he said.

That next Monday, I walked into the bank, my heart pounding but determined. I had my school ID. I walked up to the teller with frosted long red nails and eyelashes sticking straight up and so much mascara I wondered if her lids felt them when she blinked. I don't know how I did it, but I turned my nervousness into acting friendly.

"I need to withdraw some money from my account."

"You have to fill out this withdrawal slip, honey," she said.

"But I don't know the number. Here's my ID." I handed her my high school ID with my picture and signature. "The account's in my dad's and my name." I told her his name and address.

She frowned at me.

My heart started pounding in my chest. Sweat rolled

down my sides. "He wants me to withdraw four hundred dollars because it's my birthday next week and we're going on a shopping spree. Today."

"Well. He should really come in with you."

I frowned. "That's what I told him." I rolled my eyes. "But he said he had to work, and then next week he's going out of town, and this is the only day." My story made me feel so sad, all the feelings of all the times my father disappointed me welled into my eyes. I was the little girl who never got a present from her father. Never once. Joanne picked them out when I got one. Or he handed me money. "Buy yourself something." But mostly he forgot.

Her mouth turned down.

She picked up my ID and looked at it, looked at me, looked at my name on her computer screen. Filled out the number on the withdrawal slip, passed it under the window, and said, "Sign it. Put in your name and address."

She took the slip and pushed it in a machine. "How do you want it?" she asked.

I didn't know what she meant.

"Twenties, fifties?"

"Fifties, I guess."

She took some bills from her drawer, and counted them and slid them to me. I folded them in half and stuffed them in my jean pocket. "Thanks," I called as I left the bank.

I knew just where I was going.

*

I went to the piano store and it was still there. There was even a red sign saying *clearance*. I'd dreamt about it since I first saw it when I came to pick up some sheet music months before. I walked by the store and peered in the window to make sure it hadn't been sold. A keyboard. On sale. Slightly used. It had everything: sixty-one full-sized keys that felt like ivory, 128 instrument voices. Imagine that. Over 180 rhythm styles, five-song memory with sixteen tracks for each song. I could be my own orchestra. I could be my own rock band. I could mix and remix any sound I ever heard or imagined. And it was on sale, for 350 dollars.

The man recognized me. "So you've come back, huh? Better get it fast. Someone else is interested. Might be coming by to get it today."

I was just a teenager, but I knew bullshit when I heard it. Even so, I pulled the wad of fifties out of my pocket, counted out seven, and handed them to him.

"And do you want the stand? That's another hundred."

"Maybe later."

He put the instruction booklet on top as he boxed it up.

On the bus home, I placed it in the seat beside me like it was another person, keeping one hand on it.

My father never said a thing to me. Probably never even noticed.

Mom wasn't home when I got there. I unpacked my new possession and started playing. It had an earphone jack, so Mom couldn't hear me practice. I had figured out how to be a teenager. Play my music, then I could block out what was going on around me. The keyboard with the sound world at my fingertips and earphones so I heard nothing but what I played. My perfect escape.

Mom saw it in my room, frowned, and asked, "Where'd you get that?"

"Dad gave it to me for my birthday."

"When? Your birthday was half a year ago."

"Last month." I shrugged and looked away. "You know Dad. He's always late. Or forgets. It was on clearance." I knew she'd never ask him. She can't bear talking to him. And then I asked if she wanted to hear my latest song, and she listened, but soon her eyes started shifting with preoccupation.

"That sounds great, honey."

It was the automatic praise that parents assign their child when they're not really paying attention.

She stood up, and left to do all the things she had to do.

I didn't tell Aaron any of this that first day. The month before Levy was born, I dyed my hair back to my natural color and told Aaron everything. I was still haunted by my dad's philandering. Since then I've put platinum and bright red streaks in my hair—makes me look better on stage. And that's what matters now.

*

So that's how I met Special Intent. That's where we were: him painting with a roller and me with an itty-bitty brush. That's how I came to be living in Detroit, as it fell down around us, hanging out with my keyboard, my man, his people, and our brown-skinned, ringletted, big-eyed, long-lashed baby. That's how we came to be on the verge.

You never know what wonderful thing is going to happen next, even when everything seems so bad.

And then he says to me, while our beautiful Levy beats out a rhythm with his fork, "Babe. You never know what wonderful thing is going to happen next." Proving that despite my mistrust, our thoughts are aligned.

CHAPTER TWO

A Changed Man

Sky

Troy and I don't make love that night. By the time he gets home from work, he has chills. "I think I'm getting the flu," he says, as he drags himself up the stairs to crawl into bed.

"Daddy, see what I did!" Rachel holds out her hand and pulls him down the few stairs he's climbed and points to her potty. "Look. Looky." She opens the lid.

The pail is filled with more pee and a few poops. "Hey. I'm so proud of you." He leans down to pick her up and twirl her around, but his spin is only a half turn before he stands her on the ground. He reaches out a hand to steady himself and I realize how ill he is.

"She saved these all day to show you." I turn to

Rachel. "Now we can put them away and say bye-bye."
I carry the pail, and Rachel and Troy follow me.

"You happy, Daddy?"

Troy squats so that he is eye level with her. He reaches
out a hand to caress her hair. "I'm proud of you, Rachel.
I'm so proud of you." He looks up at me. "Just like
Mommy. Setting goals and not wasting time."

Rachel grins, leans into him, and wraps her arms
around him. When she touches his shoulder, he recoils,
but then relaxes into her small embrace.

I hand the pail to Rachel and watch as she pours it
into the toilet, her hand steadied by Troy's. She flushes,
then waves as the whirlpool carries her treasure away.

She tries to kiss him and he pulls back. "I'm not feeling well. Don't want you to catch it, sweetie." She runs
through the living room and opens the glass door.
Standing on the balcony, she presses her lips against the
glass. Her mouth forms a pink splayed flower. She
remains there, mouth flattened against the glass, as Troy
bends down and presses his lips on the other side. For a
few seconds, the glass separates their mouths, and then
Rachel makes the kiss-pop with her lips and Troy stands.

"I kissed you, Daddy. I kissed you!" she squeals.

When he takes off his shirt, I notice the red, swollen
area of flesh has spread from under the Band-Aid and
threatens to cover his entire shoulder. The rash reaches
down an arm and to his lower back. When I peel off the
Band-Aid, the pimple oozes stringy pus and a thick,

bloody paste. I touch the hot skin around it, and Troy shudders.

"It hurts when I touch it?"

"No, your hand feels like ice."

"Urgent Care is still open. We're going."

I pack Rachel a peanut butter sandwich, coloring books, her blanket, and Maddie, a bunny whose fur has been mostly loved away.

"Maddie needs her backpack, Mommy." Rachel struggles to strap a miniature pack over the bunny's arms. I throw in a juice box and some apples, grab a book, and off we go.

I don't tell Troy I lost my job.

I don't tell him how scared I am.

I tell myself I'm being ridiculous. They'll give him antibiotics and he'll be better. He's young and healthy.

At the triage desk, they ask him a few questions and take down our hospital card number. Our family physician is part of this system, so they have access to all our medical records. The nurse, a woman with a sad mouth, writes down his symptoms.

"He has a fever, and a sore on his shoulder that seems infected." I put my hand on his cheek.

"Daddy sick," Rachel announces and then nods to affirm the fact.

The nurse points us to the waiting room. "We'll call you." The room is more than half full. Two other families huddle around the tables. We step over the legs of a young man sleeping with his jacket as a blanket and sit on the three chairs next to him. Rachel pulls out a coloring book and crayons and begins to color.

The waiting begins. I wonder if I should tell Troy I lost my job. He tilts back in the chair and folds his arms around himself. "I'm cold," he complains. I ask if there's a blanket they can lend him, but the triage nurse says, "They'll take him back in a moment." I glance at the families in the waiting room and figure that means Troy has jumped to the front of the line. It worries me more.

"Devon," the nurse announces.

The youth slides his arms in his jacket and ambles away. I feel sad he's alone. But maybe he wants to be. Maybe he has some STD. I move away from the seat he'd been sitting in.

Rachel colors a rocking horse. She can't stay in the lines yet, but scrubs the paper with red as though brightness is enough.

"Pee-pee, Mommy," she says.

I take her hand and look for the bathroom. "Good for you for remembering." I'd forgotten.

In the bathroom, she looks at the adult toilet and then looks up at me with her brows together and her mouth in a straight line.

"I'll hold you up, how's that?"

I put my hands under her arms and hold her until she's finished.

"I did it. I did it right in the big girl's potty."

"You're amazing," I tell her.

I wash both our hands, using lots of soap to wash away any germs from the hospital.

When we return to the waiting area, Troy is gone. The sorrowful triage nurse directs me to his cubicle. A male nurse squeezes a blood pressure bulb, and then the thermometer in Troy's mouth beeps. A thermal blanket covers him. The nurse pulls out the thermometer and looks at it.

"103.8." He writes down the number and says, "And your blood pressure is low. The doctor will be right in."

"I pee-peed in the big potty, Daddy," Rachel says. "Like the one you and Mommy use."

"I'm proud of you, sweetie." Troy forces a grin.

"Daddy sick." Rachel hasn't bought his fake enthusiasm.

"Yes. But I'm still proud of you, and if I weren't sick I'd be jumping up and down for joy," he tells her.

She tries to crawl up on his hospital bed using the bars as a ladder. "No, sweetie. I don't want you to catch what I have."

A woman with red curly hair past her shoulders enters. "Hello. I'm Dr. Shapiro. So. Tell me about this sore."

Troy tells the story as she examines it with gloved fingers. "We'll need a biopsy to run some tests."

"You think it's a spider bite? It looked like it might be at first."

Dr. Shapiro carries a laptop and opens it on the small shelf that juts out from the wall. "Could be." She starts scanning Troy's medical chart. "I see you had a sinus infection back in September."

His summer cold started in June and still stuffed up his nose in August.

"Dr. Grey put me on some antibiotic, cephalosporin, I think." Troy tries to sit up to establish more command and adult presence in the small room. "Was that it?" He turns to me.

"Yes. It's here." Dr. Shapiro taps the computer screen.

She seems to be about our age. Her nails are polished with clear gloss, and small gold hoops grace her ears. She stands to reexamine his shoulder. The swollen area has grown since we left home. His flesh is deep purple and thick bloody pus trickles, dissipating in the curly hair on his chest. Her face is smooth and unlined as she asks, "Can you raise your arm?" She reveals no alarm or disgust.

Troy raises his arm only chest high.

"Well. First we'll need a biopsy and some blood to see what infections you may have. Meanwhile, we'll start you on an IV of an antibiotic, vancomycin." She turns to me, "Do either of you have any open wounds or any similar pimples?"

"I don't." I'll examine myself carefully when I take my next shower. "I haven't noticed anything on Rachel."

"A booboo here," Rachel holds on to the edge of the

hospital bed and lifts her knee. The doctor views a scrape healed long ago into a thin white scar.

"That must have hurt."

Rachel's eyes well with the memory as she nods her head.

The doctor opens a cabinet and retrieves a surgery kit, leaves the room, and returns with a syringe. "This will numb it for awhile," she says to Troy.

The male nurse enters carrying an IV pole and asks, "Which do you want, the right or the left?" He wiggles the IV tube back and forth.

"Left, I guess." Troy lies back on the flat pillow, chest exposed, the pus, an orangey trickle, close to his nipple. Troy's voice is faint, and the pale green blanket covering his lower torso and legs smooths the edges of his body so that he appears smaller, as though he is fading into the mattress.

I met Troy when we were fifteen. That summer, we were best friends. He hung out at my house all the time, like we were brother and sister, except that Tara sprawled on his lap and Mom was never grouchy with him. One day, we ran into each other at the pool. The pool was within walking distance of my house and my friends and I had begun to use it as a place to flirt with boys and see who you'd have a crush on that week. I was with Marissa and Jennifer and as we smoothed baby oil on each other's bodies, we looked at the boys already in the high school we would attend in the fall. Boys who had started to shave. Boys with thick necks and broad shoulders and cupped butts. Boys with a certain swagger and yet a vulnerability that kept us unafraid. Or maybe scared us a bit. They all did except for Troy. Troy didn't scare me. So Marissa, Jennifer, and I nestled into towel-covered chaise lounges, plugged our MP3 players in our ears, and pretended all we wanted was a golden tan, and to read the latest magazine.

I heard Jennifer say, "Wow. He's hot. You sure he's just your friend?" and she poked my arm with her elbow. I opened my eyes and sat up in the lounger.

There was Troy.

I'd never seen him with his shirt off.

He strolled in with two friends, his back turned to me, as they looked around for three chairs together. They couldn't find them, threw their towels on an empty table, and walked toward the diving boards.

I leaned back on my elbows.

The sun sparkled the water with diamonds.

Troy climbed the stairs to the high dive, strode to the edge of the board, and turned his back to the pool. His arms at his sides, he stood motionless, except to gently test the springiness of the board.

The three of us watched, leaning back on our elbows, our stomachs slicked with oil, our toenails and fingernails glossed and painted a pearl pink. I held my breath. He raised his arms shoulder height.

(That arm that he can't even lift now. That arm with the pus running down it.)

I noticed his chest expand as he inhaled. And then, in one effortless motion, he flexed his knees and sprung from the board, arched his back, and flew through the air.

There was a stunning quiet as the entire pool galley stopped chatting, paused between bites of hot dogs, and put down their newspapers. The action froze.

The tips of his fingers pierced the surface of the water so gently it made no sound. He cut through like an arrow, arms and legs together, back arched. Underwater, he flipped a somersault, then stretched with the breast-stroke. When he reached the edge, he placed his hands on the lip and, in one motion, heaved himself up, swung his legs through his arms, and stood. Water droplets studded his body, then slowly slid to the cement.

Troy still hadn't seen us.

"I didn't know he was a diver." Marissa pulled a scrunchie off and combed her hair with her fingers, fluffing it full around her face.

"Yeah. He's hoping to make the varsity team next year." But I didn't know he was that precise, that graceful, that in control of his body. How had I not seen this? How come he had not talked about it more? Maybe I just hadn't listened.

He still hadn't noticed me. The boy who dove next made a belly smacker. "OW! That hurt just hearing it!" Jennifer rubbed her tummy.

Back then, Troy was just a few inches taller than me. Then, his body seemed like a slightly different version of my own. He was just a buddy, without the competition and cattiness of a girl.

"You sure he's just your friend?" Jennifer asked again as she applied sparkly lip gloss.

I shrugged. He started to walk toward the stairs and, finally, saw me.

He grinned and I laughed.

He said hi, but he didn't come over to us. He continued his trip to the board, climbed the stairs, and this time did a jackknife, once again slicing the surface so the ripples were hardly disturbed.

"Now he's just showing off." Jennifer lay back on her towel, opened up her book, and continued reading.

I lifted the back of the chaise higher so I could watch without appearing too eager.

After all, he was simply my friend. Like a brother, as I said. He even fell asleep on our couch one night. Mom was out on a date and she came home to find Troy and Tara sprawled on the sofa, and me sound asleep in a chair, the end of *Arachnophobia* playing on the TV.

I didn't have a boyfriend, but I didn't consider him a potential one. In fact, I pointed out the cute girls in our class. He never said anything. Just shrugged.

I subtly watched him do a somersault and then straighten so he thrust his fingers first into the water, another backwards swan, and then a crazy dive in which he stood facing front, turned in midair, and entered the water feet first. He practiced that three times. Each time, he swam underwater and then leapt over the edge of the pool in one bound.

I watched from behind my sunglasses.

I watched from behind my magazine.

He slid from air to water as though there were no transition, as though water and air were the same.

And then he came over to me. He asked, "How do you think my reverse somersault is coming along?"

"Is that what's that called? You looked great. I didn't know you were that good." I smiled.

"I've been working on it." He reached his hand out to me and tried to pull me up.

"What? I'm reading," I pleaded.

"Come on. Don't you want to try it?"

Now, I don't like heights. I can swim laps, but I still remember the burn of a belly smacker when I was ten.

He pulled me up to the low board and helped me get into position. I stood facing him on the edge, his arms on my shoulders. "Look into my eyes. You're going to sail through the air. Keep your chin tucked down and your fingertips will slice through the pool."

I noticed freckles across his nose and the cowlick that sticks straight up at the top of his head. I had never seen him so serious, so earnest.

His palms were warm on my oily shoulders.

I licked my lips.

I looked down. Sprinkled across his chest, sparse but obviously present, was downy hair. Brown, reddish brown. Soft.

He's a man, I thought for the first time.

I was embarrassed by the thought.

"Now, turn around. And turn your body into a C shape."

I faced the pool, standing on the edge. He was behind me, his warm hands on my shoulders. My arms were stretched over my head. "Bend down. Arms first. Stay in that C."

I followed his instructions.

"That's right. Great, Sky. You're going to do a great dive. You'll see. Now just keep going down, and tuck your thumb into your other palm."

I did it and curved lower, and saw my knees.

"Now your hands are one. Good. Keep your legs together."

I felt myself tipping.

I plunged through the space and, before I realized I was that close, my fingertips hit the cool water, then my arms, my head, and my legs. I remembered to keep my legs together.

Troy beamed as though I were a child taking her first step. It is the same smile he awarded Rachel ten years later.

"Wow. That was great. You should join the team with me!"

I rolled my eyes.

He dragged a chaise next to mine, and again I noticed the hair on his chest.

"I think Jennifer has a crush on you," I whispered while Jennifer stood in the concession stand line.

"You wanna go again?" He didn't hear me.

"She says you're hot."

"Come on, let me teach you how to bounce and then you'll go higher."

"Don't you want a girlfriend?" I pressed the issue.

"Want to swim some laps with me?"

"Nah, I want to finish this article on Britney."

He stood and walked to the edge of the pool.

His buttocks flexed and relaxed in his blue swim trunks. His suit was spandex divers' trunks, so I could see the curve of his separate cheeks. How embarrassing.

Now, with the aqua blanket covering his legs and hips, and his chest bare, I notice again the coat of hair on his chest, and his arms.

An IV is in his wrist.

Sometimes, he jokes about his bald spot that grows at the top of his head and has almost resolved the problem with his cowlick.

"Men with hairy bodies are more likely to go bald," he said.

"They are?" We were in the bathroom sharing the mirror. He added gel to the few strands that remained of his cowlick while I rubbed lotion on my legs.

"Yep. Read that somewhere."

"I don't care if you're bald." I like the way his hair feels under my palms, under my fingertips, but I don't care if he's bald. His smooth head would feel nice, too.

But I do care, oh how I care, about the pus dripping from his shoulder and matting the hair on his chest.

As though feeling my wish, Dr. Shapiro takes a swab of the pus and closes it in a tube, and then wipes the rest away with an alcohol-dampened gauze.

"We'll do a biopsy and a quick blood exam. Meanwhile, we'll see if that IV will bring down your fever and lessen the swelling."

She leaves the curtain slightly open and I pull it shut.

Troy closes his eyes and shakes his head. "What a waste of a night. I wanted to work on the trial next week, and just spend time with you and Rachel."

"You *are* spending time with us."

"I'm here, Daddy." Rachel sits in the chair in front of the doctor's desk and pulls Kleenex, pretending to blow her nose. Then she grabs a latex glove and tries to put it on, but that task is too complex and confusing. I roll up the cuff of the glove and put it on her hand. Ghostly plastic hangs from the ends of her fingers. She flaps them, "Look, Daddy, I have long nails."

I know how ill he is by his absence of wit or comment.

"There's so much else we could be doing. Even if it's only eat leftovers and watch TV reruns," he says, looking at Rachel and me.

I squeeze his hand.

"Why don't you and Rachel go home? I might be here for hours. I can take a taxi."

"You want us to leave?"

"No need for you two to spend God-knows-how-long in the emergency room."

"I want to be with you."

"How are you going to work tomorrow if you're here half the night?"

Oh, right. The next day is Tuesday. On Tuesdays, Rachel goes to day care at eight and I start work at eight-thirty.

"Don't worry about it." That's all I say. "You just concentrate on getting well." In a week, in a few days, this will be over. Ten days of antibiotics and our life will resume as though this night has never happened.

Except I no longer have a job, and Mia's dead, I can't help but think.

Troy's eyes close. His breathing is shallow. Perhaps he's fallen asleep. Rachel's ethereal fingers color a snowman purple, and down the hall a man moans, and my heart starts pounding in my throat, neck, and ears.

An hour later the nurse returns and takes Troy's temperature and blood pressure. Troy seems to have fallen asleep, but immediately complains that he's still cold.

"I'll bring you another blanket," the nurse says as he writes down the numbers in his chart.

"How's he doing?"

"His temperature is a bit up."

"Higher than it was a few hours ago?"

"Higher than it was." The nurse leaves and, a few minutes later, returns with another blanket. "This should warm you up." He stares at the ceiling as he opens it up and flies it over Troy. It falls around him.

"Aah, that feels good," Troy sighs.

I touch the blanket and it's warm.

We resume waiting. Rachel gets cranky, so I pull her to my lap and read from the book I brought. She twists and struggles, momentarily distracted from her exhaustion. I decide to sing her the lullabies Mom sang to me, "Summertime" and "All Through the Night."

Finally, she snuggles into me and pokes her finger in her mouth.

"That's nice, honey," Troy says. I sing to him as much as I sing to her. My voice is husky and I can barely keep a tune. Tara's musical talent comes from her father, not from our mom.

I slide Rachel into her own chair and settle in the hospital cot next to Troy.

"What if I'm contagious?"

"Then I already have it." I nestle my head on his shoulder, the one that isn't oozing pus, and slide my hand under the cover and feel his flesh warmed by the blanket and his soft curly hair.

"I love you."

He squeezes me with his good arm. The one with the IV in his hand. "Always and forever," he says.

The doctor enters and I bolt upright, as though I'm doing something I shouldn't be.

First Dr. Shapiro takes Troy's temperature again while asking him how he's doing, and then takes his blood pressure. She looks at the thermometer. "Well, your temperature continues to rise in spite of the vancomycin, and we got the preliminary lab results. It looks like you may have picked up a staph skin infection."

"From a spider bite?"

"I don't know what it's from. It looks like it's MRSA, which means you could have gotten it from anywhere. Fourteen percent of people carry the bacteria for community-associated MRSA." She rewinds the tubing from the blood pressure cuff and returns it to its holder. "That means people who are not in a hospital or a nursing home."

"He hasn't been in a hospital. Oh, we visited a friend in one. Or rather I did." Could I have brought this home from Mia's hospital room? A knob in the bathroom? The handle on the water fountain? Brushing up against an infected lab coat? Did I give this to him?

"Or it could be from a gym . . . do you work out? Play a sport?"

"Basketball. But not in a gym."

"The germ is in lots of places." She places her hand

on her hip. "I noticed that you were on antibiotics for that sinus infection. That particular antibiotic seems associated with the growth of this infection. It lowers immunity to this particular bacteria." Her words are slow and her voice is deep. She meets Troy's eyes and then mine. She scans Rachel curled into a ball on one of the chairs, her thumb in her mouth and the other hand, still clouded with the latex glove, tucked under her chin. "It's probably best for us to admit you and continue to drip in antibiotics and fluids and monitor this infection. Meanwhile, we'll get the complete lab results and see if we can tailor a medication for that specific germ."

"Can we catch this? Could I have brought this home from my visit to the hospital and given it to him?"

"We'd have to do further testing on you to know that. For now, you should take your daughter home. Both of you take a shower and wash carefully. Check to see if you have any open sores, no matter how small. Clean them. Put antibiotic ointment on them. Cover them. I'm glad your daughter has at least one glove on," Dr. Shapiro laughs.

I don't want to leave Troy. But I want to keep us safe.

"Best to leave your toddler at home tomorrow."

When we leave, Troy watches Rachel as though his heart is being torn out. I blow him a kiss.

"Bye-bye, Daddy," Rachel says. And then she kisses her

fingers and, with several flutters, waves the kiss to him as far as her arm extends.

Troy kisses his palm and blows it to her.

At home, I give Rachel and me both a shower. I search our skin from inches away. No cuts. No pimples. No mosquito bites. Only a smattering of freckles.

I tuck Rachel into her crib and go to the computer. The antibiotic that Troy was given for his sinusitis may have made the germ immune to other antibiotics. Then, the infection would be more virulent and could penetrate his body, creating infections in his bones, joints, blood, heart, and lungs. He could die from bacterial endocarditis or pneumonia. He could develop blood poisoning, cellulites. Nineteen thousand Americans die of MRSA every year. More than of AIDS.

But he's young. And healthy. His immune system will fight this off.

It's 2:30 a.m. Only 11:30 Eastern time. I call Mom. No answer; she's probably with Jim. I leave a message and then call her cell phone, but it goes immediately to voice mail.

"Call me as soon as you get this. No matter what time." And then add, "I'm okay, but Troy's in the hospital."

I lie in bed as fear races through my body, my heart throbbing in my neck and ears. I can't sleep. Maybe my fear will keep him safe.

CHAPTER TWO

A Changed Man

Tara

We're on the bus, and I love being on the bus with the crew. It's so cool—we each have our own section and there are beds that open from the sides, and a table with seats to sit and play cards, work on the computer, or practice. Aaron, Levy, and I have our own little area. Red Dog, Smoke, and T-Bone share a section. This bus is nicer than the one we took to Atlanta and New York. I've unpacked, and settled us into our home. There's a skinny shelf for Levy's toys, books, and road grader. I put the prism in the window, and rainbows sparkle all around when the sun hits just right. An electrical outlet by the table is available for the keyboard and laptops, and we have a microwave and fridge. Just like a camper. I had a friend once who lived in Coachville and I loved the perfect miniaturized snugness. Everything you needed was there, just smaller, nestled into each other, and stripped down. It contained only the expedient. And then there's the sense of flexibility—you could move your tiny house anywhere you wanted, on any whim.

Besides, it's good practice not to have a lot of stuff.

We don't even really need costumes. Or I guess my costume is my streaked hair. We're allowed to—no, supposed to—look like real people. Not like actresses, who have to be perfect and beautiful all the time.

Though sexy is good. Sexy is very good. And I have a sequined black body suit and a fuchsia one, which matches the streaks in my hair so the lights bounce. The dudes wear street clothes.

Anyway, we wake up and stop at McDonald's. I get sausage biscuits with egg for all three of us and hash browns and coffee for Aaron and me, and milk for Levy. We squeeze ketchup over almost everything. Levy swishes his hash browns in it and licks it off. I add hot sauce to mine.

We drink orange juice from our fridge and get a coffeepot going.

There are leftover double chocolate chip cookies that I made before we left Detroit. I don't know how they made it through the Chicago and Minneapolis concert.

"Those cookies aren't stale?"

"Just dip 'em in milk," Smoke says. Smoke is dark-skinned, almost pure black, and unbelievably, he has blue eyes. As soon as I met him, I saw that his eyes were the color of blue-black ink. "Never saw a dude of your complexion with blue eyes," I said. We were all together rehearsing "Prohibitions of Prison" then.

Aaron and Red leaned closer. "Hey, how'd you get those?" Aaron asked.

"Those some kinda lens?" Red guessed.

Smoke just shook his head and said, "Born with them."

"I always assumed they were like mine," Red said. "Like black people's. And I've been knowing you all my life."

Smoke is a big dude, extra large, and repositions himself slowly like he's carrying weight that's more than he can bear. He moves as if he considers each step.

He's one of those people who says very little but when he does, people listen.

His slow, disinterested exterior vanishes when he plays his drums. Now he plays a hand drum, a djembe, and his fingers move so quickly they're a blur. During his solo, his hand plays the bass and slap simultaneously, or so quickly that you don't get the rebound. And when the rhythm is slow, the world hangs in the space between the beats and that drum of his resonates in my heart. Smoke went to school with Red and Aaron, and grew up around the corner.

T-Bone is the newest member. Poreless skin and liquid

eyes. Tall. A rim around his lips like a Benin bronze sculpture. The girls go crazy for him. He has a great singing voice, and can do slow gospel style, too. Aaron met him at Sissy's church, the Shrine of the Black Madonna, where they sang for the boys' choir. T-Bone was working with another crew, tried singing with us, and stayed.

Red Dog is Aaron's brother from another mother. By that I mean they grew up together, know each other backwards and forwards. Absolute loyalty and love. It's like if I wanted Aaron, Red came with the package. And Red had to accept me in the mix. Not an easy thing to do. Because a white girl in a rap crew is way weird. Controversial, you might say. They have to deal with me. Deal with me dealing with all the girls drooling over the crew. "You're just, like, notches on their belts," I tell the crew. As if they'd mind.

"I'll take that notch," Red laughs, like I meant to say something nasty.

"Or you're potential support for some baby and an easy way to make a living."

Aaron shoots me a look to quit being such a mom. Later he says, "They grown ass men. In order for this to work, you can't tell them what to do."

I know he's right, but I guess it's whatever teeny part of me that's like Sky. I do think of the consequences, the worst-case scenarios, even though half the time I disregard them because they don't seem worth passing up what I want to do. I guess that's what the crew thinks, too.

Now, Aaron can kind of be bossy sometimes. Controlling. Sometimes he's a boss for me, my protector. Like, when we started happening, Special Intent just said, "Tara's with us. She's the music. And she's my angel. Ain't none of this happenin' without her. She's our key. You got a beef, let's hear it or leave."

They looked at him and then at me. He's the only one who would ever think of me as an angel.

"Key. That's a great name for her," Smoke said. And that's how I got my name, Key, or Li'l Key.

"She knows what's up. She'll deal," Aaron said. That meant I was supposed to be cool with the bitches and the pot. No one in the crew does any hard drugs. Not that I know of, anyway. No cocaine, either powder or rock, no heroin, no X, no crystal. They smoke some weed, but not around my baby. That was clear from the get-go.

And then Special said, "Another thing. We're not going to be takin' everybody on this tour. Just us. This is professional. Besides, if we spend all our profit on keeping people in motel rooms, we won't be able to do what's right by us or them."

But sometimes Special says something and there's a look in his eye, a set of his mouth, and I know he's unmoveable. Like telling me to butt out of the crew's business. Like, once I asked him, back when we were first living together, "Where're you going? When'll you be back?"

He stepped back and narrowed his eyes slightly. "I just

got outta jail. I'm not signing up for no bars." His voice was measured. "I'll be back when I get back. You want me, call." He slid on his shoes.

I was dashed with cold, but planted my feet solid and tilted my chin, reaching for my spunk. "Man, I'm not controlling you. Chill." I nodded and lowered my voice. "I'm just wanting to make my own plans."

His eyes softened.

And then I pursed my lips and pitched him a sly grin and said, as cocky as I could, "And I, like, want you in them."

Aaron laughed then.

"You got my number, T."

But I haven't asked him where he was going again.

He said, "You know I wouldn't do anything to screw us up, right?" I guess that was his way to promise me fidelity. I guess he was feeling my distance.

We were in our apartment, Levy sleeping in his crib, both of us watching his fingers twitch slightly and his eyes slide under his lids dreaming. We stood there in awe of what we had done, making another human being. It still seems like a miracle to me, even when Levy is crying or screaming.

I guess I put myself in the middle of a storm of my own worst dread even messing with a good-looking rap star, knowing there were countless girls wanting to spread their legs for him. So I protect myself. In truth, I'd protect myself regardless. That's the only thing I learned from my dad.

So I say to him, "I'm my father's daughter. Two can play that game. And I don't want to play, I'll just be gone." Now, that's true. I'm always ready to bolt.

He asked me to marry him when we were in Atlanta, right after the concert, while the crowd was still stomping and screaming and he was charged with their excitement and his own success. "Marry me," he said in his bossy way.

I knew the women we'd have to wade through who would be jamming their hands in his pockets and sliding them down the back of his pants just to get to our bus. "After the tour is over." I tested him. Testing myself, too.

"Good idea. We'll get married in our new house."

Anyway, in our bus we're a family moving around the USA together.

I finish up my coffee and gaze out the window at the flat earth we're riding through, so horizontal the land is like the sky except different colors.

Smoke plays with Levy, trying to teach him how to draw.

Aaron has grabbed some paper and is writing. I know he can't hear anything except the words in his head. His writing looks like a map from outer space, because he arrows in new ideas in oblongs. I read his words upside down.

I don't know why, but there's something compelling

about watching him create. I don't have access to his mind, and oh, how I want it. I guess I obtain a window into his soul by observing his thoughts drip out of his fingertips. If only I knew what was in his mind, I'd know exactly how safe I am.

Occasionally I long for the classical stuff I played for so many years. And today is one of those times. The Iowa landscape looks like the day after one, the day before God started decorating the world. So I stand up, get my keyboard, and plug it in.

Fauré's *Requiem* feels perfect for Aaron's lyrics. The notes vibrate from my keyboard and pulse our bus, and I hum the voices, the melody, that accompany them.

And then Special Intent adds his final lines,

In this game
With death callin' my name.

As though old Fauré has inspired him. He reads his song and says, "Hey. Let's do this. See what you think." Smoke, Red, and T-Bone gather around us, Levy under Smoke's arm.

I stop playing to listen.

"No. You keep doing that, whatever it is."

"Fauré's *Requiem*. It's, like, about Jesus's crucifixion and resurrection."

"Perfect," Special says, "Amazing."

And he starts the hook, and I tease in the music,

humming the voice melody softly. And Special raps the chorus and we end together on the last line, the one with death calling his name, and I do the *Ahhhhmmmmen,* like it's the end of the world or the fresh beginning. Who knows, who ever knows, what way it's going to go?

And the crew, man, they're quiet, glancing at each other and shaking their heads. "That's tight. Too cool, dude," T-Bone says.

"Gettin' away from straight-up rap," Red says.

"We don't have to fit in somebody else's box. We make our own," Aaron says.

"Sure, with a baby-mama and the baby in tow." T-Bone wanted to know if he could bring his baby-mamas (he's got two of them) when he heard Levy and I were on the tour.

Aaron said, "Yep, when they can play or do something significant. When they can do a keyboard better than Tara. Or rap as well as one of us." That shut T-Bone up, but I know it's salt under his skin.

Smoke says, in his slow and lazy voice, "Mixing cultures together gives some staggering product."

Special looks up at me and smiles. "We keep getting better and better."

"Let's put some Africa in there." Africa is the name of Smoke's djembe. And we go at it again.

We work on it through the plain, through what's left of the cornfield. Under a heaven that is pale blue, almost white, but absent clouds, the green stretches out to meet it like a sea ... and we're the only ones on the road, me and my crew, my family, as we work on this song about our Detroit.

And then in between the line about vacant lots, my cell phone rings.

"Mom?" I walk to the front of the bus so the crew can keep working.

"Tara, where are you?" When she says my name first in a sentence like that, I'm alarmed. Her voice is trembly and yet hurried.

"Iowa, I think. On the way to Denver."

"You okay?" It's not a question as much as a demand for me to relieve her.

"Yes. Why? What's up?"

There's silence. I think the call is dropped. "Mom?"

"Tara. I have some news."

I know she means bad news. I sit down a few seats behind Thumble, our driver.

"Okay. I'm ready."

"It's Troy. He's in the hospital."

"What happened?" I immediately think a car accident.

"He has some kind of infection."

"What?"

"One of those antibiotic-resistant bacterial infections. A flesh-eating bacteria. Looks like it's in his lungs and bloodstream."

I didn't think they were real. Something made up for science fiction movies, or to scare people into staying away from each other. "Sky and Rachel? Are they okay?"

"Yes. But Troy's fighting for his life."

"Sky . . ." She's been through so much. "It's not fair."

I hear Mom breathing. She's not pacing, I can tell that too.

I was just five when I first met Troy. Sky had everything: Mom's favor, Troy's attention. Good grades. Straight blond hair and a golden tan. Her spectacular gray eyes stopped everyone in their tracks. I never take them for granted. And by the time she met Troy, she was playing with eye shadow and each color—green, brown, or mauve—brought out entirely different tones.

My eyes are just plain brown, hazel maybe.

And she had the coolest two friends, Marissa and Jennifer. Marissa was a cheerleader with brown ringlets and Jennifer was the high school tennis star. The three of them hung out together, so they were never lonely, and did all the things I wasn't allowed to do: wear makeup, shave their legs, go out on dates, go downtown by themselves, go dancing. I snuck around outside Sky's bedroom door listening to them, until she caught me and complained to Mom. For a while after that, they had sleepovers at Marissa's house.

I heard her tell Mom she hated me after she caught me eavesdropping on her sleepover. Mom said it's just the way of sisters. Sibling rivalry, it's called. I puzzled over that. I tried out saying *I hate you* to her, but my words fell limp, without any enthusiasm. I wanted to be like her, with a life that was effortless and flawless.

Though I guess that's not true now. Guess that's not true since the miscarriages. Though when she learned that Rachel escaped the genetic curse, everything went back to the smooth predictability Sky always manages. Until Mia died, that is.

I hear Mom clicking her tongue with anxiety.

"Can I talk to him?"

"When are you getting to L.A.?"

"Three more days. A day to get to Denver ... we're going nonstop, and then the concert, and then a day to get to L.A."

"I'm taking a flight out tomorrow to be with Sky and help out with Rachel."

I stand up, hunt up my backpack, fish around it for a pen. "What's his number?"

I write it down.

"Mom. He's young. And healthy. He'll be okay."

"Please don't give me that 'young and healthy' nonsense." I know Mom's thinking about Sky's dad and his death from pancreatic cancer at thirty-four.

"It can't happen. It just can't happen. Sky can't have a father and a husband die before they're forty. The odds, the math is against it."

I start crying.

Mom doesn't say anything.

"Troy's like my brother."

"I wanted you to know what's going on and that I'll be leaving for Los Angeles today."

I guess she won't be coming to my concert. "Maybe by Friday, he'll be better."

"I want to come to your concert. We'll just have to see . . ."

Troy is more important. I know that. I know that. But Sky always takes precedence over me. My pregnancy with Levy was dwarfed by her miscarriages. It's always about her. And because she's so damn good, she gets the sympathy; and because I've never been the good kid, but the weird, rebellious one, she gets the sympathy. Mom would say I isolated myself, but I felt pushed out.

I don't mean to whine. I'm happy with how things are now. All those sad, lonely times strengthened me to do what I'm doing now. But sometimes, I miss being as important to Mom. I thought at my concert, for that one night, just one night, all my family would be there to see me. But one way or another, I don't get that.

I consider flying to L.A. as soon as we hit Denver, but I can't leave the crew or skip the concert. I have contract obligations. "I'll come to see him as soon as we get to town." I know Mom considers that putting myself above family, but she doesn't understand what Aaron and I are carrying.

I try to explain. "We have to do this concert because we're responsible for the entire crew. They can't do it without us, and we have legal obligations."

"Well. I have to finish packing. I'll call you when I get there."

"Maybe there's something we can do to help."

She's quiet.

"I love you." But she hung up. Or the call was dropped. I don't know which.

I stay near the front of the bus, the gang still fiddling with the transition between hook and verse. They laugh, and I feel their excitement and cheer.

I moved out as soon as I told Mom I was pregnant. I saw the expression on her face, that worried, what-should-I-do-now expression that threatened to fizzle away my joy. I knew what she thought, how crazy and self-destructive my relationship with an ex-juvie con-vict, black dude must be. She said our dream was "immature nonsense." That's what she said. So when Aaron said he had a car I could use to go back and forth to high school for the two weeks before I graduated, I packed up my keyboard and some clothes, and was gone.

Aaron rented us a small two-bedroom apartment down the street from his mom, Sissy. The one we're still in. I called my mom to tell her.

"Where are you?" She was surprised I was calling.

"You got your wish. I moved to Detroit."

"Not my wish." Her tone was forced.

"You won't have to worry about me."

"What are you talking about? Of course I'll worry about you."

I imagined the list she was making in her mind. A list of my failures: Not yet graduated. Pregnant. Black lover. My grades, which were A+'s in Music, English, and Art but C-'s in Math and Science. Inconsistent. Under-achiever. Now, Mom isn't racist, but she wanted me safe and middle class, and the fact that Aaron is black and from the 'hood made that unlikely, especially since he had been incarcerated and wanted to be a hip-hop star. You can imagine our conversations. They went like this:

"Don't you want to go to college?"

"No. I want to be a musician."

"You can study that in college. You just have to get there."

"I'm going to learn by doing."

"Others can teach you shortcuts. Why do you have to do everything the hardest way possible?"

Standing on that corner in early June, I said, "I was waiting to tell you about the baby. I'm all excited that Aaron and I created this new life along with all our songs."

She said, "Don't you recognize the peril you, and your baby, could be in? You refuse to accept that your actions affect other people."

I knew she was pacing. She and Sky pace when they're

on the phone and I saw her, her white hair held back by a barrette, wearing her diamond studs, walking through her living room.

"This isn't about you. I don't play my music because of you. I didn't fall in love with Aaron because of you. I didn't decide to have this baby because of you."

"No. You want to do things your way regardless. So tell me, what did I do wrong?" she said.

I twisted the cord around my finger. "Give birth to a child who loves music more than herself, more than you, more than anything?" I coiled the cord around my wrist. "Marry my father?"

She was silent.

"Maybe I'm selfish like him. Maybe I just don't want all that society B.S. There're other ways to live. Maybe I just want to be me, do me." I released the cord and slapped at the bug on my leg, smearing my own blood over my calf. "These mosquitoes are killing me."

"Where are you?"

"I'm calling from a pay phone because I didn't want you to worry and my cell was out of minutes." You'd think she'd see all the love and consideration in that.

Her voice shifted, lost its barbs. "Well, I guess I did everything wrong with you."

"It's not you. It's me. I'm totally different than you and Sky."

She held her breath, hunting for the right thing to say. "I thought you were a terrific kid. Such talent. So smart.

A little too precocious. I always felt you rejected me and didn't want to be like me."

Whenever we talked, I flitted on the surface, or avoided her with relentless music practice or school or seeing Aaron or friends. Hiding what was really going on in my life. "What bullshit. Whatever, Mom." I was about to hang up the phone. I heard the rush of traffic sounding like waves on the beach. More gently, I whispered, "No. You may be right. That may be just what happened." I was angry with her because she couldn't keep my father. Angry at my father who didn't bother with me. When I didn't have that intact, normal family, I just threw it all away. Decided I'd be for me. Alone. "But I couldn't be like you without losing me."

"This is the first time we've had a meaningful conversation in years." There was silence, and then she added, "Since you dyed your hair black."

"See how much better this is going to be? I move out and we have the first decent conversation in years. Here I am standing in the middle of the street, being eaten alive by mosquitoes, talking to you. Doesn't that tell you something, Mom?"

"That you care."

"Shit, yeah."

"You'll start living your life, you and Aaron. You'll see if that dream can come true."

She was trying to give me something, but she didn't get it. It didn't matter if we ever hit it big, it just mattered that I create. "I got to hang up. The mosquitoes are eating me alive."

"I love you. Come and get the rest of your stuff, let me give you some furniture and make that apartment a home for the three of you."

"I love you, too, Mom."

And next time I saw her, she seemed happier about the baby and asked what she could do for Smidgen. She handed me the silk flowers, quilts that my grandmother made, and a set of dishes and flatware that she had bought. As though she was proving her faith in me, she said, "You know, you'll always be my baby," and held me very close, and I wrapped my arms around her and got the hug from her that I'd always wanted.

Maybe for her, the worst had happened. What moms fear: a pregnant teenage daughter in what seems like a precarious, insane relationship. And the worst wasn't so bad.

I hear the crew working on the lyrics. I get the eerie feeling sometimes that I can predict the future. Not exactly, but too often the songs we write come true. They happen. And occasionally later, in the middle of a performance, Aaron and I look at each other and realize our words have come true ... and the music, my music, sometimes drives Special's words. Like it did today.

We're a pair. And for a few seconds, I feel safe. Not alone anymore.

Unintentional universal connections. Amazing.

CHAPTER THREE

Before I Was Alive, Where Was I?

Sky

Troy attempts a smile when he sees me and lifts his hand. He seems smaller, as if he's shrinking into the bed and being swallowed by the sheets. I kiss his forehead.

"Rachel?"

"Mom's with her. Allie's coming tomorrow."

"Good," he whispers. He motions for the water glass and I twist the straw so he can drink easily. After a few sips, he sinks into the pillows, exhausted. His breakfast sits on the tray over his lap. Plastic lids cover the plates. The flatware remains wrapped in a paper napkin.

"You should eat. Want me to feed you?" I push the

tray over his bed and lift one of the covers. Scrambled eggs, toast, juice, and fruit cup.

He picks up some egg on his fork, holds it there and then, shakily, brings it to his mouth. I fluff pillows behind his back. "There, is that better?"

Troy nods and continues slowly moving the food from his plate to his mouth. After a few more bites, he says, "Enough." The rash has spread all over his body; his arm and hand are dark purple.

"I love you," I say.

"I know. And you know I love you, right?" He wheezes between the sentences.

"Of course." We stare into each other's eyes and say this to each other very slowly, as if we've never said it before although we've told each other *I love you* a thousand times. This time we add *I know* as though we need to always remember.

I try to make my voice casual, as if this is just as ordinary as the other thousands of times we've told each other *I love you*. Even when we were just friends. Every time we separated. Every night before we went to sleep.

"Sky. Listen. You're the one that always wants to be prepared." He motions for the orange juice and I hand him the glass, but he makes a face after he sips it. "I know you and Rachel should be okay financially, especially with your job and skills."

"Shhhh." I pull my chair closer to the bed.

"And everything is set up in terms of insurance for

you both. If the worst happens, I want you to go on and love someone else."

"Troy. We're going to be sitting on a porch somewhere watching Rachel's children. You're going to get better. The antibiotics will kick in, your own strength will kick in." I don't want him to express any negative possibilities. I don't want him even to think them.

He lifts my chin up so I meet his eyes and says, "Be free. Be open."

Tears run hot down my cheeks. He closes his eyes and wets his lips with his tongue. I touch his burning forehead. I tuck the blanket around him and sit and watch him breathe. He seems spent.

And then he opens his eyes and says, "When's Tara coming?"

"Tomorrow, I think. The concert is the day after."

A smile tugs at his lips.

He seems to fall asleep. I pick at his fruit cup. I'd subsisted on granola bars until Mom arrived. The specialized antibiotic doesn't seem to be making a difference.

At least Rachel is safe. She has no infections.

I watch him inhale, wait for him to exhale.

He has longer periods in which he sleeps, almost unconscious. Like when Rachel was a baby, I check to make sure he still breathes.

And then he wakes as though he wasn't even asleep.

I sit and watch him.

Sometimes I crawl next to him and sleep with him.

Only then can I sleep. Our vacant bed panics me. Even the sound of the sea doesn't lull me. I tried sleeping on his side of the bed, but that didn't work. I moved back to my side and placed pillows where his body would be. If I'm exhausted enough, I can sleep a few hours like that. I thought of bringing Rachel in bed with me, but didn't want to disturb her. Since Mom arrived, she's been sleeping on his side, but I'm so restless I wake her. So, I move to the couch.

Last night, after Rachel was in bed, Mom and I sat around the table, drinking wine. Remnants of a take-out dinner were still in containers. I couldn't eat much of it. Mom's eyes were pale, the mascara worn off, her lipstick gone. She shook her head and started a story: "When you were little, maybe a few years older than Rachel is now, while your dad was still alive, we were making breakfast.

"You were stirring herbs into the eggs. It had rained the night before and the birds swooped wildly in a dish of water. You stopped and asked where I was when I was a little girl. I told you with my mom and dad, Grandma and Grandpa. You said, 'I don't remember. Did I know you then?'

"I shook my head. 'You just know me now, as your mom.' I resumed slicing bread, thinking that I'd answered your question. But that answer made you sad. Your mouth turned down, your little chin trembled. 'It's unfair.

Unfair. You know me when I was a little girl. A baby even,' you said.

"I told you, 'I had to be a big grown-up woman to give birth to you. So you didn't know me as a girl because you weren't alive yet.'

"You became upset. 'Not alive? Where was I?'

"I put my knife down and slid the bread in the toaster oven. 'It was before you were born. Before you were even started.' I told you as gently as I could, but tears rolled down your cheeks in big single raindrops." Mom closed her eyes and said, "As a kid, you cried the biggest tears. Tears as big as my pinkie nail."

Mom has a remarkable memory of my childhood. Or at least everything that happened before Dad died, as though each moment is frozen.

"I told you, you must have been waiting to be born. 'Just think,' I said, 'even when I was a little girl a part of you was inside me.' I tried to comfort you." Mom shrugged.

"Then you asked, 'I was always with you? Inside?'

"'Yes. The start of you. And when you were ready, my body pushed you out into the world. Remember the pictures of you being born?'" Mom gazed at the wall behind me as though she saw the scene replaying there.

She chuckled. "You grinned and said, 'Oh thank you, Mommy. Thank you for my body.'

"But then you had another thought. 'You pushed me out? Out of your body? Oh, why did you have to do it?'"

Mom spoke in a little-girl voice, my voice of long ago, "'Now I'll never get to be a little baby again. I'll never be inside you again,' you said.

"Once you were born you could only grow, become an adult, age, and die. Kids teach you to review the world. I told you, 'You won't be a little baby again, but when you're grown up, a little baby can grow inside of you and you can push her out and be a mommy.'

"'You'll come and see my baby?'

"'Of course. I'll want to see your baby just as soon as it's born.'

"That seemed to satisfy you."

Mom grew quiet then, and I wondered why she told me that story at just that moment. Sometimes Mom's stories are inspired because she has a sweet memory she wants to share. Sometimes her stories are a message or warning. Why hadn't she told me this after Rachel was born? And then she added, "You always wanted everything fair and even." She shrugged and took a sip of wine.

Maybe she was reminding me that once you're born, you're bound to die. And we don't all get the same allotted time. The ultimate, and inevitable, unfairness.

Troy wakes up and asks again, "When's Tara getting here?"

"Tomorrow, I think." Why does he keep asking about her? "Why?"

"I want to see her. I talked to her. I think it was last night."

I lie next to him and don't say a word.

"She's like my little sister."

"No. She had a crush on you." I laugh, "Before I did."

"She was just a lonely kid and got more and more into her music," he says.

"I see it as the other way around. She cared about her music more than any of the people in her life."

"It was inextricable from her."

"Like your diving?"

"No. I liked to dive. I didn't *have* to dive. I didn't have to dive to live. And besides, I had you. Our planned life together."

"Tara has Aaron."

"Not really. She doesn't let herself." And then he falls back asleep.

And so do I. At last I sleep. And then I bolt awake, scared something had happened. I lean up and place my hand on Troy's chest. His breath is shallow. But he still breathes.

In the afternoon, I roll the back of the bed up, turn on the laptop I brought, and call Mom.

"How's he doing?" she asks.

I don't answer.

"Oh. No better." Her voice falls flat.

"I thought he could talk with Rachel on the computer."

"Okay. Let me get everything ready." A few minutes later, there she is on the computer with Rachel on her lap. "Hi, Mommy."

"Daddy's here. He wants to talk with you."

I put the laptop on Troy's tray and then scoot next to him. "Can you see us?"

"Hi, Daddy." Rachel grins, and then almost immediately the smile is gone and her brows are together. "You still in the hospital." Her mouth turns down. Maybe it's because she's a kid and all kids are like this, but her expressions seem to reveal the soul of the emotion. Her woebegone face is enough to make anyone cry.

"Yep."

Rachel scans the room, and her eyes rest on the IV with the tube snaking into Troy's hand. "Daddddyyyy." The word trails off, lost in the distance and despair.

Mom whispers something to her.

"You feeling better, Daddy? When you going to come home?"

"I don't know, sweetie. How's your potty training going?"

"I pee-pee in it all the time. I'm a big girl now."

"Good! You know I love you, right?"

Rachel nods; I see her nod.

"I'll always love you."

"You going to come home?"

"Say it. Say 'Daddy always watches over me'."

"You always watch over me." Tears course down

Mom's face. Rachel is focused on us, her parents in the computer monitor.

"Mommy?"

"I'm right here," I say.

"When's Daddy coming home?"

"I don't know, sweetie. As soon as he can." I smooth my face.

"But I'm here with you now. I'm always with you. I am inside you." He points to his head and his heart. "And I will always be there loving you." Troy's voice is soft.

"Okay, Daddy." Rachel darts a smile that fades immediately.

Troy turns his head so she won't see his tears. And then says, "Well, Daddy has to get his rest now." He stares right at her. "I love you, Rachel."

She reaches her hand to the monitor and touches his cheek. Very gently. We see her palm, the faint creases as she reaches for her father, we see the stroke Troy can't experience. "I felt that. I felt your fingers on my cheek."

He kisses his palm and places it flat against the screen. "Did you get my kiss?"

She nods solemnly.

"Bye bye, sweetie."

Her fingertips remain on his image.

Troy closes his eyes and turns his face to the side. Tears squeeze from under his lids.

I move in front of the screen. "I'll be home soon, darling. You having fun with Grandma?"

She nods her head. "We're going to the playground on the beach." And once again her joy vanishes and she says, "I miss Daddy." She swerves from her child's joy at life's newness to growing apprehension.

"He wants more than anything to be home with us. For us all to be home together. To go to Aunt Tara's concert."

Rachel grins. "See Levy!"

"Yes, in a few days, you'll see Levy."

The infection spreads into Troy's other lung. His arm is swollen and cracked. They consider putting him on a respirator. He refuses. He wants to be able to talk to Rachel and me. To his parents when they get here.

"When are they coming?" he asks.

"They're on their way. You talked to them, didn't you?"

"Yesterday."

"You want to call them?" I reach for the phone.

"Not right now."

I plead, "Let's try the respirator. Just until the medicine kicks in. Give it that chance."

"No. There's already oxygen going up my nose." His words are wispy. "The doctor didn't think the respirator would make a difference."

"We've got to keep fighting."

"I am. I have." And then he falls asleep.

*

When I go home that night, I see Rachel's kiss still pressed in the glass, her lips smeared, and the imprint of her fingers. On the other side are Troy's. His sweet lips still there, as though forming a kiss for the world.

I'm too tired to cry. All out of tears. I'm too tired to talk. I fall asleep on my side of the bed, the covers over my head.

CHAPTER THREE

Before I Was Alive, Where Was I?

Tara

So as soon as I get to L.A., I visit Troy. It's late at night, but I walk right in. He's sleeping, and I'm careful not to disturb him. I sit in the chair next to him and listen to the machines. The monitors hum. The IV drips into his arm ... drip, drip, drip ... setting up its own percussion along with his breath. It's as though I travel into his lungs with each intake.

He looks awful. Now, Troy wasn't a good-looking kid, but I still thought he was the cutest boy in the world. Sky and Mom were a duo, so close it was like they thought the same thoughts together and saw the same world. Maybe because they had gone through so much together when Sky's dad died, and had that perfect life until then.

Seven years of bliss. Imagine that. Seven years of just being a happy kid with nothing gone wrong. A mom and a dad who *liked* each other. They even told stories of going camping and to the ice capades. Imagine that.

Not that I feel sorry for myself. It's funny how bad things sometimes have good consequences. And me feeling left out was one of the reasons I played my piano so hard. I could accompany myself and I didn't need them. Or any friends.

But with Troy, I was just a kid. Ordinary. Not the kid whose cheating dad broke her mom's heart and spoiled Sky's life. Just a kid.

And Troy paid attention to me. He liked to hear me practice. He tried to teach me to dive. He was a welcome relief in our family.

He grew to be a more handsome man than he ever was as a boy, tall, with an easy smile and a nonchalant way about him. But maybe it's just what I said before. I love him so much that he looks beautiful to me.

That's what makes it so hard to look at him now. His cheeks are sunken. He's a peculiar color, something in between gray and blue. He sounds a little like Darth Vader when he breathes.

I wipe away a tear. And just sit with him. I breathe with him, but he breathes too fast and I can't keep up.

And then he jerks awake.

"How long have you been there?" He wets his lower lip and purses his lips together in a gesture that I associate with him and welcomes me home, even to this miserable hospital room.

"I don't know. A while. I didn't want to disturb you. Think I may have fallen asleep for a while."

"How's the tour?"

So I tell him about the tour. I tell him about Chicago and Denver and how cool it is being on the bus. I tell him how much work we're getting done composing new songs, and how Levy is having fun. At least he's with us. "Tomorrow, or maybe it's tonight already, is the one in L.A."

"Is someone filming it so I can see it when I'm better?"

"Someone always takes a video."

"I don't want to miss it."

"I want you there. I want everyone there." I think about my family—Mom, and Sissy and Allie, and Sky and Rachel and Troy—ready to come to my concert and that being stolen from me.

He shifts his head to me, and I see how huge his eyes are. "What's it like, Tara? Tell me. Being on stage like that." That's what I like about Troy. He simply asks what he wants to know about your life. He doesn't hide or assume anything.

"When you go out on stage, and the people are screaming and the lights are blaring so all you can do is hear them, can't see them except as shadows, there's this feeling." I try to explain it, "I don't know if there's a word, it's excitement—no, exhilaration. But, like, both sides of it at once—fear and thrill. The people are *there* for me. For Special and me. For us. And so I feel like I'm hot shit. Or extraordinary or great. But then I know I'm just me doing me. I don't believe any of it is real. I'm merely little old Tara. But as soon as I play that first note, I become Li'l Key and Special and the crew and we're, like, in our zone, doing like always. Each time a little different. Each time we hear something new. Pull out something new. The crowd provokes us, gets different juice from us."

He's quiet except for his breathing, and for a minute I think he's fallen asleep on me.

"I got it. The same feeling as before a difficult dive, except with a crowd's excitement, too. You don't get to dive in a coliseum, after all."

"Nope. Except at the Olympics, I guess. But, you know, the audience, like, makes it easier because they hear and see what they came for. They *project* their wishes and needs on you. They're ready for the party, and they're the ones that help bring it on."

We're quiet for a few seconds while the machines thump and wheeze. "Figure I'd ask you the same question. What's it like being here? Being sick with this weird bacteria."

"Hmmm. You're the only one who's asked." He stops to breathe. "I'm scared shitless. Terrified. But don't tell anyone."

"Me, too, Troy."

"Nothing's working and everything's getting more difficult." He gasps. "Each breath is a chore. Shit. I have to think, remember how to roll over. And I'm not sure what I dream and what's real. You're real, right?"

I reach out and touch his arm. It's cool and dry. "Feel that? I'm really here."

"Isn't it night? How'd they let you in?"

"I just walked in, came to your room. Lousy security, I guess." I shrug. I don't know what to say to him. I'm not prepared for this. Not even prepared for seeing him so sick, let alone him telling me he's frightened.

"You don't seem terrified. You seem like you, except weak."

"I don't have energy for my own panic. And I try to think good thoughts, positive thoughts like you're supposed to, but these bleak ones go on anyway. So I lay here suffering about Sky and Rachel and feeling like I've let them down by being sick, and even more if I die and am not there to help Rachel grow. And I know Sky . . . She hasn't gotten over, not really, her father's death. All our dead babies. Her friend Mia's death." All these words at once exhaust him, and he closes his eyes.

I sit. I'm here to listen, I guess.

"You'll take care of Sky?"

The question surprises me. "I'll try. But she won't want me to. And she has Mom."

He shifts so slowly. I can see how exhausting movement is.

"I'll try."

"Don't let her make a monument out of our love by mourning. Help her to make a monument to our love by loving."

"No one can replace you." The IV releases another drop. "I love you, Troy."

He nods. "You're my little sister. How's she doing, do you think?"

"I haven't really talked with her. She's always here. Mom's enjoying Rachel, but I thought I'd keep her with Levy for the next few days so Mom could focus on Sky and you."

"You're generous."

He says this as though it's a message not just about this act, but a bunch of them. A stance in my life. Generous as though forgiving.

"I want to help as much as I can. Sky's my *sister*, Rachel is my niece. I love them. It's easy."

"Of course," he says.

"Sky would do it for me."

He doesn't say anything. Sky complained about me to him when we were kids. But I know the bristly and off-handed way she treats me is her way of avoiding her real feelings. I know this because of something that happened a long time ago. Before Troy, when I was five.

Dad hadn't shown up to pick me up for our usual weekend. I stood in the living room, looking out the window, then sat on the porch stairs, walked up and down the block, but no Dad. Mom was out on a date. Sky had to watch me until Dad came, then she could go to a sleepover at Marissa's. I waited, but no Dad. It must have been late spring or early summer, because I was outside. It got dark. Fireflies came out. I thought about getting a jar and catching some to amuse myself and so I didn't look stupid sitting on the stairs, my cheek in my fist, staring endlessly into the road and jerking at the sound of any car.

Sky made us breakfast for dinner . . . cereal probably, or eggs . . . and watched TV and talked on the phone with Marissa.

I slumped back outside. Now even the fireflies were asleep. Maybe Dad got in an accident, I thought. I ran to tell Sky. "Maybe something happened to him? Maybe he's in the hospital?" My excuses became reality. "What if Daddy dies?"

Sky huffed with annoyance, got off the phone with Marissa, and called his number, but there was no answer. "He's probably out with a woman."

"I'm scared," I told her. I thought about playing my piano, but Sky hugged me tight to her. She rocked me like Mom used to. This was a surprising and remarkable gesture. Even though she was bony and it was hard to mold into her, she felt good. I ignored the pinchy bones and knobs of elbows.

"I know, let's go for a walk," she said.

"Really?" A walk in the dark. "What if Dad comes?"

She knelt down. "He's not coming. Get it? He's doing

something else that's more important to him." She jabbed her temple with her finger as though pushing ideas into my brain. Her pupils were wide and the rim of her gray eyes surrounded them like a halo. "We'll go to Magic Mountain."

"Wow. Okay." This was a different sister. "You think this is okay?" I really was asking if she'd stay this nice.

"Yes. I'm your babysitter. I can say. Scared of the dark?" she teased.

A little, but I wasn't going to admit it.

There were heavy trees above us. The cool night air smelled of some sort of spring flower. We were out in the middle of the night, no one knowing where we were, and shivers fluttered my arms.

We walked to the park and climbed Magic Mountain. Now I know it's just a big hill where they dumped some dirt so kids could sled down it, but then it seemed huge, especially standing at the top with the park receding. The distant streetlights stretched the shadows from the slide and jungle gyms across the field below me.

Sky was nonchalant.

"You don't care, do you?" I asked.

"Huh?"

"You don't care if Dad is in the hospital or dead. You hate him."

"I don't hate him. He just doesn't have anything to do with me. He's not *my* dad. He's yours. He married Mom and made a big mess of her life and left you both."

It's true, I knew it then and know it now. I'm sorry I didn't begin with more fun, love, ease. All that good stuff. I try to make it different for Levy.

Sky lay back and said, "Look at the stars."

There was no moon, so they were as bright as they can be close to a big city and lavish across the heavens. I cuddled in close. "You're so lucky," I told her. "So pretty, and you have such cool friends and you get to go to parties and do what you want. Have sleepovers. I don't get to do anything. Everyone bosses me around. I hate being the youngest."

"You'll get to do all those things when you're as old as I am."

"I wish Mom would have another baby. Then I'd be the big sister."

We gazed at the stars. Off in the distance, a dog barked.

"You want to hear a big secret? A really big secret that I've never told anyone?"

"A secret?"

"You won't tell anybody, will you?" She whispered in the dark, shushing the words so their substance grew.

"I promise."

"I wish my dad was alive even if he didn't show up. Even if he was unfaithful and fought all the time with Mom. I think you're lucky."

I held my breath. And turned her admission around in my mind.

"Don't ever tell Mom."

I shook my head. "Promise." We lay on the top of the mountain looking at the sequin stars. Ruts from winter's sledding poked our backs. "I love you, Sky."

"I guess you'll be the youngest and I won't have a dad. That's that. It's unfair."

"Yes."

"Unfair," she said again.

"You want to wait here all night and see the sunrise?" I asked.

Sky tried to figure out if that was okay. Taking a walk in the dark was as exciting as she could get. Now that I was here, I wanted it all. If I were her age, I wouldn't have hesitated. "Mom'll be home. She'll worry."

The stretching sky pushed down on my chest. I couldn't imagine my dad really caring about me. Sky knew her dad loved her. That seemed better.

But then this light came, a streak of yellow-orange-red fire in the dark. "Look." I pointed to it. "What is that? Where's it coming from?"

"I don't know," Sky said. "Some reflection from some-where."

"It's on your hair," I told her. "Your hair's on fire."

She slapped her head and laughed. And pointed to me. "It's down your nose, a stripe. Half of you is orange. Like war paint or Halloween. You should see how pretty you look."

"You, too."

We danced our hands in the smudge of light, watching

them blaze. Watching the color change and flicker over our fingers. "Look. I have a red foot," I squealed.

"I like your orange eye and cheek."

"Hey," I said. "Wishes do come true. We got our sunrise in the middle of the night. Maybe that's why they call it Magic Mountain."

With her arms wrapping her knees, she looked just like Mom, but smaller.

I touched her bright hair and my hand glowed.

I laughed. And said, "We're the orange sisters."

"The Orange Sisters," we said together and high-fived.

When we got back home, Mom was still on her date. And Dad had not called or come by to pick me up. In fact, he forgot me for the rest of that year. Maybe the one after that, too.

I never told anyone Sky's secret.

Now I look at Troy, who seems to have fallen asleep, or maybe he's just resting before he coughs out the next sentence, and I know how dismal it will be for Sky if Troy should die. I know better than anyone. Her childhood tragedy replayed through the generation like an inevitable curse. And last month her friend Mia died. A nightmare that reoccurs and, worst of all, there's no waking. Just the endless reel of loss.

"Troy," I say, "you don't need to worry about Sky. I'll

take care of her and the crew will help. They're about nothing if they're not about family. Family is all. So we'll just scoop Sky and Rachel up into our crew and help them through." Except for T-Bone, that's all true. T-Bone is just into T-Bone and the women who rub up against him. "She's got Mom and, like, all her friends, too. A huge extended family."

I don't know he's awake until he says, "That's what I need to hear."

"But you've got to fight. Reach inside and grab your strength. *Visualize*." I'm too young for this. Usually I think I can handle everything, but I'm too young for this. "I love you so much. I couldn't have grown up without you in my family." Tears run down my face, but I don't want Troy to see me crying. But why not? He needs to know that he's loved. "You know how important you are to all of us, right?"

"Hey. Think about how important I am to me." His voice falls off as though he's asleep. And then he stirs and says, "I'll miss myself."

I spend the day with Rachel and Levy while the crew sets up the concert. Sky and Troy's rented condo in Venice is across a walkway from the beach, a view of the sea from the windows. The condo is on the second and third floors. I take the kids to the beach and we walk in the sand, feel the water on our feet. Rachel takes this all for granted, it's her front yard, but this is the first time

Levy has seen the sea. I show him how the water is salty, and tell him it's so big it stretches all the way to China. We walk along the shore and Levy notices my footprints in the wet sand. "Look," he says, "you're leaving marks."

"Yep, you are, too." I point to his small imprints, his toes rounded like Aaron's.

"How's it do that?"

"You squash the sand down," I tell him.

He presses a foot down and carefully lifts it. Rachel follows suit. Then he walks looking backward, watching the pattern our steps make, evidence of the three of us, marching across the beach. He turns. "Look what's in my foot, Mommy." A stone is imbedded in the sand at the ball of his imprint. He reaches down, picks it up, and hands it to me.

"Oh, it's shaped just like a heart and it's deep red, too."

He grins at me.

I hand it back to him.

"For you, Mommy. My foot found it for you."

When we walk back, the tide has washed our footprints away. "Where'd they go?" Levy asks.

Rachel points to the sea. "Gone there."

"A wave made the sand new again," I tell him.

Levy's lips turn down and then he smiles. "I'm walking in water," he laughs.

We keep making new footprints. Troy's last words buzz in my mind. I imagine him laughing. I imagine him sitting up and eating his breakfast. I still haven't seen Sky, but gave Mom a quick hug. She said she'd try to make the concert if Troy was doing better. Otherwise, she'd stay with Sky.

"I understand."

Of course. This time, it's what I would do, too. Troy's illness and helping Sky is more important than my biggest concert, the culmination of all my hours and years of lessons and practice. The reward for Special's and my work. There will be other concerts. Maybe even bigger ones. But, then again, who knows? Maybe I'll get hit by a bus tomorrow and she will never have seen me. And Troy will recover.

We walk along the boardwalk edged with palm trees on one side and shops selling beach clothes, T-shirts, medical marijuana, and tattoos on the other. A man in a green hat wears a sign, *World's Greatest Wino. Jokes and Songs*. A little bit later, a man holds cardboard up with marker saying, *Kick my ass for a dollar. I'll also accept food-weed-beer*. We enter a restaurant with a red awning called Small World Books and Sidewalk Café. The kids swirl corn chips in mild salsa, dropping splotches of it on the table. Rachel hands a pacifier to the mom of a baby that dropped it. She does this almost solemnly, holding it so she hasn't touched the sucky part.

"You're such a sweet, gentle girl," I tell her when she crawls back up to her chair.

"Shanks," she says.

"'Thanks', she said 'thanks'," Levy interprets.

At first I couldn't understand a word Rachel said. Levy translated for me. Now I understand her pronunciation, but Levy still enjoys helping. Rachel looks at me and bites her hamburger. She has a delicate compassion that's a contrast with Levy's there's-the-world-let-me-grab-it approach.

Outside the restaurant, a white dude with a black T-shirt and panama straw hat plays keyboard and sings Billy Joel songs with easy control of the instrument and a voice that teases out sorrow in the lyrics. Even with the breeze and the sound of crashing waves, his voice captures interest. He's a good-looking man, probably in his forties, and I'd imagine him with a full-time gig in a piano bar or upscale restaurant. He takes off his hat and walks back and forth among the diners asking for money. I give him five dollars and he nods to us.

Then a woman with gray hair twisting from a low ponytail sits down at a rickety upright piano. She slides the sleeves of her baggy purple shirt to her elbows and plays flawless Chopin. It's the same piece that I played for my last piano concert for the high school orchestra. She tilts her face to hear her own notes. Her face is lined, her nose prominent. I wait to hear if she accomplishes the tricky spot, the part that I struggled to play smoothly. Her fingers slide through the measures.

I watch her and shudder.

A wind comes from nowhere. The palm fronds rattle like snakes.

*

On the way back to Sky's condo, I buy orange eye shadow and, before the concert, cover one side of my face.

"What's with the orange?" Special asks.

"It's for Troy. Troy and Sky."

"I've been thinking about him all day." He frowns at me.

"Sky and I are the orange sisters. I'll tell you the story later."

I shoot him a look and he adds, "This concert. I mean, we're from Detroit and this is L.A. We could go either way."

I slip on a black sequined tank top with spaghetti straps, and jeans. Silver stilettos, too. "The new one will bridge it." I pull a strand of hair over one eye.

"Wow, you look hot." Special nods at me with that unmistakable sexual interest.

I check on the kids; they're both asleep on the couch in the dressing room. Levy has his arm over Rachel as though he's protecting her from what this night might bring.

Before we start, I peek from behind the curtain. The house lights are on and I see five empty seats in the front row. Five seats for Mom, Sky, Troy, Allie, and Sissy. None of them are here.

Oh, well. What I expected. I know Mom needs to be with Sky and Troy tonight. That's most important. I tell myself, *You've got to get your spirit up. There's a show to do.*

Your most important one. This is about you and Special and your life. You have your music. I straighten my shoulders. *I have to do what I need to do.*

And then I see Allie. Of all Mom's friends, she's the one that I feel closest to, and she was supportive of me and Aaron from the beginning. Her hair is fluffed up, and she wears jeans with rhinestones on the ass pockets and one of her crazy tie-dye tops. She's trying to look hip, but her shoes throw her cool off. She strides down the aisle by herself like this is where she belongs, plops down in the front row. Straggling behind her are three kids, wearing the requisite sagging jeans, white T-shirt, and baseball caps, who sit next to her. She gave the other three tickets to fans waiting in line. Good for her.

"Allie's here," I tell Special.

"By herself?"

"Looks like she made some friends." I point to her and the three decked-out youngsters.

"They're some lucky kids."

Allie's not Mom, but she's the next best thing. "I'm grateful she came."

Aaron huffs air out and says, "You deserve that and more. A lot more." He puts his hands on my shoulders and turns me toward him. "Babe. You got to put the shit away. Ain't nothin' for the rest of the night but us and our sounds. Us," he says again, "and our music. That and loving them," he nods toward the audience. We have to love them for them to love us, he says.

And as if on cue, here comes Sissy, sitting on the other side of Allie. She arrived straight from the airport. I watch as Sissy and Allie greet each other. How do they know each other? I guess from the Christmas cookie party, the cookie exchange that Mom has had my entire life. Mom invited Sissy right before Levy was born.

The first time I met Sissy was in the middle of the night. I was with Aaron in Detroit; we'd spent the day working on lyrics and then went to St. Andrews to do some freestyling. A perfect spring day and evening, until we walked back to his car. Flat tire. And he didn't have a spare. And it was late, way late. Everything closed late. He shrugged and said, "I guess you're coming home with me."

Now, home was his moms. "Why don't we, like, rent a hotel room somewhere?"

"You have extra money? Moms is just a mile away."

I looked down.

"What, you afraid to meet my moms? You going to love each other."

I'd never met any boy's mother before. Except Troy's, and he doesn't count. Of course, I never really had a boyfriend before Aaron, either. So we walked through the quiet night. It was near Easter, and one house had plastic pastel eggs hanging from tree branches.

And then we came to a red brick house, with a porch in front. Gray trim. Aaron rang the doorbell. "We need to let her know you're here."

Sissy answered, tying a sash across a turquoise chenille bathrobe, her hair in pink rollers. The foam kind.

There I stood. A white girl with black hair and silver hoops in my nose, eyebrow, and all down each ear.

"Moms, this is Tara. She's a surprise."

"Well, come in, Surprise." Sissy smiled and then stepped aside so we could enter.

"My ride got a flat and I'm already using the spare. I can't get Tara home."

"She can sleep in Shana's room. We'll take care of this in the morning." She turned to me. "Your moms know where you are?"

I shook my head.

"Don't want to worry her to death. Let her know. Better to wake her up."

She'll never believe the flat tire story, I think.

"I'll talk to her, if you want." Sissy must have read my mind.

Sissy didn't blink an eye at a Goth-looking white girl standing on her step in the middle of the night. She put me in her daughter's room, now the guest bedroom. Embroidered forget-me-nots and daisies graced the pillows' edges. A crocheted afghan of giant violets was folded at the foot of the bed. The dresser was laden with perfume bottles, some with atomizers. I couldn't help squeezing the orangey bulb to smell the aroma.

Aaron's room was at the other end of the apartment, and Sissy slept in a bedroom between us.

She just ushered me in and welcomed me. Life was whatever came at her next. And she accepted it with grace.

The next morning, she fed us shredded wheat, took us to Discount Tires, dropped us off at our car, and drove to work. Aaron drove me home.

I trust Sissy's love and friendship as much as anyone's.

Now she's settled in her seat next to Allie, and they're turned to each other talking.

There's the customary hush, and the DJ takes the stage and starts playing, and the spots come on while the house lights dim. As soon as my soles feel the vibrations, fear and thrill run up the backs of my legs, up my spine, down my arms. I flex my fingers.

"I love you, babe," Aaron says to me, and then turns to the crew. "Let's do it. Let's scoop up that love. Let's go."

We stride on stage and the house screams. We start with "Prohibitions of Prison" to get the audience revved up. And then Special gets serious. He quiets the crew and takes the mike. "My folks is in the hospital going through it in L.A. tonight. And so I want just to take a moment to think about Troy." He bows his head and then says, "To think about *all* the peoples not doin' as well as we are." Amazingly, the throng quiets, as though they're in church instead of at a concert. The audience is the usual decked-out group, evenly split between black and white kids. They're our people. Usually they're screaming for us, pumping fists in the air to our beats, singing the lyrics they know. Their excitement hits my throat, pumps my chest.

This quiet, Aaron's mention of Troy, catches me unaware, and my sense of buoyancy switches to grief. I clench my eyes.

"This his favorite song." Special turns to the crew and says, "Believe in Me." He nods at me and I start up the soft music. When he gets to the hook, *I'm gonna love you past, Your hurt, Your pain,* I think of Sky and how brave she'll have to be to let someone in. I think how hard it is to let Aaron in, and we haven't even been tested.

I refocus on our music, the loving lyrics written when I was pregnant with Levy. I become the keyboardist, watching Special for his cues, keeping an eye on Red because he sometimes gets off on his own and needs me to follow. As usual, T-Bone is bumpin' and grindin' for the babes. Now the audience is tall dancing shadows jumping to our beats. Special is drenched in a sweat that turns his skin molten bronze, dancing as he sings since he can't stop moving. Me either, but I'm tied to my key-board.

When we start the new song, "Recession," I get to play Fauré. I start at the beginning, with that long note that's as perfect as a lonesome train whistle, and let it blanket the venue, dark and empty and lonely because oh how I need this music, oh how I need its cleansing. T-Bone's fabulous voice carries it with me. Special starts on the hook, the

audience stamping and screaming by the time he gets to
how can I change in this game with death call'n my name. He
never says that as a question, but a statement.

During the yelling, he steps to me and whispers, "I
wrote something for tonight while you with the babies
and we worked it. You just play that bullet track or the
car screeching when it seems right."

"Aaron, I . . ."

"You can do this, babe. Just feel me."

Special holds the mike and starts,

I heard it through the grapevine
Performing in California
Was like strolling through some land mines.

I put in the bullets that I'd sampled. Out beyond the
blaring lights, I sense the audience wary and waiting. Is
he really going to get up on *their* stage, in The House of
Blues, and brag about Detroit?

And then he raps the verse:

When the world is ghetto
We all in the same gang.
Bangin' the same thing.

He's talking about unity, trying to demolish the invisible walls that split the people. This could go either way.
And from the great void, the audience starts cheering.

If this the life you live
You gonna accept it.
Because it's hard as can be when you young and black.

A barrage of bullets.

That's what goes on in the city of Boss Angeles
And it feels like home because
Detroit is just as scandalous.

Now, he has—we have—completely won the audience. Detroit and all. White chick and all. Brother in the hospital putting a blanket of terrifying sorrow covering all. I end with Fauré's first note and let it play over all of us until it's just about to die.

And then a final single gunshot.

Done.

I hold my breath in the silence. And the audience starts cheering.

Perfect.

Special winks at me. He raises the mic to the ceiling and then reaches it out to the audience so they can hear themselves.

"Feel your power. Feel YOUR power," he bellows, and then nods so the entire crew aims their mics for the throng, a tsunami of cheering, stomping, screaming, yelling.

The word *power* is exaggerated until it's a tidal wave. I

can't help myself, I sample it. And then play the notes back loud as the sound system will let me.

The audience and the speakers both throb *Hear our power. Hear it.*

Wow.

Holy shit!!!!

It's our best concert. I'm dripping wet with the thrill, sadness, exhilaration, pride running down me. Dripping with *Hear our power.* And for a moment, I am one with Aaron and our audience. I feel the love. The particular love and the universal love. I am not simply and only my music.

And then, sadly, I know it's time, and I turn down the volume until it whispers. And finally fades away. And we stride off stage, the audience still screaming, hollering for more.

"We can't top that," Aaron says in the wings. "Leave them wanting more."

We're done.

Slowly the audience gives up, turns its back on the stage, and trickles from the auditorium.

I'm alone again. Even as close as Aaron and I are on that stage and as powerful as this concert we did together was, when it ends, there's that feeling that was with me as a child.

CHAPTER FOUR

Unpredictable

Tara

When Aaron steals a moment to hug me, we quiver with invigoration and pride. Security attempts to limit the post-concert throng backstage to a list we've compiled, but people push through to cluster around the crew. Usually no one pays attention to me since most of the swarm is girls wanting to take an artist home for a roll, and security lets the pretty ones through. They're hoping for leftovers. Occasionally someone arrives from the press. Occasionally the interviewer is looking for some action, too. Our record producer is here, holding forth proudly while a dude in an NY baseball cap takes notes.

Sissy hugs us. "I'm so happy," she says to Aaron. "My son, my baby boy knocked it outta the park, honey. Outta the park." Her eyes gleam with pride. She squeezes me tight and almost lifts me up with her enthusiasm. "Tara, you were fabulous. Your range! I didn't know that little body of yours could belt it like Aretha."

"Just for a note or two." I hold on to Sissy, missing my mom. "I'm so glad you got to see us."

"Your mom woulda been here if she could." She squeezes me extra for her, then adds, "You made her proud, too."

Allie enfolds me. "It was such a thrill to see you. Ah, Tara, you're so accomplished, and what charisma! Aaron and you both." She sweeps her arm, "All of you. I remember you as a toddler and now, look at you . . ." Her voice trails off.

We've never had family backstage after a concert. My two separate selves are brought together. It's disconcerting, almost embarrassing. The sexy me, the flaunting me, the flirting and representing-for-the-audience me is so at odds with the family member, the daughter. The little girl Allie knew with the knobby knees who plunked away at the piano and was ready to vomit before her first recital. The messy housekeeper Sissy rolls her eyes about. All those other versions of me. But maybe this is what adults take for granted. We're all complex as we juggle and play out different aspects of ourselves.

"Your mom wished she were here. She really wanted to come, Tara." Allie's hands are on my shoulders, and she stares straight into my eyes as though willing me to feel

Mom's love and pride. "But she couldn't leave Troy and Sky. Not tonight." She shakes her head slightly. I don't want to ask how he is. I don't want the exhilaration from the concert to vanish, but as soon as I think that, it sinks like a balloon losing air. "How is he?"

Allie presses her lips together and pulls the corners down. "Otherwise your mom would have been here."

"What happened to your friends?"

Allie frowns. "Oh. You mean those dudes I gave the tickets to? They're off doing whatever's next. They loved the concert, though." And then she adds, as though she almost forgot, "Troy's parents arrived. They're at the hospital, too."

"I don't know them well. They, like, moved to Florida right after Troy graduated from high school."

Levy and Rachel have woken up, and they run onto the wings of the stage. I pick up Levy and spin him around and then do the same for Rachel. "Whheeewwww!" I sing as I turn her and she giggles. The three of us stand off to the side while the crew and Allie and Sissy move to a table laden with food and beverages. Levy sees it, runs toward it, and Rachel squirms out of my arms and runs after him.

Then I see King standing there, a phalanx of dudes behind him forming a wall between me and the others so I'm cut off and shielded. King walks without making a sound; he doesn't arrive, he transports himself. He glides. I've never seen him in person, let alone close enough to touch. His smooth skin seems formed from brown porcelain. Liquid black eyes. He's oiled with decades of money and protection. Decades of people fawning over his celebrity, putting a polish on him. Decades of people anticipating his every whim and wish so he concentrates only on his lyrics and music and makes money for his people.

He stares right at me as he floats toward me. "Li'l Key, You've got quite the scope." He's taller than I'd imagined. He's in great shape for a man in his forties.

For years, I've listened to his music. In person, this close, his voice has a vibrato, a depth the best sound equipment is unable to capture. Hot honey. A voice that I've tried to mimic with my keyboard.

"You were, like, in the audience?"

"I was." And he tilts his head toward me. "And I appreciate your skill, your training, and your, ah, creativity. How you span worlds." He flexes a smile and warmth radiates.

Could I ever take his voice for granted, or would I always be more aware of its sound than his words? Now, I struggle to focus on his meaning. "Thank you. I just do what I do. Who I am."

He looks me up and down slowly and I prevent myself from squirming under his scrutiny. "Hot little shorty, too. Very. With your own swag." He nods.

"Thank you." I guess you say that when someone tells you you're sexy. Or at least when King does.

"I like the orange." He's dressed in a gray silk suit without any sheen. I catch a glint of ruby cuff links when he moves his arm.

"That's new tonight." I know I'm being an idiot, another stupid starstruck fan, and I need to get my wit back.

"Hope that's not all that's new. Tonight." He wets his lips with his tongue. "You might consider doing you with me."

But the way he says it, I'm not sure if he's talking about having sex with him or singing with him.

I back up.

He reaches in his pocket and pulls out a card, flips it against his nail. "Think about doing a few tracks with me."

I lift my chin to seem bold.

"Loyalty is my middle name. We could see where, exactly where, you and I could take it. I could use a talented keyboardist with a voice and sass."

Just then, Levy breaks through the line of suited men and runs to me.

I pick him up. "Daddy lookin' for you. He go, 'Where Mama?'"

"Oh, you Special's baby-mama." As though that discards my music.

"He's my baby-daddy." Annoyance returns my spunk.

He laughs. "Sparky. I like that." He lifts one eyebrow. I swear to God he does. Just one, and keeps pinning me with his eyes. "You think you're crucial?" He speaks that very softly, seductively, so that his words and his tone are at odds.

I hear what he's saying. I'm used to taking care of myself. "Hey. We're doing great, our star is rising. And you? You're telling me you're ultimately selfish." But he's fanned my lack of trust.

"No, I'm telling you, take care of yourself. I could give you a spotlight. You could help with a little highbrow edge and some crossover. YOU." He nods when he says *you* but adds, "Li'l Key. The unpredictable one."

I don't know what would happen if Aaron changed or if the congruency of our goals and dreams shifted. Right now he's the leader and everything for us gets better. Maybe I'm allowing our desires to match, squashing my own voice.

"You decide if you want to be with me for awhile. See what we can do. Just a little or a lot."

He turns and saunters toward Aaron and says something I can't hear. The dudes block them from my field of vision. He shakes Larry's hand. Larry is the entertainment lawyer who Troy hooked us up with. I wonder if Larry is King's attorney, too.

And then King strolls back to me, lifts my chin with his forefinger, and examines my face. "Yep. Hot as hell and a musician. And unpredictable. That's for me and what I'll be doing next."

"What about Special and the crew?" Maybe I could cut

some grooves with him or do a few stadium concerts and bring along Special and the crew in some way.

"I already have a crew. I need a keyboardist with a voice."

I'm not sure if I've been hit on or hired. I still can't take the very tone of his voice for granted.

He slides away, leaving the auditorium. Even his walk is sexy. He doesn't need to open a door. He doesn't need to think where he's going next . . . he simply faces where he wants to go and his boys make his way. But at the door, he turns to me and flicks his finger as though he's tipping an imaginary hat. Spins and dances out the door. Other than the honor of his request, the affirmation of me as an artist, I don't know how I feel about him. He's sexy. But so what?

"What he want?" Aaron asks.

I shrug. "What he say to you?" I slip King's card into my back pocket.

"Said we did a great concert. And you a diamond in the rough. That he was going to take you away from me."

I laugh.

"Said it like I don't even know what a blessing you are." Aaron narrows his eyes slightly. "I know, babe. Believe me. He just worried about us as competition. Trying to break up our strength, you know?"

I shrug. I don't know if Aaron is reading King's strategy or trying to block his play. Trying to make it seem like it's not about me, but about him. "Not sure if he wanted to have sex with me or play music with me."

"Both. He wants both. Who wouldn't?" He says it like he's my friend and not my lover.

The man with the NY baseball cap is from the *L.A. Times* and wants to interview Special. While they're talking, I get some fried chicken and mini carrots. I haven't eaten since lunch with the kids at Small World Café.

T-Bone stands off to the side, his thumb hooked in his waist, leaning against a post, some pretty cocktail in one hand, watching the action. There are three women surrounding him. One with white hair and fake tits and jeans low enough to see her belly ring. Another traces the edge of his ear with her fingertip. The third just stares at me with green lenses and fake eyelashes as if her eyes watching what T-Bone sees will prove her empathy. He examines me with these three choices around him, calculating his next move. He's the prettiest one of all. For the first time, I wonder if he's really down-low, he's so pretty and so perfect. Or maybe he'd die if he knew I thought that.

Allie talks with Smoke. The man from the *L.A. Times* comes over to me and asks about my training. Turns out he studied classical and recognized the requiem notes. So I tell him what I tell everyone. I grew up boughie in Ann Arbor and my dad was able to pay for lessons. Lucky me. I remarked that that was the only thing my dad ever did give me. Lessons and genes. But the interviewer thought I meant the jeans I was wearing and that my father bought my clothes.

Fat chance.

I don't even know if my dad knows what I'm doing. He's only seen Levy once. But the lessons I appreciate.

By then the mass of people have gotten what they came for. Or recognize they aren't going to get more. T-Bone leaves with the three babes. Red Dog leaves with some women too. Smoke is married and has a little girl. He doesn't play around on her. Not that I know of, anyway. Perhaps, I assume every man is like my father. So it's Sissy and Allie and Aaron, the kids, and me. The kids pull the curtain ropes. Then eat what's left of the fried chicken and chocolate bars. They'll be up all night from the sugar and caffeine.

I inhale and ask the question I've been avoiding all night. "How's Troy?"

Allie glances at Sissy and shakes her head.

"It's twelve-thirty," Sissy says.

"I think they'll still be up," Allie replies.

Finding a quiet place isn't hard. I just go to the dressing room. I pick up Rachel's bunny, Maddie, and sit her on my lap and push Mom's number.

She answers immediately, as though waiting for my call.

"How's Troy?"

"How was the concert? I so wished I could be there." Her voice is low and soft.

"Fine. Great. Our best one. How's Troy?"

I hear her intake of air. "He passed, Tara. Two hours ago." Her voice is soft, whispery.

Right while we were singing the song about Detroit.

"Sky and I are still with him. And his parents are here."

"Did they get to talk to him?"

"He slipped into a coma right after they arrived. As though he was waiting for them."

"I should come."

"No. Take care of Rachel and we'll stay here until they take him for cremation."

It seems to me that Rachel should say goodbye to him. But maybe that would be traumatic. It seems to me we should all be together at a time like this. But I'm always on the side, never part of the main action. I think of King telling me to take care of myself. How do I do that exactly? And then I get an image of the gray-haired lady playing Chopin in the street.

"Can I talk to Sky?"

"Here she is."

"Hi."

She doesn't answer.

"I was with Troy last night. Did he tell you?"

Silence.

"I'm sorry. So sorry. I love him." Tears clog my throat. "I'll always miss him. Is there something you want me to do?"

My questions are met with silence.

"I love you, Sky. My heart goes out to you. To all of us. Is there anything I can do for you?"

Then Mom's voice says, "She can't really talk."

I hold Maddie. The bunny has silky ears. I'm not sure what to do. Nothing, I guess. Take care of Rachel. Tomorrow we go to Las Vegas.

"You want me to take Rachel to Vegas with us?"

"No. Why don't you come by the apartment before you leave?"

"Okay. I'll see you tomorrow morning, then."

Maddie's paws hold a carrot in front of her mouth as though she's taking a bite. Her eyes are shiny black cabochons that give her a look of wisdom. I press her to me, fold myself around her, and cry.

"I'll miss myself," Troy had said. *I'll miss myself.*

I'll miss him, but there's a part of me that's lost now, too. I miss myself.

Next morning the Entertainment section of the paper blares a headline, *Detroit Captures L.A.* The review mentions a new twist to hip-hop music, expressing a profound lyricism and new unity. A tight crew that works as one to bring a fresh sound and consciousness to the scene. Healing old wounds, Motown rises again. I'm mentioned for my depth and pizzazz, my tone-filled hooks and unpredictability that are an earmark of creativity. I don't think of myself as unpredictable, but that's the second time in twenty-four hours I've been told that. But me, I don't always know what I'm going to do before I do it. I told you that already. I read the review and think, Aaron and I don't need King. But do I?

We take the tour bus to Sky's. The crew waits while Aaron, Levy, Rachel, and I go in. Mom has dark blue circles under her eyes and her lids are swollen. As soon as she sees us, she places a fingertip over her lips and whispers, "Sssssh. Sky has finally fallen asleep."

Mom looks pale.

Rachel bursts with an eagerness that Mom's caution can't contain. She calls, "Mommy! Daddy!" as she runs through the house.

Sky's sleep is going to be disrupted.

Mom's and my eyes meet and then she looks away, sits down at the dining table, leans her head into her hand and twirls circles in her hair, a gesture of comfort and anxiety that I've seen throughout my childhood.

"Has Sky made any plans?"

I want to see her. But fear of her reaction prevents me from waking her up, hugging her. Crying with her.

"There'll be a memorial service in three days."

"Are you staying with her? Sky's going to take a few weeks off work?"

"Sky lost her job."

"I didn't know."

"It just happened. The day Troy went into the hospital."

Mom sits and I stand trying to help, but helpless.

"We haven't made any plans. But I have to be in Chicago next week to speak at a conference." Mom trains other insurance agents in sales and marketing.

Rachel runs back to the family room, calling, "Daddy, Daddy."

Levy tugs at Aaron's hand. "Here's Daddy."

Rachel glances at Aaron and then runs back upstairs.

"Someone needs to say something," I say.

"It's Sky's place," Mom replies.

I'll miss myself, Troy said. The refrain keeps throbbing in my head.

Maybe what I do next is wrong. Mom sits worrying circles on her scalp. Levy holds Aaron's hand. Sky is in her bedroom, sleeping or hiding. Unavailable while Rachel runs around the condo searching for Troy. Sky's condo, in spite of all the chaos of the last week, is neat. Brown and aubergine pillows fluffed on the sofa. The DVDs in the entertainment center perfectly stacked. The kitchen counter clear and all dishes, glasses, and appliances put away. External regulation maintaining order and calm. Outside the sea stretches across the world. I grab Rachel's hand as she runs by me. Rachel is not my daughter, she's not in my care, but I can't bear her frantic hunt for her father. I grab her hand and kneel down so our eyes are even.

"Daddy still in hospital?"

"I have some sad news, Rachel."

She looks at me with those spooky gray eyes Sky has.

I wonder if she already knows. Sometimes we don't want to know things we already know. I hold both her hands in mine. And then grasp her close to me so she can melt into me. "Daddy's gone," I say into her ear. "Daddy loves you very much, more than the whole world, and he wanted more than anything to stay with you, but he's gone. That's why Mommy and Grandma are so sad. Why we all are so sad. We miss him already." I start crying.

"Daddy come back tomorrow?" She nods as though to reassure me.

"No, Rachel. He can't come back."

"Ever?"

"Not ever."

And then Rachel starts wailing. I hold her tightly. Mom gets up and hugs her, too. Levy comes over, and then Aaron, and we kneel around Rachel, embracing her while she screams.

Sky must hear these wails. They must penetrate her wall.

CHAPTER FOUR

Unpredictable

Sky

I don't remember any of it. Not really. I just remember that he went in a transition as smooth as one of his dives. Ready ready ready. Poised in position. A minute bounce and a plunge with barely a splash. Just a finishing breath. Troy broke through to the other side as if entering water and then sank deeper. He divided existence so it didn't know it had been disturbed.

Hardly made a ripple. Hardly made a sound. Yet the dive is complete and the difference profound.

The doctor asked me, did I want an autopsy? It might help them understand how the bacteria took such hold on him. She said something about one in a million, very unusual, so young and seemingly healthy.

He'd been through enough, I told her. And I held his cold hand.

Until Mom pulled me and said we had to go home. I had to sleep. They needed to take him.

So I did. I did what I was told.

I had a million things to do, to arrange. I completed what I could and let Mom do the rest. Mia's husband, Marc, came. He knew just what to do, her death still so recent. He made the decisions. Got a place for the memorial service. Wrote an obituary. Called and emailed Troy's friends, basketball team, and law firm. Our classmates. All that. He knew. He just looked at me and shook his head. Shook his head. I don't remember him even saying a word. And Mom tried to support me, be with me. Only she knew where I was, where I'd been. She'd been with me through Dad's death and now this. I list the calamities: My dad. Three miscarriages. A stillbirth. Mia's death. My job. Troy's death. I think of putting them in my iPhone; then maybe I'll quit going over and over them in my head. I hit the note button and there's my old shopping list: dish detergent, eggs, coffee, fabric softener, olive oil, cherries, almonds. I haven't bought any of it.

My father's death. Three miscarriages. A stillborn. Mia's death. Troy's death.

Am I being punished?

Have I done something wrong?

I sit at my window and notice a small bump on the

framing that forced ripples, long dried, in the paint. The grain of the wood runs underneath the paint swirls created by the imperfection.

I study these two separate patterns, the wood grain, once living, and the frozen paint wrinkles. I consider the ripples in the water that Troy made when he dove, and the stillness of the air after he drew his last breath. I envy the visible evidence of movement in the paint, in the grain of wood. I stare at the molding and wonder about the connection. Or lack of connection. I get lost for hours in my own thoughts.

An ambulance siren blares. It comes closer. He's gone already, no reason for an ambulance now. For a minute, my heart picks up as I have the thought, maybe it's coming for me.

I curl up on my bed.

Rachel comes to cuddle with me. She pushes me to respond. But I lie there. She peers into my face, I feel her doing that, but I don't open my eyes. Her fingers caress my cheek. I can't bear seeing her. Feeling her breath on my face is hard enough.

Off in the distance I hear wailing, but that has nothing to do with me. And then quiet returns. And then the lump that is Rachel is next to me, on Troy's side, trying to curl around me. Her little arm rests on me. I smell her sweet baby-oil smell. And chocolate.

And then one day I'm handed a box and told, very

softly, gently, "Here they are. His ashes." I open the lid and see some gray powder with lumps in a plastic bag. Soft as feathers. Troy?

But I don't put it down. I hold it.

And everyone is there. All these people. Allie. And Sissy. And Tara, who just hugs me and cries and says something about how she promised him she'd take care of me. Aaron and his friends. A big very black man with blue eyes.

He holds me in his big bear hug and smells of some fresh scent and says, "I've been where you are. I understand." And then he looks at me with those ink-blue eyes. I almost see heaven, and Troy in there. In those eyes. And I just look at them like I look at that glob of paint, trying to discover something.

The table is covered with food that people brought. Strawberries, cantaloupe, cherries, grapes. The colors seem gaudy. I can't imagine eating anything so lurid. Plates of yellow plastic-looking cheese and crackers. Lasagna. Pasta salad. Chicken salad. Potato salad. Lettuce salad. Tabouleh salad. Tomato and mozzarella and basil salad. All greasy, oil-slicked, and slimy.

Disgusting.

I smile, but it feels like I'm baring my teeth at the world.

I won't shake anyone's hand.

Aaron comes to me, crouches down. "Troy and me went to the Palace to see the Pistons and, because all the traffic was rerouted, we ducked through an alley taking a shortcut. In the alley, a man was beating up a woman. She lay on the ground while he kicked her in her stomach.

"Troy jumped out of the car. Together, we scared off the attacker, and then took the woman to the hospital." Aaron stands in front of me. I sit on a chair. Troy's ashes are on a shelf and I stare at them while he talks.

"Troy acted when he saw something wrong, when most would walk away." Aaron nods. "He reminded me that people can be good, unselfish."

I wonder why Troy never told me this story. Probably something else was going on. Maybe we were home after one of my miscarriages.

One of Aaron's friends sings about a sparrow. His voice is alone in the void, just him singing about God looking after a sparrow so He looks after me, too. I don't believe it, but I want him to keep making the sweet tones, lonely like a train whistle at night.

Stuart, my ex-boss, tells me how sorry he is. Terribly sorry. He says it like he's guilty, and that confuses me. "You didn't make him die by firing me," I say. "That much I know." After that, Stuart leaves.

Troy's colleagues tell me how much he loved me. Tell me what a fine lawyer he was and what a fun colleague. I hear all that.

Troy's parents stand, arms hanging limply, their only child gone.

I won't hug anyone.

I might make them sick. I might give them a horrible flesh-eating bacteria.

Most leave.

People tell me a list of ridiculous things: Time will make this easier. In a few years, my life will be as though this has never happened. The universe sent me Troy's death as a learning experience. It will make me stronger. God wanted him more than I did. God doesn't give us things we can't survive.

Some just tell me they're sorry for my loss. That's the best. But it doesn't matter much either. Sissy tells me I'm strong. I'll be okay after awhile. I want to ask, how long is awhile?

Muddled piles of discarded scraps of lettuce and chaotically arranged bright orange cheese are scattered across the table. Naked pokey-looking grape stems lie there.

Tara takes care of Rachel and Levy, tries to find a program on TV. Mom and Allie shift uncomfortably. "You know I have to go, right? In three days. I have to fly to Chicago," Mom says.

I think I nod.

"I'm worried about you. I don't want to leave you. I called Rosie."

Rosie is Mom's friend. Rosie runs her husband's legal practice and is his paralegal.

"She's pregnant and can't put in the hours to run the practice. You could share a job with her." Mom looks into my eyes to learn if she's getting through to me. "You could work there until you pass the Michigan bar."

I nod. She's bringing this up now because she doesn't want to leave me unless I'm settled. She doesn't want me to be alone with Rachel. "You think I should move back home and work with Rosie."

"It's one of your options," Allie says.

Mom looks up at Allie. "You only have Marc here, now. You just moved here a few months ago. You don't have a community here. At home you have us. And Marissa and Jennifer. Old friends."

That's not Troy's and my life. I don't have that anymore. I don't have my life anymore. We moved here from San Diego to be closer to our jobs and Mia.

"It's too complicated," I say. "I can't figure it out. What's best, that is." I realize my speech is disconnected but don't know how to make it hang together any more than I can make sense of the words people tell me, or the hideous food.

"Well, we'll pack you up. Thank God this was just a rental. You can break your lease."

"We'll drive you and your furniture back home," Tara says. "If you want, that is . . ."

I can't stand the expression of worry on Tara's face. That and her swollen lids and wet eyes.

"I'll help. I can stay and help every step of the way," Allie says.

"Allie will drive with you, in your car," Mom says.

"Smoke will drive a U-Haul with your furniture, clothes, toys, and stuff. That way you'll have all your things." Tara crouches in front of me, watching my face for an answer.

"You can put them in my basement. Until you get an apartment," Allie says.

"We're driving pretty much the same route on the rest of our tour," Aaron says.

"You and Rachel can stay with me," Mom says. "You won't be alone."

But I know that's a lie. I'm alone, now.

"At least until you get your own place."

It doesn't make any difference. I don't know if I say that in my mind or out loud.

"We can't leave you and Rachel like this. Here. Alone," Mom says.

Whatever you think is best.

"You and Rachel will be with people who love you. And you'll even have a job if you want one," Allie says.

I see her smile, how hopeful her eyes look. I notice her white teeth.

How did it get like this?

How did I get like this?

I hold the gray box on my knees and then shift it closer to my chest.

What did I do wrong?

The Metal Man

Tara

After Troy's death, everything hangs. No one knows what to do. Sky just sits, not talking. She doesn't tell us what she thinks. We suggest options, but she watches us as if our words don't make sense.

She doesn't pay much attention to Rachel, just looks at her sadly. Sissy and Mom and Aaron and I try to fill in the gaps. Levy seems to be the only one who helps, because Rachel forgets and laughs when she plays with him.

Sky stares at the window, the pattern on the carpet, Troy's ashes.

"Well, we have to get on with our tour. We have the Vegas concert in a day and then we're back on the road two days after that." I use Aaron's voice when he's being the boss and controlling the crew. "If you want to move, you have to be ready in three days."

Mom shoots me a look.

"What? That's what we have to do. People rely on me." I meet her eyes.

"What do you want?" Mom turns to Sky. "To stay here, or do you want to come home?" No one is pleading and suggesting anymore.

"Whatever you think is best." Sky stares at the box on her lap.

"Well then. We'll move you back to Ann Arbor. Back home."

And as if someone pressed a play button, we all started moving. And as I help her pack, I think about my own opportunity with King. I pay attention to myself in the spaces between caring for my sister.

The truth is, I wasn't a virgin when I met Aaron that day at Habitat for Humanity. Nope. He knew that, of course. After we got to know each other, while he was still in prison, I wrote and told him. He wasn't either. He'd done it with several girls. I hoped all that was that, over and done. I hoped after Levy was born I could feel safe. I don't know why. My mother wasn't safe after I was born. Now I know that nothing is ever over and done. The past is always the present. The past is the future. This is what happened:

I was at Blue Lake, which is a music and arts camp. My teacher suggested I apply, and so I sent in a CD, and damn if I didn't get a scholarship and get bounced up to the advanced class. When I told him, my father said, "Those lessons I got for you are paying off." But he didn't come and see me. Not any of my recitals or performances.

I was excited about being with kids who were like me.

But they weren't. They went because they wanted to go to a camp. Or because their parents pressured them so they'd be accepted into advanced band or orchestra so they could get into top-notch colleges. Or to get the kids out of their hair so they could go off to New York, or Toronto, or Paris. The girls were all perfect, with manis and pedis and long glossed hair. More like Sky than me. I concentrated on the classes and swimming in the lake.

Then I meet Horus. His name by itself would make him an outcast. He wore paint-encrusted clothes and granny glasses. Curly hair that made a messy halo. He was studying writing along with painting, and we had a composition class together where he sat isolated from the rest of us. We ambled side by side to the cafeteria for a lunch of baloney or peanut butter sandwiches and lime Jell-O. He put his head down and ate. I made patterns in green globs. One evening we ended up sitting on the edge of the lake. Turned out he was a scholarship kid, too, from Ypsilanti. He painted brightly colored, disembodied people. One painting was an arm painted in super-realism and a tree.

"This place sucks, don't you think?" he said.

We were under a small rise by the lake. The other students drifted to the cafeteria. He was painting clouds with houses nestled in them.

"I feel so fucking weird." I talked to the clouds he'd just painted. "The other girls. Well, they've got it easy. A bunch of princesses playing with music." I pulled up the hood on my sweatshirt.

"I never pay attention. Besides, it doesn't matter. I'm here to learn and we get the same benefit. Maybe our time here is more treasured." He tilted his head, a smile at the corners of his mouth as though he knew something about me I didn't.

He studied me, I licked my lower lip. "What?"

"You'd be kinda cute if you weren't so square. You need to be messed up." And then he took my hair out of its ponytail and ruffled it till it was sticking all over the place and pulled out my tucked-in shirt. "That's better."

"You think I look too nerdy, huh?"

"Not anymore." When he pushed me, my arm yielded under the motion and I rocked to the sandy grass. He leaned over and kissed me abruptly and briefly, before I could decide what to do, before I could push him away. I lay there, his dark eyes glinting at me through his glasses. And then I shut my lids, pushed my palms into the sand.

I felt him hesitating, not sure what to do next, but I wasn't going to stop him. He leaned over me, touched his mouth to mine. Tentatively. My lips parted and I tasted the texture of his tongue. He wrapped his arms around me and squeezed me to feel my flesh through our shirts, and my heart quickened.

The bell clanged. We jumped up, walked to the flag-pole. All the campers held hands around the circle and sang, *Day is done. Gone the sun*, while the flag was pulled down.

The melancholy notes hung over the grass while he squeezed my hand. My palm was sweaty.

"Hey. Let's meet later. About midnight. Over by the boats."

"Even though I'm so square?" I laughed.

There was no moon or reflected city lights; clouds obliterated the stars. I snuck out of my cabin, holding my breath, careful not to step on the squeaky board. I shut the screen door slowly so it wouldn't slam. Once I was out and down the path, I saw the open field. Empty except for the trees and the flagpole. The lake was a void, the hulls of the boats humped logs. Horus was not there. I stood beside a canoe and listened to the water swish against the shore, feeling foolish and discarded.

Then he was beside me and hugged me. "You smell like baby powder," he said.

"You don't like it?"

"Reminds me of my brothers and sisters."

I leaned away, trying to see his eyes in the dark.

"Like home, I guess."

A few hours ago we were comfortable and easy. Now, I was—he was—supposed to do something, but not sure what. This was too set up. I wasn't timid about sneaking out, but now what? I was happy to simply be with him, and then he grabbed my hand. I touched the base of my throat.

"You're so fragile, so small." He wrapped his fingers around my wrist.

I hate the fact that I'm small. It makes it easier to be overlooked, not taken seriously, like I'm a toy.

He kissed me and I pressed into him. I had to stand on my tiptoes to reach his lips. That act, my yearning displayed by standing on my toes, made me confront my own vulnerability, and realize the risk I was taking.

His arms pulled me to him, his hands slid over my back, my face, our mouths still together. My breast. I was surprised at the tingles his fingers produced. Now I take all those reactions for granted. But then it was as if I was studying myself. I didn't stop him, maybe this was why I met him, the reason I stood in the dark on my tiptoes. So he slid his fingers under my bra, my nipples hard, my breath now gasping between my teeth.

I wanted him to embrace me and comfort me, but I couldn't name the pain that needed solace. It was a kind of home I'd never felt.

"Horus?" I whispered.

"What?"

"Ohgod. Nothing." I pressed closer and slid down his

body to stand firmly on the sand, and my movement stroked him.

"You feel so good," I told him. "You, like, smell so good," but I didn't know if speaking would dissolve our mood.

"You're so sweet," he said, as though I was a child and he'd been here before and knew exactly what was coming next. He accidentally scratched me or poked me with my own bra buckle, so I unhooked it. Luckily my shorts were elastic and he slid them down to my ankles, trapping me, and I had to kick them off. He didn't take off his T-shirt.

It hurt, but not too much. I couldn't spread my legs wide enough. I figured it would be easier with a stranger. Not be so scary. But why did he move so fast? And then it was over. Was this it?

Afterward, he lay on top of me, not wanting to move. Perfect. His pounding heart felt like mine, like we only had one.

We'd both done it. I guess that was what it was about. Mom said it makes you feel closer to each other. Afterward, I guess I did feel closer to him. But closer like we had done something wrong together.

He looked down and saw the darkness of my blood. Black even in the night. "You never did this before?" he asked.

I swallowed. "Could you tell?" I held my breath. "I mean, I've fooled around, but I haven't done this."

"It makes me trust you more." He stopped and thought. "You just wanted it out of the way?"

"Something like that. This isn't your first time?"

"Nah. But it's always new. Different," he said.

I wondered, was he my boyfriend now? "So?"

"So."

"You don't like putting yourself out there?" I said.

"I thought I already did."

Then I got it. "We're gonna have a good next week," I said.

He laughed as though he'd established power, but I wasn't sure exactly what he'd won. I thought, *Oh my God. I'm in that club with all my girl friends. I'm not a stupid virgin anymore.*

The next time, he took his time. My motions were almost as vigorous as his and afterward, he held me close. I realized something and tried to put it into words, but I didn't have them then, or now. Something about what drives us, but not just us, the circling of the earth in the sky. The mighty force of sex and the subsequent vulnerability of love. I had the world before me. And the risk of tragedy.

"I'll score some rubbers. I didn't anticipate this."

We're safe. I'm about to get my period, I thought. *We'll be together for the week*, I thought. *And who knows? Ypsilanti isn't that far away.*

He laughed and kissed my chin. Then my eyes.

*

At breakfast, the next morning, Horus sat with one of the perfect girls. He leaned forward and said something, and she laughed. He didn't see me, or didn't acknowledge me. I don't know which.

That afternoon, I saw him strolling toward the office in his painted jeans. His head was down and he seemed preoccupied. The canvas with the clouds was under his arm, a duffle bag in the other hand.

I thought of calling out to him and at least saying hi, but watched him walk away.

That night, I heard he went home. I wondered if he was caught sneaking out and was expelled. I concentrated on my sloppy joe. Later, I heard there was an accident in his family and that was why he left.

He never told me his last name. And I never told him mine.

My period came the next week. I was okay. But I knew then that men were risky. What was he but a cute dude who had sex with me, and the next morning was with another girl. Just like my father. And then gone forever. Like Sky's father. I focused on my music. I was awarded the solo piano performance in the final concert.

And I learned that if I held myself back, it made them want me more. So I learned to move fast and leave them quickly.

That was the summer before I met Aaron. And when I met Aaron, he was in kiddie prison, he was safe. He wrote me lyrics, letters detailing how he wanted to take me to the zoo and the park, and take a canoe down the river. How he wanted to kiss me, undress me. All that. But he was where he couldn't cheat on me. It was a relief not to have sex and stir up vulnerability or face the possibility of actually gaining love and losing aloneness. "You're a wimpy choice," I told him before we started heating up.

He was amazed that a white chick from Ann Arbor would find a black kid in prison the cowardly choice.

"I, like, don't have to worry about you cheating. I don't have to worry if we'll really work out. I fault myself for being such a chicken," I wrote him in one of my letters.

"I'm not exactly in my comfort zone, either. I never thought this would happen to me. Feeling connected with someone from a different world, as though we were one soul in another life somewhere, sometime. Feeling exposed. I'm not like this with other people. Only you. You could hurt me. You could actually devastate me."

I didn't know what I was going to do next. I wrote him: "Don't expect me to just stay home playing my keyboard all the time. I'm going to be hanging out with my friends."

He wrote back: "You do what you can. I'll do what I gotta do. But don't want to hear about you with no other man."

I have to remember that. He was safe for me. I was

never safe for him. And it was never about sex. Not really. Not ever. That just brought us even closer. And with him, it was as though we always knew each other's body and we were home at last. At last.

He asked me to marry him when I told him I was pregnant. Me seventeen and not yet graduated from high school.

"Don't want to mess our good thing up with expectations," I said.

"You want to be my baby-mama, or you want to be my wife?"

"I want to be my own baby-mama." Didn't want to rely on anyone or assume anything was permanent.

I think about this while I box up clothes for my sister, and drive to Vegas with Levy sound asleep in the back. I have to remember who Aaron is, really is with me, because at the Vegas show, my dressing room is filled with six dozen orange roses. Each with a different card: *Have a gr8 concert. Thinking about U. My unpredictable 1. I'm ready, r u? Looking 4ward to our music. U got the swag. What's next?* King doesn't sign his name to any of them. He knows I'll know they're from him.

Aaron narrows his eyes when he sees the flowers. "What you tell him?"

"You know, like, I told you."

Levy runs and grabs me around the legs. "Mommy. Mommy." I pick him up and squeeze him to me, inhaling his scent. "Butterfly!" and he flutters his long lashes on my cheek, tickling me. I wind his soft curls around my fingers.

Aaron shakes his head, "What's going on?" His hand sweeps around my dressing room, and then points to me, to Levy, to himself. "You going to risk all this?"

"I haven't done a thing." I stand there, Levy on my hip, my fingers buried in his hair, my legs planted strong, meeting Aaron's glare. "Don't be paranoid."

After the concert, in all the Vegas hubbub and buzz, Aaron talks in the corner with one of the babes hunting for some action. He stands inches from her, and she slides her fingers into his front pocket. Yep. She sure does. My neck pounds in fury. His back is to me as he leans into her.

And then there's King. Right there again with his army of fit dudes.

King revolutionized hip-hop, embraced gangsta rap, and caught the wave into crossover, owning himself and his own record label, bringing on new talent and developing them. He created his own clothing label, too, *King Kloz*. Baggy clothes for men, and skin-tight half-there clothes for women.

He asks if I got his flowers and what's on my mind.

There's so much going on I can't begin to sort it all out. I could escape everything . . . Troy's death, Sky's sadness, rushing back to Venice Beach after each concert to help Sky pack while she just sits staring into space with Troy's ashes on her lap. And now this tug-of-war between Aaron and me.

Before I went off to try to help Sky, Aaron held me close. We were in our bus and he threw the pencil he was using to write lyrics down on the desk, so happy to see me. "Hey, babe. Is it working like you want?"

"I don't know what Sky's going to decide," I said into his neck.

"I didn't mean her. I meant us. This. Our crew. Our family. Us."

"It's better than I thought it would be." I snuggled close to him and then told him the rest: "That's the truth. But it's a taste of how amazing it could be. How far we could go."

"We'll get there," he promised.

I got very quiet and he could feel me stiffen.

"I'm not going anywhere, babe," he said. "Unless you push me away."

How did he get so wonderful, so mature? Or was it all some game?

Now, standing there with King in front of me and some woman hitting on my man, I think about how I could escape all this and simply focus on stardom.

Just then, the woman with Aaron points at King. Aaron turns around and our eyes meet. He only sees the piece of me that isn't hidden behind King's large body. But when our eyes meet, I recognize sorrow in his, a sickening look that lingers. He told me once I was his angel. A miracle. I helped him believe in his own dreams, the strength of our team.

I look up at King and say, "Look, dude. My brother just died. I'm ... well ... I'm at sea." I glance at Aaron and he leans toward the woman. He's shifted so I can only see his back, but I know he's close enough to smell her, to feel warmth from her body.

Something has been stirred up by Troy's death. Even if everything is fine with Aaron, I have a more vivid fear of being left, being alone again. There's a greater sense of my own vulnerability and my importance to Levy. King's attention hints at a way to solve some of that and have complete freedom. He might be right. I may need to prepare to take care of myself and Levy.

King tilts his head and shrugs, under a matte black jersey jacket with a stand-up collar, his own label. "You're young, just starting. Don't you want to see where you could go? Beyond being part of a crew?" He waits for me to say something, but I don't. "You could be mega like Beyoncé, or have Madonna power and solo stardom. Go places you haven't even dreamed. You just need to be developed, directed. I see it." He points to his eye. "And you need it." He points to me.

"What do you get?"

"A cut. I'm a businessman." He raises his eyebrows. "And some fun." He strings out the word so I can make the fun be anything I want.

I don't want to slam doors. I meet his eyes and turn my voice as intimate as I can backstage with the crew watching. "I have a sister to take care of, and my family is ...

well . . . counting on me. I need time. Can you back off while I sort things out?"

He slides his palm so that his fingers touch mine and his electricity courses through my arm. He nods. "You have my number. But just like you're unpredictable, I'm impatient."

"A month. Can you give me that? I need to finish up this tour, get my sister and her daughter back home. Sort things out." I nod to the entire crew. "Then I'll call you."

Smoke watches.

T-Bone is watching, too.

Red Dog's eyes shift from me to Aaron.

I've disrespected Aaron in front of his crew. I inhale and roll my shoulders back. No, maybe they'll respect me more as an artist rather than the baby-mama tag-along that Aaron stuffed down their throats.

But not with King holding my hand and making it look like it's about sex. Not with his melty dark eyes looking at me. Not with his lips, full and dotted with freckles. He licks the lower one and purses them together, a gesture that Troy used to make.

I drop King's hand and step back.

That night, I say to Aaron, "You gonna be a prick? Going to flirt and carry on with some other woman and make all this worse? I can always get another cheating son-of-a-bitch." I don't want a bad boy. I want a good man, one who loves me, who's honest with me, but that's the scariest thing of all. In a way, a jerk is a chicken choice. It doesn't carry the risk of hope.

"Looks like you already got one next in line." My back is to him, I'm about to crawl into bed, but then he turns me to face him. "I'm here, aren't I?"

"He wants to make me a star."

"I want us both to be stars." He spits the words out.

"I, like, told him to back off. I'm here, too." I thought Aaron was that all-the-time loving, forever man. Sky thought that about Troy too, and he died. They die or they leave: either way you can't rely on them. I think again about Sky's and my conversation on Magic Mountain.

"He better watch himself. He's stepping on my toes."

"I'm not *your* territory. He's helping me be me." I point to my chest. "It's a business proposition."

I know Aaron worries that we won't become what we've dreamed, that I won't be by his side. I'm vital to it all. Integral to his dream. He considers me almost as he considers himself. I wonder if it's in the width of that *almost* that it all falls apart. As we stand there facing each other these thoughts flash, and I know I'm at a pivotal moment. For the first time, we are really tested.

"Not that I trust you after what I saw tonight, anyway." With a father like mine, how could I trust any man? But I'm not going to throw us away. I want to see where this new place leads. And so I say, "I love you." I don't say it casually like we do every morning and every night. Like we say it instead of hello and goodbye. I say it slow and deliberate. I reach my hand up to touch his cheek. And say it again. "I love you."

He wraps me in his arms and holds me tight to eradicate the flesh that separates us.

The next day, I return to L.A. to help Sky pack. Allie is off visiting a friend. I start on Rachel's toys. Levy is with us. The two children pick up toys and drop them in the box. "You want this one?" I ask about a Sesame Street toy that doesn't pop up anymore. Rachel nods, Levy throws it in the box. I try to make it fun, talking in the voices of the stuffed animals. The kids get into my game, and pretty soon the plastic toys tell us, "Bye bye, I'll see you in Ann Arbor." Levy sings about each plastic ring, "I'm a ring wanting a bigger ring. Here it is. Here it is." And then drops the complete tower of rings in the carton. I label each box; Levy scribbles pictures on the cardboard.

"Will Daddy be there? In Ann Arbor?" Rachel looks at me, crouched among the few toys that are still unpacked.

"No. Daddy's gone." I say it as softly as I can. "Except for your memories."

"I want my daddy." Rachel's lower lip trembles.

I don't know what to say, so I just continue packing. And then I say, "Me, too. I miss him, too." And Rachel comes to me and pats my shoulder. And we hug each other. Levy joins in.

Downstairs, Mom packs up the kitchen while Sky slowly wraps the plates in paper. I swear it takes her ten minutes for each plate. She stares into space. Lost in her thoughts, distracted by visions.

I make myself coffee.

"I can't figure it out."

I know she's not talking about her plates. Sky has been making statements like this for days.

Sky examines her hands, turning them back and forth. "I brought it home from my visit with Mia." She then nods. "I didn't mean to." Her voice breaks up and she starts crying again.

"No." Mom puts her hand on Sky's shoulder. "It was that medication that weakened his immune system. It was an extraordinary, one-in-a-million reaction. That's what the doctor said."

"Why look for a cause, a reason? It's just bad luck. Really terrible, sad, tragic bad luck." I finish wrapping the plate Sky began.

Tears dribble down her cheeks. "It can't be just fucking luck." She chokes on the word. "It's unfair. There has to be a reason. I hate every living man just for being alive."

Mom stacks the plates in a box. "I guess you should have agreed to that autopsy. Then we might know more."

"Another of my mistakes," Sky says, bitterly.

I smear peanut butter on whole-wheat bread and then cover it with raspberry jam Mom made last summer. The peanut butter is homemade from honey-roasted peanuts and the jam is flavored with almond Torani syrup and extract. It's the best peanut butter and jelly in the world. I carry sandwich halves to the children and leave a plate of them on the kitchen counter for us to eat as we work. No one but me touches them. Sky has forgotten about food.

"Am I being punished?"

"For what?" Mom says.

I know sins are secret, sometimes just thoughts or wishes. "Wouldn't it be great if all the evildoers got punished and the rest of us, who try to be good and fair and just, only reaped rewards?" I nestle a plate on top of another.

"*You* just get good things. Success. Money. A man who is still alive." She says this with more energy than I've seen since Troy's death. "*You* get it all, regardless of how much fear and turmoil you've created."

I bite my sandwich and wrap another plate, ignoring her anger. I'm not going to fight with her. Not now. My heart goes out to her.

But she won't stop. "You were such a bitch."

"That was years ago. I was a teenager."

Her fist pounds the kitchen counter. "You get away unscathed. Unpunished." Her eyes are narrowed.

I bite my lower lip and consider what to say. Any other time, we'd be at it. I'd say, "*You're* jealous of *me*? Well, it's a turn of the screw because I envied you my entire childhood, followed you around, was pushed away like the ugly duckling, the pesky, nerdy, annoying little sister. And you were mean and resentful." That's what I would have said. Any other time. I'm surprised she envies me. And I guess a part of me is glad. But I can't fight with a sister whose husband died a week ago. So instead I say, "It wasn't just luck. I worked hard for my success. You know that." I struggle to maintain an even tone. "I just haven't felt the need to make everything nicey-nicey." I hunt for the proper words, grab more air, and measure my voice: "I haven't conformed to everybody else's ideas of how *I should* live. And I'm sorry you've had so much tragedy and I've had better luck. And maybe I'm the one that *deserves* the tragedies because I was such a terrible teenager." I stop. I'm not going to justify my decisions and my actions to her. Not now. "But you've had it all, Sky. And you and Troy made a wonderful life for each other and together. You have an incredibly sweet and beautiful daughter." I don't know if reminding her how good it was is the right thing to do.

"Why me? Why am I being punished?"

Sky thinks I was, or am, a bad daughter. But maybe Mom was wrong for not accepting me. She never paid attention. For me, it just was the way it was from the beginning. "Each of us did what we had to do. And it is what it is now."

"Please, girls!" Mom warns in the voice she used when we were children.

*

Later, Mom and I finish up the kitchen, wrapping glasses. Rachel and Levy watch *Yo Gabba Gabba*. Sky stares at the TV.

Mom says, "When you were a baby, I rocked you to sleep and you sang a song. A two-note song. 'Ah oh ah oh ah oh,' you sang over and over." Mom's voice imitates my infant tones. She stuffs paper into the bowl of a glass and nestles it beside the others in the box. "You were just a newborn, a tiny thing, but you sang that little song. When I put you in your crib, you continued, 'Ah oh ah oh ah oh.' You sang yourself to sleep." She gazed off in the distance as though my tune conjured up a newborn me. And then she turned to me. "You did that for years. The music comforted you. I didn't. It was always the music."

I don't know what to make of this. I don't know why she told me this then. As though I had my music, and I didn't need her? Is she jealous of my music? Is she telling me how unneeded she felt as my mother? I busy myself encasing a wine goblet. There was too much going on with my father for her to be happy with me. I had to learn to comfort myself. Thank God I could make my own music.

I was lonely even then, even as a little baby. We don't exist without each other. What are we but animals with language? And what is the point of language if it isn't part of a connection with someone else?

The Metal Man

Sky

I'm in the car with Allie, driving from Los Angeles. I don't know if this is the best thing, going back to Ann Arbor. I was happy here, in San Diego and L.A. But I can't seem to make a decision and there's no point in sitting in that rental without a job, or friends.

I'm without a plan. A goal. I don't know what I want or what I should do. My life has been ripped out from under me. I don't recognize it anymore. Or me. Not without Troy.

I used to know where I was going and why. I wanted Troy, I wanted to be a lawyer, and then I wanted a baby. I got all that. And lost two out of three. Well, I still have my degree and can pass the bar in Michigan.

I won't be alone.

I'll have Mom and all her friends. Tara, for whatever she is worth, is close by. Jennifer and Marissa are both there.

But Mom might try to take over.

No. I just have to draw lines.

In Venice, at least I was with Troy.

And I feel like I'm leaving him.

Our life together seems a long time ago.

And just a minute ago.

Rachel is in the backseat. When I turn to look at her, Maddie is on her lap and the dress-me monkey and turtle face her, spread out on the seat. Maddie acts as a teacher, telling them they have to be good. Can't mess up their toys. Must pee-pee and poo-poo in the potty. Rachel has been so good with her toilet training. I haven't paid enough attention. I need to give her more praise and support.

As we drive away, a woman stands on the side of the road. At first I assume she's hitchhiking, or begging for money. When we get closer, I notice that she's a middle-aged woman, dressed in a creased pair of pants and a tucked-in printed blouse, her short hair neatly coiffed. She holds a poster that says, *You must have self-respect to earn respect*.

And then we're out of the city on I-40 and a sign says it's 2550 miles to Wilmington, Delaware. The other side of the country. From the Pacific to the Atlantic. There are messes of tangled dusty shrubs beside the highway.

Maddie says, "*I know you don't like it, but it'll be okay.*"

Turtle answers in a squeaky voice, "*No it's not! No it's not! No it's not!*" Behind them, out the rearview window, I see our U-Haul and, when we round a bend, I see the bus with Tara, and Special Intent, and Red Dog, and T-Bone and Thumble inside. What peculiar names, like characters from a make-believe world as bizarre as whatever goes on in Rachel's mind that allows Turtle and Maddie to talk.

I think all this while staring out the window at the curving, looping road, still hazy from L.A., the landscape strung with rusty power lines.

I'm glad Tara's on the bus. At first we thought we women and the children would ride together, but Tara wanted to stay with Aaron. Maybe later we'll switch up. But right now I'm glad it's only Rachel and Allie in my black Honda Accord. It has only 50,000 miles on it and was tuned up a month ago. It should be able to make the trip without a problem.

"How ya doing?" Allie asks. Usually I like to talk with her, but I glance at the mirrors, making sure my furniture and clothes are still behind me.

"I don't know." I look out the passenger window.

"It'll get better."

"That's what everyone says." Troy's box is on my lap. I place my palms on either side of it.

Even Allie, who usually has words of wisdom and advice, doesn't know what to say to that. So she watches the yellow line. It's flat desert. Rectangular bundles of hay stacked on top of each other and covered with blue tarp, just in case it rains. But it doesn't look like it rains much.

I'm reassured by the sight of the U-Haul in the side mirror. As though the truck with its burden of sofa, TV, books, desktop, clothes, toys, high chair, mattress, dining table, and crib are Troy. Maybe Troy's DNA, minute bits of him, are scattered in the mattress, on the sofa. Mixed with mine. A nail clipping maybe. I picked up his brush, woven with his hairs, from the bathroom counter. It smells like him. Then I saw him standing in front of the mirror, trying to slick down his cowlick and complaining about going bald. He existed only in my seeing, and immediately faded away. And I was left holding his brush. I tried putting it in the box with his ashes, but it didn't fit.

Allie extols the scenery. It looks bleak to me. Southern California in the winter, without a hope for the wipe-away cleanliness of snow.

I glance back again to make sure the U-Haul is still there.

"Everything is safe. All your things are okay. Smoke seems like a conscientious driver," Allie reassures me.

Smoke's driving is comforting. I stare out the window. I don't know how long, how many miles. I just stare.

My cell phone rings. It's Mom asking me how I am. The worry in her voice exhausts me. She's at the conference. She doesn't like being away from me.

"Allie, Rachel, and I are driving." That's all I say. And then Mom makes a loud kissing sound.

Allie and Rachel invent a story. I half listen as they take turns narrating. Rachel's characters vanish. One to Chicago. One to a hospital. Allie invents new ones.

When my iPhone rings again, I jerk.

"Hey, you see the signs for the amusement park?" Tara sounds enthusiastic and excited, as though we're simply on a road trip. "It's just ahead. We thought we'd stop. Stretch our legs. Let Levy and Rachel go on some kiddie rides. We need something to eat. Something besides my trail mix and apples. What do you think?"

"I'm not hungry." She's such a child. An amusement park at a time like this.

"Oh." Tara's voice deflates. "Let me speak to Allie."

Allie nods and then says, "Okay. I could use a break, too."

"I have to pee-pee," Rachel says. "So does Maddie."

"Well, we'll stop then."

We come to a stone wall. East is directly ahead, and sun blares through the windshield. We drive down a skimpy road. The amusement park is empty.

We enter a different world, a perfectly groomed forest. Trees shade the ground; their branches exit trunks at exactly the same parallel distance from the earth. Nothing grows underneath them. The trees are stiff and the breeze dead as though it's not a forest, but a stage set from

Disneyland. Our shushing car wheels on the blacktop make the only sound.

Allie pulls to a parking space, where weeds have grown through cracks in the split tar. The U-Haul and bus pull beside us and stop.

I look around. "Everybody is gone."

Rachel tugs my hand. "Maybe they're over there." She points, and then Rachel and Levy run down the road.

Aaron, Red Dog, and Smoke go with them. I watch as the adult figures obliterate my daughter. I shift and see her arms flap as she runs, her hair flying in the wind she makes.

Tara looks at me and frowns. "You okay?"

"Yeah." I walk down the road, examining my toes moving in my flip-flops and listening to their slap with each step. My chipped red toenail polish seems so garish. So unkempt, as though a harbinger of the evils of sloppiness.

We enter a clearing, a cluster of low, modern buildings in front of a lake mirroring the sky. The lake's edges are perfectly curved and outlined in red brick; the contour forms soft bays and inlets. On the far side is a Ferris wheel, tilt-a-whirl, and carousel, all as immobile as the trees. A concession stand waits to serve hamburgers and pizza and Dairy Queen.

The rides remain motionless; as though expecting a flip of a switch or a wind to start red, blue, and yellow spinning, whirling.

We're the only people.

Taller than any of the buildings, maybe three stories high, is a metal statue of a man. One foot is planted on a pyramid that is at least five feet high. His bearded chin juts over a clenched fist; his other hand rests on his hip, fingers spread. He's formed from metal rectangles, small ones for his fingers and chin, large ones for his chest. His expression is confident, bordering on angry, as though he's determined to rule.

He must be the king of angels because a circle of them, each shielding a small garden, surround him. They're almost as tall as I am and armored with stiff wings, breasts of metal cones. Warriors? Avengers? Amazons? I envy them for their rigid autonomy. Everything soft and flexible has been hardened.

Rachel and Levy run between the angels, looking up at their unsmiling faces, poking at them, and then skipping to the next one. Rachel comes to me. "What's this?"

I shake my head.

The lake glitters silver to the sky. I examine the steel man. He's a monument to something. Maybe the artist who made him.

The men wander closer to the Ferris wheel. Maybe they can make it spin. A merry-go-round of tigers and elephants, alligators and zebras, and gigantic robins and dogs is off in the distance. The animals still have most of their vivid hues, but the paint is chipped in random splotches so they all appear spotted.

I stretch out on the ground, beside the lake. The grass is brittle and sharp. I cross one ankle on a knee; one hand cradles my head, the other rests on my chest. Rachel runs back to me, lies beside me, and cuddles into me, resting her head on my shoulder.

Rachel's eyes close and her body molds into mine, yearning for whatever I can give.

The sun must be over our heads now but under the clouds.

"This is scary," Rachel says.

"Yes." Tears wet my cheeks. The giant man reminds me of how far away and absolutely gone Troy is.

A huge bird pecks at the dirt and feathers the air with long eyelashes, steps delicately over a tuft of grass like a ballerina. It cranes its neck at us, blinks when it notices something strange in the flowerless forest. Daintily placing its feet on the earth, it undulates its long neck as it stretches past us.

It seems as out of place here as everything else.

"Look at the ostrich," Tara points. "What's it doing here?"

We watch it tiptoe around, flexing its neck and fluttering its lashes.

Rachel closes her eyes. The steel man watches over us. Unbelievably, she falls asleep. Just like that. Like she needed my arms to relax. We lie there while everybody else strolls around the lake. I listen to her breath.

She jerks awake beside me and wails.

"Honey?"

"I had a bad dream." She rubs her fists in her eyes. "We ate dinner. Daddy sat in his chair. He said, 'Oooh, sweetie. I'm so proud of you.' We ate macaroni."

I rub circles on her back. "That sounds happy."

"It isn't true." She screams out the word *true*. "Now Daddy's gone."

I didn't know how nice they were till they were gone. Simple family dinners.

The ostrich picks its path between the stiff angels, jerking with each sound. An angel holds her palm up as if waiting for a present. The angel's metal wings curl dangerously.

"Was I bad, Mommy?"

She asks the question I ask myself. After our baby was born dead, Troy brought me ice, fed me slivers of it. Smoothed my brow. Cried with me. When he left, and then Mom, I lay in the room by myself. I heard babies crying in the rooms next to me. Saw them in their cribs as they were pushed to their moms' rooms. My breasts hurt. *I'll give anything, do anything to have a healthy baby. That's all I want. A healthy baby. I'll give up everything else. Just give me this.* I squeezed out tears and begged. Prayed.

The sound of all those babies' voices made me remember Tara screaming bloody murder in her crib. She was angrier and more desperate than the infants being wheeled as fast as can be to their moms. The year before, when I was in third grade, the girls in my class voted my mom the prettiest mother.

And then came Tara. As I lay sore from an episiotomy without a baby to ease the pain, my eyelids swollen from tears, one night came back to me. I came home from school just before Mom arrived with Tara, about two months old. Back then, Mom was manager of a cell phone store, Verizon I think. She gave me a one-armed hug, unbuttoned her blouse, opened the flap on her bra, and began feeding Tara.

I looked away. Mom's face was puffy, her arms thick and flabby, and she still had a pouch where Tara had been. No one would vote her the prettiest mom anymore. She smiled at me. "Tell me about your day, sweetie."

Turning away, I grabbed a can of soda and popped the lid.

"How was school?"

I drank the soda.

"Would you get me a can, too?"

I handed her a cold can, and she shrugged. She couldn't open it because she was holding Tara. I opened it for her. And then sat down, shifting my chair so I couldn't witness Tara's hungry mouth gobbling her up, her little fingers splayed out on Mom's chest. Mom smiled and tilted her head back. "Aaaah." Her voice was relaxed and at peace, as though she'd been waiting for this union.

In the old days, we'd snuggle on the couch after school and talk. Or play a game.

"Do you have any homework?"

She asked me habitual questions and I answered them mechanically. Yes. No. Whatever. Some math, but I'll do it after dinner.

"You need me to quiz you on your spelling words? Don't you have a test tomorrow?"

"Sure."

We made dinner while Tara rocked in a swing, watching us with a finger in her mouth until she dozed off.

I set the table. Mom looked at her watch. "Wonder where he is. He knows I have to go back to work to close up."

I knew already. Kids haven't learned to hide unpleasant truths from themselves. Stephen never did what he was supposed to other than his job. And that seemed to be mostly conning people into buying stuff they probably didn't really need. Even as a child I saw that.

She called Stephen's cell phone, but no answer. She called his work, but no answer. So this night, this night I'm remembering while I'm lying here alone in a maternity ward with a dead baby taken away, Mom had to leave me at home.

"I'm going to have to go. Stephen should be home at any minute."

I rolled my eyes, and she pretended she didn't notice.

She asked, "You know how to warm the milk up, right? There's a bottle all ready in the fridge." She opened the door and showed me four bottles.

"You'll be okay, won't you?" There were dark blue circles under her eyes. I noticed the dark roots where her streaked hair had grown out.

"Sure."

"I'm right around the corner. You know the number, right?"

I nodded.

She grabbed a tube of lipstick and smeared it on without a mirror. "Is it okay?"

"Yep," I lied. It was above one lip slightly, so she appeared lopsided.

"You'll be okay, I'll be home as soon as I can."

"Yep," I lied again.

"If you need me, call."

So she left.

Tara slept, her head falling to her shoulder like her neck was broken. Her index finger was wet from her mouth. I brought my face close to hers looking for Mom, but I just saw Stephen in her brows, her defined cupid's bow, and her widow's peak. A heart-shaped face, they call it.

I turned the TV on to watch *The Cosby Show* and wrapped myself up in an afghan that Mom knitted, the one we used to snuggle with, and curled it around my knees and sucked on some hard candy.

And then, just near the end of the show, Tara started screaming. She didn't wake up gently, but furiously.

Maybe she had a bad dream.

Anyway, I grabbed the bottle and ran it under hot water.

Her shrieks intensified.

The water wasn't warm yet.

I touched the plastic bag of milk and it was still cold.

Tara hardly gave herself time for air, she was so angry. Not soft and loving like she was with Mom.

And then the water became hot, and sure enough the bag was warm. I tested it the way Mom showed me on my wrist and it didn't feel cold or hot, so I guessed it was okay. I unbuckled the strap around Tara, her little arms hitting my face.

"Stop that."

But she just kept bawling as I pulled her from her swing and settled her on my lap.

I put the nipple in her mouth, but she was so busy howling she didn't even know I was giving her what she wanted.

I guess that's still true of her. She doesn't yet realize she's getting what she wants—she's too busy looking to make sure it's there.

I squirted milk in, our mother's milk, and she felt it, and clamped her lips around the nipple.

Quiet. After awhile she made a little humming noise in between sucks.

The Cosby Show was over. I'd missed Dr. Huxtable's lesson.

I looked down at Tara, her eyes closed again, her sucking slowed. Her arm was now flung away from herself. She wore a soft pink–and–white fleece one-piece. She nestled close to me and it felt good. Yes. For that one second, I didn't mind the awfulness of feeding my half sister my mother's milk.

Then the door slammed. Stephen was home. Tara started howling again.

"What are you doing to her?" he demanded, his thick eyebrows twitching.

"Nothing. I was just feeding her."

He grabbed her from me.

"Well, do it right," he ordered. He looked in her face, snatched the bottle from me and stuck it in her mouth. "Stop it, baby," he demanded.

She started nursing and he said, "Okay, then."

He smelled funny. I didn't know the smell. I'd never smelled it before, I don't think.

And he handed Tara to me and left.

I put Tara in her crib.

And went in my room, to read *The Babysitter Club*. I read how Kristie eventually accepted her mom's second husband, but I knew that wouldn't happen with Stephen. I had tried, but he bossed me around. "Don't put your feet on the sofa." "I can hear that Walkman from here. You'll be deaf by the time you're thirty." "My God,

Marnie, are you letting her out like that? In that skimpy T-shirt and shorts?"

Was there anything good about him? He was good-looking. He read a lot and had a lot of knowledge but thought he knew everything. He taught me chess and proceeded to beat the pants off me every game. "Not going to let you win. That doesn't teach you anything," he said and raised one dark eyebrow. Even the good things about him had a bad side.

I was falling asleep, and Stephen was in the shower, when Mom got home and ran up the stairs. "I know where you were!" she yelled. "You can't do it. I'll still smell her on you."

Their bedroom door slammed.

"You aren't you anymore," he told Mom, his voice loud, but even.

A few minutes later, the front door slammed and I could hear Mom sobbing.

Yes, I thought. *Get rid of him. Let's go back to how it was.* Back in the days when Mom hugged me as soon as she saw me, kneeled down and picked me up and swung me in a circle. *How's my beautiful Sky? How's the sweetest little girl?* She tickled my tummy until we both laughed tears. When one of my drawings was posted on the school's bulletin board, we celebrated by walking to the Dairy Queen for sundaes.

I hear her tiptoe into my room and feel her look at me. I pretend to be asleep. Maybe she'll kiss me. Maybe she'll snuggle with me.

But then, Tara woke screaming, and I knew it would never be like it was.

My life was over.

This was what I thought about the night my baby was born dead.

Then Troy returned with a huge bouquet of tulips and daffodils, *Joy* perfume, and Cherry Garcia ice cream.

"We'll just keep doing this, Sky. We'll play the statistics and eventually we'll hit the wonderful fifty percent." He kissed my forehead and placed his head on my pillow.

I may have thought my life was over, but then I found it again in Troy.

"I promise. We'll have our baby," he said. And we did. Rachel.

He was so good to me.

This was what I thought about in a dead amusement park, lying under a tree with mean angels surrounding me.

I know it will never be like it was and I feel sorry for the little girl Sky. And I feel sorry for the adult Sky. And I feel sorry for Rachel. It will never be like it was.

"Was I bad, Mommy?" Rachel asks again, bringing me back.

"No, sweetie," I muster.

"Did Dad do something?" Rachel continues, insisting on a reason.

What did we do? Come to California. Know Mia. Want a baby. Play basketball. Get a sore throat. That's all, I think to myself. I loved him. I dared to love him and he died. "Your father was a good man. Illnesses aren't punishments. Some things happen without a reason." But I'm not sure I believe that. "Or we don't know the reason."

She shakes her head as though it's useless. Such an adult gesture for such a small child.

The ostrich flicks a foot at me and a butterfly lands on his head.

Then Allie and Tara and the rap crew return. "None of the rides work. There're no open bathrooms there, either. We went in the bushes."

"No food. No bathrooms. No rides."

"Hey. This place is a trip. It's crazy. Like an abandoned Hollywood set," Aaron laughs. He always looks at the bright side.

"That's what it is. Somebody else's dream gone mad."

They laugh, slap each other's hands, and bounce with energy. "We're wandering around in someone else's dream. I wonder who he is," Aaron says.

"I'll bet you'll write a song about it," Tara says.

We get back in the car and I say to Allie, "That place is as crazy as I feel." It's probably the most lucid statement I've made in over a week.

"You're struggling to make sense out of what's

happened." Allie turns the key in the ignition and the car hums. "I remember when my dad died. He was forty-four and I was nineteen when he dropped dead of a heart attack. For six months after that, I wandered around saying 'Life is meaningless.'" She shakes her head. "I couldn't figure out why he died right in the middle. I couldn't *conceive* of someone not being able to finish his own story, his own life."

"I didn't know your dad died young, too."

Both of her hands are on the wheel and she turns her head to back out of the parking space. Her features are very relaxed; she's not smiling, or frowning.

"Not as young as yours. Or Rachel's. People survive these sudden losses. When you hear their stories, you're amazed at their resilience and fighting spirit."

"You think Mom's recovered?"

Now we're behind the U-Haul and bus. I like it better that way. I can see them.

Allie watches the road. She presses her lips together, considering what to say. "What do you think?"

"Oh. One of those therapist answers."

She laughs, but waits for my reply.

"Mom doesn't cry about Dad anymore. But . . . I don't know. I don't think Stephen helped. Mom accidentally landed herself in a hurricane." It's peculiar trying to see it from Mom's viewpoint instead of mine.

We're both quiet as we watch the landscape.

Then Allie continues, "A lot of people are like that.

They can't bear to be alone and think someone else will make the pain go away."

Mom and I shared our lives then and now. Unbelievably, way beyond the statistical probability, we're faced with the same tragedy as adults. Over and over. In a bunch of different configurations, the same rare, random, awful event.

I watch the U-Haul shift and sway. The three vehicles in our little caravan. And then we start seeing signs for the south rim of the Grand Canyon. White cattle wander on the plains under folded mountains.

A while after that, I don't know how long, Allie says, "But your mom is alright. More than alright. And I think she's finally found her man in Jim."

"It's taken her almost twenty years."

"It doesn't have to take that long, but mourning a major death takes an average of twenty-seven years. Imagine that. Luckily, you get to live your life while you're doing it."

I'm not talking anymore, just watching the red earth and the crumbled dusty trees. I don't know where she gets all these statistics. *Psychology Today*, maybe. Someone told me that 43 percent of statistics are lies. I guess that's a joke. But maybe not.

"But we have to mourn," Allie says.

Now, I want her to stop talking, so I don't answer.

CHAPTER SIX

All Through the Night

Tara

I tuck Levy into bed that night, just as I always do. I read "Hiawatha" and sing "All Through the Night," except I make up the words.

And then he starts his little song. We sing the notes together. It isn't the same one that I sang, that I didn't even know I sang until Mom told me the other day. It isn't *ah oh ah oh*. It's *la de la de*. So he starts his comfort music and I sing with him. Together we chant *la de la de* and, just before he nods off, I place him in his bed and gently kiss him on his forehead so his silky curls tickle my cheek. I stand beside him, my hand on his back; his chest radiates the warmth of him while his voice dims, my voice whispering until we both stop.

I don't tell Mom any of this. None of us can help who we are, and maybe it's enough that she noticed and remembered. Levy and I both find solace in our love of music. Mom had that easy connection with Sky. So much depends on the luck of how the genes sort out. And what happens to your parents along the way. I mean, it's not about you. You don't make your childhood. Life is full of all kinds of surprises.

I learned that from Sky, from the sudden switch in all our lives when Troy died. I don't totally believe he's gone, and want to call him like I did sometimes when he was at work because it was always easier to talk to him than Sky. In fact, he made my relationship with Sky smoother. But now I wonder what will happen between us. She attacked me in her condo when I was helping her. I swallowed my pride though, bowing to her circumstances. Was she angry that I was, for once, in a position to help her? I can't tell if her mourning has crossed over into self-pity.

No good deed goes unpunished, I think, listening to Levy's breathing rhythm.

That night, Aaron enters me and together we are sweet and slow. From the beginning, there's an extra intensity created by the threat of King, and by Aaron's flirtation. We stare into each other's eyes the entire time, watching fleeting expressions flash across our faces. The light is dim, so I only see the gleam from his eyes as they shine at me, and the triangle of his nose. We surge together until I get the sense that we can move forever, that once again we've tapped into the stirring of the universe.

He says, before we finish, "I always thought sex was just sex. But it's ... I don't know the word ... spiritual, mystical. As though we're meditating together."

"You said what I feel," I tell him.

"We're so right for each other, it's spooky," he whispers, his voice rumbling under my cheek.

My head nestles on his shoulder, his arm is around me, and then he falls asleep. He looks so handsome, his face open to his dreams. Nothing this good lasts, but I've thought that before and it keeps getting better.

Just before I fall asleep I think, *when will I fuck it up?* That thought is in my father's voice. I know just how to do it. How to play the games, how to destroy my own world and walk away to another one, completely indifferent to the devastation I leave in my wake. I'm hit with a crisp sense of my father's fear of entanglements, his strong desire to be alone. Maybe that's what has made me hold myself back. I tell myself I've been the jerk. Better that than the jerkee. Then, King's face with a slight condescending smile shows me the way to be like my father. I don't want to be my mother, so maybe being like him is the better option.

I understand what goes on inside me, and I accept it. But that doesn't seem to make a difference.

*

The next morning, we're at the Grand Canyon. The crew is up and dressed. Levy is still in his PJs and I watch as he pulls on some jeans and struggles with the button. "Good job," I tell him. I think it's the first time he's buttoned his jeans. "You're getting so grown up." He grins at me, and then strolls away. Part of me wants him to stay a little baby. Aaron combs Levy's hair while I get dressed, and then we're ready to go.

None of us has ever seen the Grand Canyon, except for Allie.

"It's the number-one wonder of the world," Red said, looking at a map and realizing how close it is to Vegas.

Yesterday, we drove through red earth split with startling peaks. Sometimes the earth had caved away, as though the ground couldn't seal up a wound, and a gulch formed. Red mesas, hills with their tops cut off, looked like tables decorating the flat landscape. Not much green. Only red and pink and purple, and a sky overturned on the earth shedding clouds and rain. In the distance, bolts of lightning zigzagged from within black clouds, exhausting themselves, then flashing again with new claws.

Levy pointed at the lightning, but it had vanished. And then he noticed that out the other window, the sky was absolutely blue. The sun sent a shaft of light to the red earth. A thunderstorm and a sunbeam simultaneously.

The heavens can hold so much. Even T-Bone, usually so disinterested, shook his head and simply said, "Wow. A schizophrenic sky," with awe in his voice. We sat in our seats and watched the rain sheet down one side of the bus while the merry sun floated among a few fluffy clouds on the other.

"I didn't know this was possible," Red Dog said.

"As astounding as music," I whispered to Aaron.

"I know." He squeezed my thigh. "Amazing."

So it's a sunny morning and not too hot when we all meet above Ooh Aah Point.

And there it is: a red and beige striped wonder. Peaks stick out all over the canyon sides. Across the way there are crenulated rocks banded with color. The color ignores the juts and recesses in the cliff. I should learn to knit and make a poncho with those colors. Mom would love it; Aaron would hate the poncho. I sit on a rock, Levy beside me, Aaron on the other side of him. We each hold a hand as we consume the view.

"Hey, let's go down?" T-Bone asks.

I know going down is easier than coming up, especially with Levy. We'd all have to take turns carrying him. I glance down the path and it looks narrow, with a dropoff cliff on the other side, so I think he and I should wait. But the crew can't contain their eagerness and start down the canyon. "Don't forget you, like, have to come back up," I call.

Aaron laughs, "You don't think we can make it? Anyway, we're not going all the way down."

I guess I'd like to go, but I stay with Levy and wait for my sister and Rachel and Allie. Levy and I walk along the path that edges the canyon. The color bands meander over the cruel rock.

"Who made this, Mama?" Levy asks.

I take him as close to the edge as is safe and point to the river snaking at the bottom. "It's not a who, it's a what. That river carved this. It used to be up here, where we are, but it dug out the rock deeper and deeper till it got there." I point to the bottom.

He looks over the lip, me fastened to him by our hands, and then frowns at me as if I'm making up a story. "For real?"

The Colorado looks like a stream, like our little Huron from up here, and nowhere near powerful enough to cut rock. Sometimes truth is less believable than fiction.

"The rocks are kind of soft," I try to explain. "And we're so far away it looks smaller."

The two of us sit filled with wonder.

He picks up a rock. "Look. It has dots on it." He hands it to me.

The rock is shaped like an egg, gray with white speckles. I hand it back to him. He's making a collection of rocks. The heart-shaped one, a rough green one that somehow became smooth on one side that he picked up near the metal man. Now this one.

"You're getting souvenirs from our trip."

"What's 'venires?"

"Things that help you remember, that are part of the place," I tell him.

And then Rachel, Sky, and Allie arrive. I see Rachel first. She's wearing a blue L.A. baseball cap and mini sunglasses. It's the first time that Sky has taken any care in dressing her and she looks cute. Then I realize, Allie probably dressed her. Rachel runs to us and takes her glasses off as though the colors with the other-world-view are in them. Her eyes widen as she sees the canyon, the random straight-up mountains in the middle and the drop to the bottom of the earth.

Sky wanders on the path next to the edge watching her feet, not even paying attention to the view or us. She doesn't even say hello. I go up to her and give her a hug, "How you doing today?" I make my voice soft, trying to be extra loving.

She should realize we're ALL here helping her, but she seems to listen to private voices, to watch the world through half-shut, narrowed eyes. She doesn't answer. Troy's death wasn't that long ago, but she is still so detached. "Did you sleep last night?"

"Until 3:42. Like always." She shrugs and keeps walking.

Rachel and Levy are with Allie, who knows this path. We can all go down a little bit until it gets too narrow for the kids, so we start into the canyon. I see Special and the crew below on the switchback trails. They're bouncing down the trail, water bottles in their hands or jammed in a sagging pants pocket, half skipping, excited by the beauty around them. They've totally lost their urban cool as they run down the canyon like boys again, Aaron running free in all this glory.

It's early, and not tourist season, so we're the only people here. Down at the bottom, there are some mules. Other than that, we have the Grand Canyon to ourselves.

We pick our way down. I hold Levy's hand, and Allie holds Rachel's. We get deep enough that we have the sense of being IN it, part of it. The rim, and our usual earth, is far enough above that our existence is only the chasm. All we can see are the rocks that look so soft, almost washed with color, but are really sharp, jagged, and cruel.

Allie looks around and says, "It always takes my breath away, it's always new. I look at the pictures I take and they don't capture it. They're only a little slice." She hangs on to Rachel's hand, turning her head slowly to view the totality.

"I want to go home," Rachel says and starts crying. "I want Daddy."

Levy shakes his head and goes close to her. "I don't think he's there anymore." He doesn't say it meanly, but like it's a fact that he figured out.

Allie hugs her.

Sky walks ahead of us, examining her shoes again. The rest of us hug Rachel.

"I know what. Let's all imagine your daddy and send him images of this beautiful place and feel how happy he'd be that we're all here together enjoying it," Allie says.

"Mooooommmmmmyyyyy," Rachel calls.

Sky turns and walks toward us, her hands limp at her sides, and Rachel pulls her into our small huddle on the edge of a cliff. We hold hands. I think how spectacular that this exists. How lucky we are to live on *this* planet in spite of the tragedy of Troy's death. When we drop hands I say, "Rachel and Levy, you both are such miracles. All of us. And this place." Then I realize how sentimental and schmaltzy I'm being, overwhelmed and blown away by the splendor and the tumult of the last few weeks. As though the Grand Canyon is a refuge.

Sky doesn't say anything.

She simply turns and shuffles down the path examining pebbles on the trail.

CHAPTER SIX

All Through the Night

Sky

I don't get the big deal about the Grand Canyon. It's a big hole in the ground. Just something a river carved out eons ago. No more spectacular than mountains or clouds that we take for granted. It doesn't change how I feel. It doesn't take me out of myself. If Troy were here, he'd want us to walk to the bottom and ride the mules back up. Once, long ago in another life, that would have been fun.

So after the Grand Canyon, we hit I-40 again, 280 miles to Albuquerque. There are signs about Route 66 all along the way as we drive through dusty earth past Flagstaff to Winslow and go to the motel pool. Well, Tara and the rap dudes take a helicopter ride over the canyon. Allie and Levy and Rachel and I are at the motel.

Troy has been dead almost a month. It'll be a month the day after tomorrow. A month. It seems like just yesterday. It seems like forever. I only know it's a month because of the date on my cell.

"You'll take care of Levy?" Tara asks Allie. She ignores me. The truth is, I'm relieved no one expects much of me.

Even though it's already fall, it's warm enough that we can go swimming. Rachel has on her suit. I brought her water wings with me. Well, I think Tara packed them or Mom, just in case we were able to swim at a motel on the way home. We think we're all alone, and then here comes a woman with two children.

"Hey, Mom," the woman's daughter, I suppose, calls. "Wait."

The woman clasps towels, and a pail handle hangs from her forefinger. A boy, about five, totes trucks in each hand. A fuchsia swim ring with a bobbing sea horse's head encircles the girl's arm. The woman's hair escapes its clip and flies in the breeze. Repeatedly, she flicks her head to get it out of her eyes, but the wind is persistent.

The woman pulls three chaises around a table and plops a purple tote on one.

"When'll we eat?" the girl, who is probably eight or nine, whines.

"Have an apple, Molly. They're in the paper bag," she says pointing to the tote. Molly grabs one, takes a bite.

She puts it down and jumps in the water. The boy pushes his trucks on a band of mulch surrounding impatiens. Levy joins him.

Allie starts talking to the mom. Her name is Brooke. She's from Lansing, where she works as an art teacher. She got laid off, and decided they'd travel. They make a big deal that we're all from Michigan, that Brooke went to the university in Ann Arbor, and she and Allie talk about restaurants around the Diag and parks around the city like it's an incredible coincidence, small world, six degrees of separation. Blah blah blah. Compared to the statistical improbabilities in my life, this is nothing. Then she asks Allie what we're doing, and Allie tells her we're helping Rachel and me move back home.

Brooke nods as though she understands. They've just seen ancient Hopi dwellings at the Homolovi Ruins, nearby at a State Park. If we have the time, we should see them. In June, the kids' father took them to Disney World.

Allie whispers to Brooke, telling her that my husband died a month ago. Then I hear Allie say, "And believe it or not, we're traveling with a rap crew. Levy's dad and mom."

Then Brooke laughs a rumbling chuckle, a laugh that's more like a man's than a woman's. "Far as I'm concerned, it's a roller coaster. I'm just along for a ride. Figuring is impossible." Brooke is tall and angular, with high cheek-bones and a defined nose. Her plump lips add softness and sensuality. She is one of those beauties that doesn't need makeup.

"The 'shit happens' view of life?" Allie says as she watches the three kids in the pool.

"Exactly."

I lie on my chaise. Levy has left his truck and paddles in the shallow water with Rachel. Molly does backward somersaults and shouts, "Look, Mom, look what I can do."

Brooke sets out sandwiches and tells Molly to get the shoestring potatoes, tells Tyler to get the napkins. "Do I have to?" he grumbles as he leaves his trucks in the middle of grading a road.

"Just them; we can eat this with our fingers."

I stare at ripples of water, the fake turquoise of the pool. There's no diving board and only a few scrubby trees and plants. It must be because of the elevation and lack of rain.

"You guys hungry?" Brooke asks Allie. "I've got extra cheese sandwiches."

"Thanks. We ate lunch right before we came here."

A man arrives with a net to clean the pool. Molly goes up to him. "Hi, Mister," she says.

"I'm Martin, call me Martin."

"Okay, Mister."

"She calls all men Mister since her dad left," Brooke explains.

Molly grabs a handful of shoestring potatoes. "Can I go back in, Mom, pleeese?"

"Just in the shallow end. When Martin is finished cleaning. You both can go."

"I love you, Mom." Molly kisses Brooke's cheek. "You're the best mommy in the world."

Brooke leans back on her chaise and closes her eyes. Allie gets in the pool with Rachel and teaches her how to blow bubbles. Molly tries to teach Levy to swim. He holds on to the side of the pool and kicks his legs.

So it's just Brooke and me, on side-by-side chaises with a red and white striped umbrella between us. She says, out of the blue, "It doesn't turn out like we think, does it? We try to do everything and juggle it all so we have bits and pieces of everything. Like me, the kids, my art, and my husband. Can't keep all the balls in the air. Hell, I guess I wanted two complete, different lives."

I don't say anything. I'm examining a ripple, just one. I watch how it bumps up and then sinks, and returns and then slowly bounces to the edge of the pool. "But none of the lives would turn out like we envision, anyway," I say.

Brooke releases a bitter chuckle. She wets her lips and tells me her husband had gone to a conference and stopped on the highway, one of those little gas-up places in Nowheresville with a McDonald's and a gift store laden with souvenirs and packaged nuts and candy. He purchased cigarettes from the girl behind the counter. Brooke doesn't sound angry. Only bewildered.

"Now my husband hadn't smoked for years, but he saw this girl and bought cigarettes from her and sat in his car smoking until she was off work, took her out, and made love to her. This eighteen-year-old girl. He came home to tell me . . .," her voice cracks, "that he was leaving us, quit his job. Hell, in less than a week he was gone for good. Moved to Illinois. Just like that. See? A revolution in a day."

I don't say anything. She already knows my husband died.

A few minutes later, I say, "He was so young." I say it as though I accept it.

"I haven't been with a man since then," she tells the pool, "and that was over a year ago. Haven't even *talked* to one, let alone *been* with one."

We open up about our lives with each other because we're strangers and we're both not sure what happened. So many different ways for everything to get shuffled. So many ways to fall from the ordinary.

"It's only been a year since he left," I tell her.

"It's been an entire year and I haven't even talked to a man alone," she whispers. "I used to like sex. Like, hell, *love* it."

"Me, too." I haven't even thought of it, not once until Brooke brought it up. "He's the only man I've been with. I wonder if I'll ever be with another."

I guess nothing works out the way we expect. It's always different. I don't know if I say that out loud until Brooke says, "Yeah. Sometimes it works out better. I like being a mom more than I ever thought I would."

There are sparkles on the water like diamonds in the snow. I never saw that before, or maybe I did and didn't realize it. I struggle to remember, and then I do. I noticed them long ago when Troy was diving.

"When I was a girl, my dad used to take me to the Upper Peninsula to a cabin he had near Tahquamenon Falls. It was a cruddy cabin, slightly better than a tent. It didn't have lights, just a wood-burning stove. In the fall, he and his buddies used it for hunting. In the spring, he took me fishing." Brooke sips from a can of Diet Coke and passes me one.

"When we were up there, Dad used to say, 'Brookey, this is my dream. See this forest, see this lake, see this? Imagine, cottages. Imagine, people coming to Brooke's Lakeside Resort.'" Brooke chews on the inside of her mouth. "One spring day, I was getting dressed when my dad came back from loading the boat and he had two men with him. I figured they were friends of his. I was Molly's age, I guess." She shudders.

"What did they want?"

"They didn't hurt us. My father shared our food with them . . . hot dogs and potato chips and Cheerios. One of 'em, with a fat stomach and missing a front tooth, played Go Fish with me. I beat him and his friend teased. 'You let some little baby beat you, Tiger? Some teensy-weensy broad?' 'Shudup,' he said. When Tiger stood up, he was a lot bigger, and the other one didn't say anything more. It seemed, hummmm," Brooke hunts for the words, "not

usual, but not abnormal. My father was, I don't know, fid-
gety. We didn't even go fishing. I kept buggin' him
because it was gloomy and boring in the cabin, but we
stayed inside all day. That night, I slept with my dad and
the strangers slept in the bigger bed. And then the next
day, my father drove them to a gas station. Filled up his
car and handed them his money. A car, with a man and
two women, waited for them." Brooke falls silent.

"What happened then?"

"Nothing. We went home." Brooke's head sags, she
inhales. "We didn't go back up to the cabin after that. My
mom never liked it anyway, so my father sold it. He and
Mom built a new house outside of Paw Paw, where they
still live."

"Who were the men?"

"I think they'd escaped from a prison . . . and wanted a
place to hide. Dad didn't tell me what was going on until
I was a teenager. Then he told me he was held at gun-
point, but I didn't see guns. One kept his in a pocket, the
other in his waistband. I think Dad told me then to teach
me how dangerous the world is."

"Did it work?" I keep forgetting to eat and I notice
how flat my stomach is.

"Hell, no." She frowns.

I take a swig of the cold Coke and I feel it travel
through my body. "Why'd you tell me that story?"

"That incident stays in my mind. Hell, since Calvin left
us, I keep thinking about it."

"I thought maybe there was a message in it."

"Me too." Brooke shakes her head. "But I haven't figured it out yet. It depends on how I look at it, and I look at it in different ways at different times. Sometimes it tells me that people won't hurt me. That's when I was a kid. Sometimes it tells me that danger arrives stupidly guised, but is everywhere. You can't foresee it, but you have to be alert. That's when the kids were smaller. Now, I don't know." She chews on the inside of her lip. "I guess, it's . . ." Brooke frowns . . . "Things are not *necessarily* what they seem, but they can be exactly as they appear. We only have a piece of the puzzle and have to figure life with our one little piece. I keep trying to decipher signals that I was oblivious to. There must have been *some* sign that Calvin would leave us." She shakes her head and whispers, "Hell, I didn't even know he was unhappy."

"I brought the bacteria that killed Troy home by visiting my friend in the hospital."

"But you didn't kill him," she says. "You didn't do anything wrong any more than I did. That's the only thing I learned this year. Whatever it was that made this happen, it was inside him. It wasn't that I was a bad wife, or lousy in bed. In fact he told me I was much better in bed than the eighteen-year-old. So it wasn't that. Don't know why the hell that's even important. Guess it's not."

"We just want control," I say.

"Exactly." She blurts an ironic chuckle. "Even if we have to accept unwarranted guilt."

I try to interpret the lesson of Brooke's story.

Then she shrugs one shoulder and grabs the Coke, takes a sip, and rests it on a stomach toned from sit-ups or Pilates. "Well, we persist. That's all. Like me and the kids survive in spite of Calvin's demolition. Survive, hell, we even have fun. And I get to parent exactly how I want to. No compromising with his strict approach."

And then Tara, Aaron, T-Bone, Smoke, and Red Dog return exhilarated by the view from the helicopter. "You're not just surrounded by it," Tara says, "you get to see it, see inside the gorge, and there're enormously complicated peaks and valleys *in* it. It's ... intricate."

No one crowds my view of the pool. I'm stretched in my chaise immersed in the movement of a ripple, feeling more relaxed after talking with my new friend. Lansing is not that far away from Ann Arbor. We think alike, Brooke and I. Maybe my life isn't over. I'm beginning a new life. I'm not aware of the sun on my body or the voices of my family ... I guess they're my family ... bubbling and laughing about the canyon, about the next concert in Albuquerque. Wouldn't think a rap group would have a following there. I hear Brooke say the same thing. I'm vaguely aware that T-Bone flirts with her and I hear her guttural laugh off in the distance. If she wants sex, I'm sure T-Bone will oblige. Maybe it's easier with a stranger. There's an ebb and flow of all their voices as though I'm listening through water. Allie talks with Smoke. I vaguely hear them behind my chaise. Levy plays with Aaron beside me. I pay little attention to anything but that ripple and how occasionally there's a sparkle on it that sinks.

So everyone is there.

Rachel comes out of the pool. She grabs some shoestring potatoes and sips my Coke. She says, loud so everybody hears it, "I want Daddy."

Levy takes her hand and fastens her to Aaron, then stands somberly watching what will happen next.

"No! *My* daddy." Rachel jerks her hand away, and cries.

Aaron hugs her. Levy hugs her.

Then, Tara hugs her and Rachel wraps her arms around Tara's neck and snuggles into her.

I don't want Tara to take care of Rachel when I should be doing it, but I'm so tired.

I look away. But I know I have to do something. I get up and stride over to Tara.

"Leave her alone," I state. My neck throbs. "Don't keep taking her from me."

What I'm saying and everything that happens next is kind of fuzzy. A series of events that seem to take place in a tunnel.

"What are you talking about?" Tara's caution seems patronizing. "I haven't taken anything from you. I'm trying to help."

I scream. I know I scream only because my throat scrapes. "Mom. Troy. Calling him. Flirting with him. Sitting on his lap."

"Why are you hanging on to that? That was ten years ago. I was just a lonely kid."

Her condescending tone increases my fury. "Later, too. You two were always so close. And now Rachel. You're trying to make her love you more."

"I'm just trying to be a good aunt," she shouts. "Take care of her when you—" her face beet red as she shrieks *you*—"aren't able to. Or won't."

She's in full rage. I've never seen her this angry.

"How about *you* being thankful for what you still have instead of acting like you have nothing and the world's come to an end. How about you pay some attention to your daughter, that baby you wanted so much. How about you quit pitying yourself."

Her out-of-control anger makes me feel victorious, so I flush with surging strength. I don't know what I screech. Something about her life being easy. Something about, she goes her own way doing her own thing, ignoring everything and everybody else.

She screams back, "Ignoring? Me ignoring? How 'bout you and Mom ignoring me? How about you ignoring your own daughter now?"

And then I gasp as much air as I can and shout, "How would you like it if it was Aaron who died? How would you like that?"

And just then, off in the distance, I hear Molly scream, "Help, help! Mister, help!"

There's a splash so abrupt and enormous it soaks me.

The startling cold water on my sun-warmed, anger-flushed skin alerts me to look toward the pool.

Aaron slaps his arms frantically in the water and then dives down, disappears. And brings up Rachel.

He holds her high, swims with her, carries her above the water. Smoke helps them to the edge of the pool.

They lay her on the cement.

How did she get in the pool?

She doesn't move. She's not moving.

Her eyes are closed.

Brooke tilts Rachel's head, puts her ear to her mouth, pinches Rachel's nostrils, presses her mouth to Rachel's and breathes. Brooke lifts her head to check Rachel's chest.

No motion.

I stand over her screaming while time speeds past.

Levy's cries seem to echo, to blurt off and on in some uncanny strobe.

Why isn't she moving? My chest heaves. I grab my hair and shake my head.

Brooke forces air into Rachel's mouth again. No movement. Rachel's arms are outstretched, paler where her water wings covered her. What happened to her water wings?

Smoke kneels beside Brooke, folds his hands over each other, and presses Rachel's chest in several quick pulses.

Oh no. Please, please. I shriek.

Brooke opens Rachel's mouth, blows into it. Then Smoke resumes pushing her chest.

And again.

Over and over. I watch Smoke's huge hands bear down on her fragile torso, his fingers sheltering her ribs.

Over and over. I watch Brooke blow air into her open mouth.

Everything stops except Smoke pressing Rachel's chest. And Brooke breathing into her mouth.

Tara and I stand next to each other, watching Brooke and Smoke work on Rachel.

Rachel lies, arms outstretched, her little lips open for Brooke's air.

She is motionless.

Blindly Killing Your Own Family

Tara

The first thing that happens is this: Allie says to me, in a whispery voice, her arms crossed over her chest with a pleased smile on her lips, "Look at your sister, she's made a friend. She's coming out of herself."

And sure enough, there's Sky talking to a woman with wildly curling auburn hair and sunglasses and one of those bodies toned from scads of Pilates or yoga. Sky is turned toward her as they converse. Maybe it's easier to talk with a stranger.

"Her name is Brooke and she's from Michigan, too. Isn't that a coincidence?"

Me, my mind is still reeling from the view from the helicopter, the canyon brushed with cloud shadows

deepening its hues. The funny silence except for the helicopter's blade slicing the air, the sense of hanging in the
sky. I think I'll try skydiving one day. I say that to Red
Dog and we plan a trip to the dunes by Lake Michigan
until Aaron frowns and says, "Not my Tara, not my Li'l
Key, not my baby-mama. You too important to take that
risk." You can imagine how I feel, protected and
annoyed, loved and disrespected all at once.

So we all mill around, happy with our day and happy
to be back together again. T-Bone notices Brooke's
knockout body and slides over to her, kneels down,
stares into her eyes, and begins asking her questions as
though she's the only woman who has ever existed. I
think then Sky goes back to watching the pool while we
discuss what we want to eat for dinner, wondering what
we can find in this town. Italian? Mexican? Chinese?
Steak?

"Pizza! Pizza!" squeals Levy.

We're a bit away from the canyon now, on the road
home, on the road closer to Albuquerque, where we have
a concert the day after tomorrow. We're near Winslow,
Arizona in a national chain motel, Quality Inn or Econo
Lodge. I don't even know. The earth is a reddish desert
plain. I'm looking forward to the Albuquerque concert.
Looking forward to painting my face orange and putting
on my sexy clothes and being Li'l Key.

I think of King's proposition. I could become more
famous, make more money. I could branch out and do a

solo album, maybe. King could be a springboard to so much. In truth, lyrics keep buzzing in my head, *I'm left I'm left I'm left missing myself*, and this time the nascent song is about the shift that's happening with Aaron.

I hear a sweet, haunting melody to accompany it, a melancholy lilt surprisingly soft and gentle. I wonder if Aaron would feel threatened if I wrote and sang my own songs. Now, even *my* music is ours. I have no individual voice. Sing more, rap less. If I cross over, will he consider it a betrayal? Or is hip-hop dead and dying, and is that why King wants me to join him, needing my ease with the eclectic, classical, pop, and rap?

Rachel announces she misses her daddy and Levy tries to share his, putting Rachel's little hand into Aaron's. His face is so serious, his lips gently together, his eyelashes shadowing his cheeks when he attaches Rachel to Aaron. He realizes how much love he has, me, his dad, Red Dog and Smoke, Sissy and Mom. His big family. I'm so moved by my little guy's generosity. I kiss and hug him. I hold Rachel, trying to comfort her, and she cuddles close to me. And then she walks away from me and plays with a little boy, must be Brooke's kid.

And then everything goes crazy.

Sky jumps up from the chaise and starts screaming at me. "Leave my baby alone," she shouts.

I'm confused. "What are you talking about?" I try not to shout back. I try to keep my voice measured to deflect her rage, but my even tone seems to escalate her anger, as though my very attempt at composure enrages her.

"Rachel. You're trying to steal her from me. Make her love you more." The veins stand out on Sky's neck.

"What? She's *your* daughter, Sky." I keep my voice even and calm, aware of her vulnerability so soon after Troy's death.

"You've taken everything from me."

"Everything? What are you talking about?" She was the one that had everything, got everything she wanted.

"Just like you tried to take Troy, too."

"You can't think that there was anything going on between Troy and me. He was my brother."

"But you," her eyes are narrowed, "in your weird way worm yourself into everything and take it over. And now you have everything and I have nothing."

My heart pounds in my neck, my face heats with rage. "I've always been your scapegoat. You have Rachel. I've just been filling in because you are so—" I look for the word, but now I'm beyond anger too—"irresponsible!" I scream back at her.

"Don't tell me about responsibility," she taunts. "You're so responsible?" she snorts. "Dragging your little son around with a rap band, where God-knows-what is going on. God knows what drugs he's exposed to. What shit you are all using. You think I'm stupid? Or Mom? Or Troy? We all know. And my husband died. I'm trying to be responsible."

"You're crazy." Then I feel Levy's arms wrapped around my leg.

I see, as I whip my head around, the darkened fury on Aaron's face, incensed she's screaming at me in public and that she is accusing us.

"Don't throw your B.S. on me," I say.

But she is blinded by her own rage, and can't stop screaming accusations. "There's a fine line between a rap crew and gangs. Drugs and wanton sex."

"Oh, so now you're showing your true racist self. Have you seen any hard drugs? No. You haven't seen any 'cause there aren't any. You don't see me as I am, you see me how your mind made me up. And you act like your life is over when we're all here helping you. All of us . . . the drug-using, gangsta-rap crew you accuse us of being."

Her fists clench. She might hit me, and my own hand folds to defend myself.

"You're making a monument of your grief to prove your love for Troy," I gasp.

Aaron steps beside me. Levy's arms are wrapped around my leg to protect me from Sky's screams.

"Don't blame me for your faults. Look around you. You're still alive. And so is Rachel."

"It hasn't been a month. Not even one month. Your life is so easy because you only think about yourself. How would you feel if Aaron died? How would you feel if it was your beloved Aaron dead?" She shrieks the word *dead*.

Aaron DEAD. She shrieks the curse. An ambulance wails off in the distance. Then the alarm fades.

I inhale sharply and my chest heaves. I've gathered enough air to continue the fight.

I've thought about Aaron dying. How could I not after Troy's death, how could I not put myself in my sister's shoes? How could I not, with a father like mine? Aaron could leave for another woman, he could leave because he was bored. He could die. I've known that from the beginning. What would happen to Levy? And it's in here, in these coulds, these horrible possibilities, that King's offer gains value and desirability. He's the ace in the hole. Not King the possible lover or the man, but King the bridge to solo stardom, to security if Aaron's gone. Before Levy was born, I didn't plan ahead or worry about safety. I was a go-with-the-flow kind of gal, never knowing what I might do next. Now security is seductive, and fame is safety.

And in that space, the space of me grabbing all the air I can and these contradictory thoughts warring in my head, Aaron steps between us and puts his hand on my arm.

So what happens next is: "Help, Mister. Help!"

I turn to see a chubby girl—Brooke's daughter?—in the water, clinging to the side of the pool with one arm and pointing into the water with the other.

Aaron makes a leap—flies actually, stretched over the water—to land flat on his belly.

The resounding spray hits all of us.

He sinks in the water and brings Rachel to the surface. Swimming and carrying her high above the water. Smoke jumps in, and then they gently lay her on the cement.

She isn't moving.

T-Bone points at the three of them, Brooke blows into Rachel's mouth, and Smoke's fingers spread over Rachel's tiny ribs. Now, Rachel lies, not moving, not breathing, maybe lost too—oh God no, not that too, not that now, how could Sky survive? How could I?

Brooke breathes for her and Smoke pushes her little chest, squatting side by side, working to save her.

Sky stands over Rachel, shaking and wailing. Howling. Her rage at me replaced by terror and fear.

Levy cries and I turn toward him.

Rachel lies still. Strands of hair are stuck against her forehead. Smoke's fingers press her small chest. Brooke blows air into her lungs.

Over and over.

Time creeps on. I watch as Smoke and Brooke keep working on Rachel.

Finally, Rachel coughs. Water dribbles from her mouth. She looks around at all of us crowding her. She sits up, gasps, and wails. It's a sharp-pitched note that fades, and then reasserts itself. Almost like a siren, that high-pitched and tense.

All that in a few blazing minutes. It's slap-dash hectic

action, as though we're in one of those bizarre movies where action freezes for some people and speeds up for others. Each of us in a different time zone. Molly and her brother huddled by the bushes. Levy hanging on to my leg. Sky shrieking. Aaron's clothes, still wet from his rescue of Rachel, drip water in slow motion to the cement. Red Dog and T-Bone stand frozen by the edge of the pool, Brooke and Smoke move with the rhythm of their own breathing.

With Rachel's cry everything changes. Time resumes normalcy. Sky, Allie, and I weep with relief and gratitude. Brooke sits back on her haunches, her palms on her thighs, and then she and Smoke hug each other. Aaron and Red Dog and T-Bone clap Smoke on the back and ask him how he learned CPR.

Sky holds Rachel close. Rachel cries into her mom's shoulder. "It's okay. You're okay," Sky tells her, swaying back and forth.

Over Rachel's head, our eyes meet. Sky's contain relief and sorrow. She doesn't shift her eyes; they remain fixed on mine as she stares at me washed of rage and desperation. And then, tears stream down her face.

Rachel looks at all of us standing around her and resumes crying. Brooke pats Rachel's back and then calls her own children, the chubby girl and a little boy playing in the bushes with a truck, and hugs them close to her.

*

My sister cursed me.

I glance at Aaron and then squeeze his hand. His brows slant down, his eyes narrowed with anger and distrust of my sister for her accusations and curses.

"It's easier to be angry than sad and scared," Allie says.

"Well, that explains the emotion, not the words," Aaron tells her. Aaron and I and the crew have gone way out of our way to help Sky. I know that's what Aaron is thinking.

Allie presses her lips together and nods slightly.

Sky's arms and cries of relief surround Rachel.

"I hope those are tears of happiness and gratitude," I say, looking at her.

She glances up at me.

Her words can't be erased.

I move close, lower my voice to an almost whisper, and say, "I understand how scared and crazed you were." I try to excuse her. I try to hug both of them.

But she maintains the truth of her accusations. I consider saying, *but it isn't true, none of that is true*, but instead I say, "I'm so relieved, so happy Rachel is okay," and kiss Rachel on her forehead and kiss Sky's hand, the one on Rachel's shoulder with her wedding ring still on the third finger.

See? Everyone thinks I selfishly immerse myself in my music. But look how hard I try and how my attempts are ignored or misinterpreted. I can't do it right, so I retreat to a musical solitude, which is a mixed place. Safe. But lonely.

Then Rachel squirms out of her mom's arms and runs

up to Levy, standing close to Aaron as though she doesn't understand the mushy fuss.

Allie says, "Hey. Where're your water wings? You need to always wear them when you're around a pool or lake."

Rachel turns her mouth down. "Over there." She points to pink, deflated wings in the mulch, which Tyler has attempted to bury with his truck. Allie pulls them out, shakes them off, rinses them, and reinflates them. One has a hole in it.

"You can't go back in the water unless you're with an adult." She kneels in front of Rachel, placing her own hands on Rachel's shoulders. Now she's taking over the mom role. Sky is back on the chaise, her palms over her eyes. Her shaking chest indicates she's crying.

By now the other kids are splashing in the pool. Even Tyler has abandoned his construction project to play Marco Polo with his sister; Levy joins them, but his swimming isn't up to the task. There's a shallow end, and I take Rachel and go in. I grab Levy's hand and make a circle and dance around playing ring-around-the-rosy. When we come to the all-fall-down part, I sit on the bottom of the pool and watch while the kids fall back in the water. Rachel reveals no fear, no memory of danger. But I never let go of her resilient little hand.

Does Sky actually think I'm stealing her daughter? She should join us.

Sky sits on the chaise watching, her eyes on Rachel. Brooke is beside her. I steal glances at them. For a while,

Sky stares at us. Well, not at us, around us. She watches the water as though she expects a demon, the Loch Ness monster, a mermaid to leap up in an amazing plume and spectacular glory. We skip around the circle again; her eyes are almost on us. And then I realize, she hopes that Troy will surface, stroke through the pool, and leap out to land beside her.

I say, "Let's wave to Mommy, let's wave to Aunt Sky." At first she doesn't notice our motion, and then she does and smiles.

She smiles! I wave her to us and she enters the pool.

The four of us bounce around, the adults stooping in the water, doing another round or two of our circle game. Sisters playing with their kids; something I once dreamed about, but the joy of the moment is tarnished from the fight. Allie joins us and we bounce around the circle, making great splashes when we all fall down. Sky has a forced smile on her face, and then she takes Rachel aside and says, "I'm going to teach you how to float."

I know then the thought that got her out of her chaise. Sky recognizes she has more to lose. She captures a piece of Troy by doing what he would do. He would certainly teach Rachel the glory of the water. Sky can protect Rachel. She's aware of what she still has.

Allie comments, "She's faking it until she makes it. Just as well."

"Children heal so quickly. Forget so quickly," I say.

Allie shoots me a look. "Sometimes. Or they remember

differently. I mean deep somewhere in their nonverbal souls. You did the perfect thing. Making a game out of falling in the water. Now she has to learn both. It's not all fun. There's danger, too."

I think about learning how to negotiate the fun and staying safe from the danger. With too much security, change is avoided; with too much excitement, safety is threatened.

For the next hour, everything seems normal. Sky plays with Rachel and Brooke gets in the water. It's the three moms and the four kids giving different swimming lessons. T-Bone feigns interest, standing next to Brooke, but she isn't buying his interest in anything other than how her boobs emerge from her bikini top and how her ass pokes out of her bottoms. But I get the sense that something casual might be right up her alley.

Aaron went to the store, and has one of the motel's grills going to make barbequed chicken; it's marinating in lemon juice and herbs. Sweet potatoes wrapped in foil edge the glowing embers. Then Sky gets out of the water and goes toward Smoke sitting at a table playing Hold 'em with Red Dog, a bottle of Hennessy on the wood table. She touches him on his shoulder and he turns toward her just as he picks up his three cards. I see his hand: two aces and a jack.

"Could you do me a favor? Drive me to find some water wings for Rachel?"

"When I finish this hand." He says it evenly, not betraying the win he's about to have.

I wonder why she asked him instead of me. I think of a thousand reasons. Brooke is flirting with T-Bone, Allie is busy reading on a chaise, and Sky's probably tired of being in a car with Allie. Sky wants me to watch the kids, and Smoke helped save Rachel's life.

Why do I watch Sky so closely, as though her decisions predict, prophesy something about me? As though her life has an answer or an influence on mine? I always have. The big sister demonstrating an approach to the next stage of my life.

So I show Rachel and Levy how to take a big breath and put their heads in the water.

"Watch watch watch," I tell Rachel and Levy, holding their hands. Then I inhale and put my head underwater, holding my breath. I lift it and exhale. "Now your turn." I mimic the motions for them and they copy me. I watch as Rachel and Levy gasp and then hold their heads underwater. Levy bobs to the surface, and then Rachel.

"Good job!" I say.

Sky calls me to the side and says, "Smoke and I are going to get new water wings. Will you watch Rachel?"

"Yep."

She says, "Rachel, I'm getting a surprise for you. Aunt Tara will watch you, okay?"

She's trying. I can see it.

"Okay," Rachel grins.

*

"Let's see how long we can hold our breaths." We inhale as much air as we can and duck our heads underwater. I open my eyes and see the kids floating, each gripping me by one hand. Levy's eyes are tightly clenched; his shorts billow around his skinny legs. Rachel clasps my hand; her hair surges and drifts with water currents and our bodies. Levy lifts his head. Then me, though I have plenty of air left. Rachel floats, her hair swaying around her head, and then she surfaces. "I won," she grins.

I understand her enunciation perfectly.

"Yay, for Rachel," I sing.

"Let's go again," Levy says.

We take turns winning.

Blindly Killing Your Own Family

Sky

Rachel is okay. But that was such a close call. I'm still shaking from almost losing my precious child. I ask Allie and Brooke if we should take Rachel to a doctor. Allie asks her some questions. Brooke says we should just watch her. She seems fine. A tragedy averted, this time. Calamities are always around us, surrounding us like the canyon. I think this as I get in my car, on the passenger side. Smoke pushes the driver's seat back and inserts the key. "Where to?"

I check for a Kmart or Walmart on my cell phone's GPS and, when the directions pop up, I show him the map.

He glances at it and says, "That's just around the

corner." He pulls out of the motel parking lot sure of where he's going, as though he's memorized the town's layout.

I have a bad sense of direction. Even before, when I had Troy, I was afraid of getting lost. That's why I have a GPS in my car and on my cell. Double the protection.

"You have remarkable eyes," I say to Smoke.

"So do you." He makes a right turn from the parking lot.

He drives to a main street and we stop at a red light. "It's just that blue eyes aren't often found on someone as black as me."

I don't say anything. I didn't mean to comment on his race and now I don't know what to say. Skin as dark as his *is* unusual in the U.S., especially with blue eyes. The light turns green and we start driving again.

He fiddles with the radio. "You like country?" he asks. His bulky fingers delicately turn the knob to adjust the volume.

"Sometimes. Mostly, I like R & B and rock."

"You don't like rap much."

"It's the language. And the materialistic, sexist messages."

"That's the contrary nature of the culture. Turn the bad into something good somehow, like turning pig guts into a delicacy. We remake it, redefine it as ours instead of some shit shoved down our throats." He says this calmly, his voice soothing although his words aren't.

I resume looking at the scrubby trees in between a Discount Tire, an El Torito, a Bojo's Grill, a CVS, and a Sam's Food Mart drifting by, each chain store with a parking lot in front.

"Do you like country and R & B?" Making small talk is an effort for me, so I have to prod myself.

"I like all music. Listen, it's not true what you said back there. You need to know that."

"Huh?"

"About the drugs. Speaking for myself, I don't use no hard drugs. And I haven't seen *any* of us do that shit." He shrugs, and the motion revolves his shoulder and his arm. "We're not riding dirty. Too much to lose." He turns to me when he says this. "See, Red Dog saw shit eat up his moms and pops and learned bitter lessons. We from the bottom of the barrel, growing up in the D. You know Special did time, don't think he's about to get caught up in some rinky-ass state where dreams are dashed. Freedom and life too precious. If you listened to what we sing about, really listened, you'd know. I know it sounds like I'm some New Age dude, when I'm not. But I get high playing Africa . . . that's all I need."

I gaze out the window as more chain stores pass by.

"And as for women. Well, we grown ass men. They aren't married. Of course some of us may catch what's thrown at us. But I don't waste my time that way."

"You don't have to explain yourself."

"I don't, but I will for Tara. I'm used to people seeing

me with stereotyped eyes. But I got a lot of loyalty for her."

He didn't mention T–Bone.

"And I love that li'l Levy almost as much as my own little girl," he continues.

I don't totally believe what he's telling me. I mean, he's telling me the truth, but there's got to be another side to it. You never know what other people do, the secrets that other people keep. Levy seeing the crew go off with different women has an impact. Levy being on a bus with a bunch of men instead of playing in a park influences him.

"Levy, he's got lots of fathers," he says and smiles. "Lots of examples of what a man can be. He's a lucky little dude."

Then I think, have I protected Rachel? Her father just died. She almost drowned. I shudder. I've planned, provided, guarded, and look what she's gone through.

I see pansies and marigolds blooming under some scrubby willows.

I still have Rachel left from my life with Troy. Oh, and my law degree and experience, I add as an afterthought.

At the Walmart Supercenter, we find a bunch of water wings on sale and I buy a pink and a lime green pair for Rachel, and a turquoise pair for Levy. They're such brilliant colors they hurt my eyes. Smoke carries the bag for me and opens the door. I've missed such chivalry.

Sitting in the car next to Smoke feels safe and solid.

Maybe because of his size, but mostly because he saved Rachel's life. I tell him so.

"Along with Special and Brooke."

I don't know how to thank him. Our seat belts are firm around us.

After dinner, the kids fall asleep sprawled over each other in my room watching TV. Aaron, Smoke, and Red Dog play cards in Red Dog and Smoke's room. I smell the basil aroma of pot. Well, Smoke said they didn't do hard drugs. He didn't say anything about pot. I don't know where Brooke and T-Bone are. I wonder if Brooke and I will still be friends after my fight with Tara. I haven't thanked her properly for saving Rachel, but how do I do that? And Aaron and Smoke. Everyone saved her. Everyone but me and Tara. The people who should have done something.

In all the years that Troy and I were together, I never yelled at him, not like that. Only Tara, and that was when we were kids. But the truth is, the awful truth, after that shrieking-screeching fight, I feel better. Relieved.

I find Allie and Tara in Allie's room. Allie has bought a bottle of wine and we sip it, still full from dinner.

"Fat chicken. Look at my fat chicken!" Levy had squealed with delight at a particularly stubby piece he picked up. He licked off the sauce and nibbled the thigh, and he and Tara split one of the sweet potatoes. Rachel, who usually doesn't like chicken, ate half of my breast.

Smoke and I brought a salad bag from Walmart, and Allie got some ice cream and chocolate sauce from Circle K. A complete family meal, I thought. Aaron's chicken was perfectly tender.

"You could open a restaurant," I told him.

But he didn't smile at me. Evidently he's still angry about what I said to Tara.

Levy held out his empty plate after he finished the entire piece. "I ate the whole chickie." He laughed. His curls bounced with glee, the balls of his cheeks almost hiding his black eyes. "It's my flavorite."

"Favorite," Tara corrects him.

"No, Mommy, my favorite flavor. F-l-avorite."

"What a funny word," Aarons nods. "Let's make it one from now on."

Rachel wore her "prestnicks," even at dinner.

"What she say?" Smoke asked me when we gave her the water wings.

"Presents," I tell him.

"Yep. Tanks for the prestnicks." Rachel slides them up her arms. I forget that her enunciation isn't as terrific as her vocabulary. She wore them to dinner and the "prestnicks" are still on her arms as she sleeps curled around Levy.

Now, in the quiet night after a tumultuous and terrifying day, Allie opens the wine and pours it into the plastic glasses next to the ice bucket.

She hands us each one and says, "I always wished I had

a sister. But no such luck. I figured a sister would be another woman who shared your life, knew all about you, shared your childhood." She sips her wine. "A best friend with witnessed history and deep knowledge of each other."

"We're too far apart in age," I say.

"And we're, like, so different," Tara adds.

"We have different fathers," I say as though Allie doesn't know and as if it explains everything, though I know it doesn't.

Allie lies back on her bed, cushions around her. The spread on the bed is printed with contrasting colors so it doesn't show stains. Tara and I sit on two upholstered chairs on either side of a table. There's nothing spectacular or even interesting in this room. It is exactly like Rachel's and mine next door. Simply functional and clean. I sip my wine, and savor the taste.

"You think you guys are different?" Allie laughs. "My grandmother and her sister looked alot alike but were vastly unalike." She emphasizes the *un*. "It's one of the things from my childhood that I still ponder, and I'm amazed how one family could have such disparity." Allie shakes her head and clears her throat. She rests her glass on her abdomen and crosses her ankles. "My grandmother was German, her parents emigrated from Germany. This was back in the 1880s."

"I thought you were Jewish," Tara says.

"I am, but my mother's mother, Mum, was German

and she grew up proud of that German heritage. In fact my nana spoke German with Mum when they didn't want us knowing what they were saying." Allie chuckles, and sips on her wine. She wears a pair of knit black pants, a wildly multicolored shirt, and equally vivid dangly earrings. "Here," she interrupts her story and turns to the bedside table and lights a candle. "This'll make the room smell good. I always pack one so that I carry a little piece of home with me." Then the flare from the match ends.

"So. There were two sisters. When my grandmother was fourteen, she was sent to a hospital to be a nurse ... that's how they did it then. It was a Jewish hospital and she fell in love and married a Jewish doctor and converted. Alma, her sister, married a man she met at a German community youth meeting. They went through World War I. And then the Depression hit."

Allie stops and narrows her eyes as she looks at each of us, and asks, "You know all this from your mom ... right? ... because your grandparents were German and there's a large German immigrant population in Michigan."

"I've never thought about it like that," Tara says. Her hair is up in a bun with a clip. Shorts, a T-shirt, and no makeup wipe away ten years, and she looks like a kid barely past puberty.

"Well, yeah, we all arrived as immigrants. Even the so-called Native Americans. They just got here earlier," Allie says.

"Unless you're black, and then you didn't *come*. You were stolen and *brought*," Tara says, and I know she's thinking about Aaron and Levy.

Allie shakes her head and her earrings jingle. "Think of this. The middle of the Depression. One sister married a Jewish doctor, converted to Judaism, and lived in the Jewish community. One sister pro-German."

Allie leans back against the pillows. I glance at Tara, whose eyes are wide, her legs crossed, her fingers entwined.

"Then it got more complicated. Pup was fired from his job one week before he would be entitled to his pension." Allie shrugs and shakes her head. "He moved in, along with Mum, to Nana's. Then, Nana's youngest sister died in childbirth, and Nana and Poppy, my grandfather, adopted her toddler and the baby."

Allie interrupts herself here for a footnote and lowers her voice. "They were adopted with the condition that the girls retain their Christian last name and attend church." She shakes her head slowly.

"Then what happened?" Tara asks.

Allie crosses her legs and puts her elbows on her knees and leans toward us. Her toenails are polished with iridescent red. "My Jewish grandfather was supporting all these people—his wife's German family. Then Aunt Alma became enmeshed with the Nazis, advocating the necessity for Germany to rise again under the leadership of the Fuehrer. She started trading currency for the

Germans. Going back and forth across the Atlantic from the U.S. to Germany with suitcases of cash."

The candle flickers illuminate our faces. The blinds are tightly shut against the night. I remember drawing family trees in school and concentrating on my father's family because it seemed more mysterious. He was Irish Catholic, and that's about all I knew. I didn't pay attention to my mom's side of the family. The German side. She was with me. I had her.

"So," Allie narrows her eyes and stares at each of us. "Before the war, right before my birth, there were these two sisters. With the same father and mother. One a Nazi." Allie turns a palm up. "The other a Jew." She turns her other palm up.

"Then. One day Alma came to Nana and took her aside. The Nazis were going to win the war and conquer the U.S. 'Already we're making lists of Jews,' Alma said. 'You can save your children. Annul your marriage and deny their Jewish blood. Before it's too late.'" Allie swallows and shakes her head.

Allie stops. Her head is down. Tara and I look at each other. I can't imagine Tara and me being on opposite sides in a war. Our family squabble, which seemed so important, feels less so.

"What happened?" Tara prods.

Allie lifts her head and clears her throat. "'I'm not going to turn myself into a whore,' Nana told Alma. 'My children into bastards.'

"But Alma insisted. 'You're risking their lives for your pride.'"

"Did they keep communicating with each other?" I ask.

"Sometime during that period World War II started. Alma was still a Nazi sympathizer. She still visited her mom. I remember a holiday when we were all there. The war was still going on or just ended. When Alma arrived, she and Mum went into Mum's bedroom. Alma came out alone." Allie's earrings catch glimmers from the candle.

Outside, I hear a car pull into the parking lot. Its lights slide through the slits of the blinds and momentarily stripe the walls.

"Anyway," Allie resumes, "Alma sat on the upholstered wing chair. When I entered from the bathroom, I saw fury darkening my father's face and heard his paper crackle when he turned the page. Poppy left the room with steps that slammed and thumped as he climbed the stairs and slammed the door to his room." Allie sipped her wine and inhaled.

"Alma cried about how old and frail her mom was getting. Her mom was being supported and cared for by Jews when she, herself, supported a regime to kill us all. Her OWN relatives, because they were hers too, weren't they? Like it or not."

Now we're all quiet. Tendrils of bright streaks slide out of the clip holding Tara's hair. She looks so unremarkable. Not like a celebrity, just my kid sister.

I remember what Tara said in the fight. She reminded me that Aaron, and Smoke and the crew, were helping Rachel and me. I'm just not sure it's a rescue that I want.

"Life led them down such different paths partly because of who they had married." Allie sips her wine. "Nana figured out a way to accept," Allie's eyes slowly circle as she hunts for the word, "well, tolerate her sister's disgusting beliefs with the love they both had for Mum and the love Mum had for both of them. The love, that mother–daughter bond, was respected over horrendous political beliefs."

No one says anything, and then Allie adds, "I wonder what they talked about, that mother and daughter, when they spoke about it. Because they had to, didn't they? I wonder about the hidden motivations and thoughts that are never spoken."

"What do you think?" I ask.

"I asked Nana, and she simply said that they were all very proud of being German but then the wars came, and the holocaust."

Then Tara asks, "No, like, how do *you* reconcile it?"

I realize then that her questions stem from more than curiosity about Allie. And I understand what she's learning from Allie's story. She has moved from the security and safety of being in the white majority to the potential threat and hardship of being a minority, even though that is less now than it was twenty years ago. And because of her choice, Mom and I have a new affiliation with black people.

"As a child, I wondered how some of my kin could have killed their own kin. I imagined a German relation herding and gassing a Russian Jewish relation and neither one—the murderer or the murdered—recognizing they were relatives through me. A terrifying possibility: blindly killing your own family."

Allie stops and bites her upper lip. "But, isn't that what war really is? Aren't we really all related?"

Tara is quiet, maybe considering all the possible futures for her and Levy. "Levy and Rachel are both amazing mixtures as a result of our and our grandparents' lives. I think about that a lot. The accident of me—I mean, here I am lasting so much longer than my parents' relationship. And then the accident of me meeting Aaron."

"Yes," Allie says. "And Rachel and Levy already love each other and share such a bond. They enjoy each other and share their worlds."

How the future might tear them apart. "We don't have political beliefs pulling us, though. Not a war," I say.

"No. But you disapprove and have stereotyped beliefs about what's going on with us. All that drug shit you accused us of." Tara meets my eyes and says this without blinking, her flat tone absent of confrontation.

"Smoke said something about that, but I smelled pot in your room."

"Sure, pot, but we don't touch hard drugs. And I seem

to remember you and Marissa smoking some during one of your sleepovers. None of those dudes use hard drugs . . . well, I don't know about T-Bone. He's the party boy, he's liable to do anything for a thrill. But they couldn't afford it when they were growing up and now they have too much to lose. It's the dudes in the 'burbs who have that luxury."

"You forget I'm a lawyer. Pot is still illegal." I sit back and cross my arms. "I know the statistics. Seventy percent of drug users are white. Seventy percent of people serving time for drugs are black." Desperate to change the subject, I ask Allie, "Were they ever loving sisters?"

"I don't know. But we learn from them by using history to help us understand the present. They were more alike than they could see, and so are you two," Allie continues.

Tara and I glare at each other, then look away.

"Have you ever realized you went through the same things: the loss of a father, and a long-lasting first love?

"You don't realize it but you both bonded so strongly, so young. And being a mother is important to both of you. And you're both hard-working and dedicated." Allie counts these five similarities on her fingers. "Oh, and you're both beautiful," she laughs.

"Sky always found me annoying. She didn't want us to bond over anything." Tara has a peculiar expression on her face, as though she's thinking something else. And then she turns to me and asks, "Are you coming to my concert in Albuquerque?"

I look away. "I don't know if I could stand so many happy people."

Tara nods. "Do you remember that night we went to Magic Mountain? When we were kids?"

I struggle to remember and must squinch up my face in confusion, because she adds, "Remember, Dad didn't pick me up like he was supposed to and you had to babysit?"

"That always happened."

"We walked to Magic Mountain and sat on the top and told secrets." Tara nudges.

She twists toward me, a pleading expression on her face. And then I remember, and tears start as my father's death and Troy's death combine in a wave of anguish. I nod, my fingers covering my eyes and cheeks.

"And that orphaned orange light, the sunrise in the middle of the night, do you remember?" Tara is not deterred by my tears.

I nod.

"I thought about that the day Troy was dying and, for the L.A. concert, I painted my face half orange to commemorate us."

"Oh, so that's why you did it. It looked so cool," Allie says. "It gave you an unearthly appearance."

Allie's words break the silence between Tara and me.

"You know, you'll always have each other. If you want each other," Allie says. I know that she told us the story intentionally.

"But look at Alma and Nana, did they have each other?" Tara pushes.

Allie shakes her head. "At Mum's funeral, Alma wailed out her guilt and sorrow, wailed to bring the heavens down. Nana tisked and said, 'People who mourn the loudest have done the least.' But through the years the war was forgotten. The Nazis were viewed as an aberration. Alma became a Republican and campaigned for Eisenhower. So did Nana. But I don't know if there was forgiveness. And of course no one ever forgot. Even I, two generations later, haven't forgotten. But they were sisters regardless."

Tara turns to me. "I love you. I've always loved you."

I don't say *I love you* to Tara. I'm not sure I've ever said it to her. I have to peel away layers of sadness and anger and resentment. But then I creep toward something I know is the truth: "I envy you. I've always envied you."

"Really?"

"The secret that I told you. That your father is still alive."

Tara huffs, making a snorting sound, "For whatever good that is."

"Alive means there is a possibility for reconciliation. When you're dead, it's over."

Allie sits crossed-legged on her bed, watching us. Now, I smell the sweet vanilla from the candle.

"But you *know* your father loved you," Tara says.

Yes. "And I know Troy loves me." I inhale, turn to

Tara, and say, "Your life is so easy. You played against the odds and won, and I played it safe and lost."

"You haven't lost," Allie and Tara say together.

"Troy's gone. But *you* haven't lost. You still get to decide what you do next. How you live out the rest of your life."

"I've had no determination in what's happened."

"But what you do next, *you* do," Tara says.

Why does Tara think she knows so much when she's so young? I guess because she's been alone so long, since she was a baby. And I feel sad for her, for the first time. I look at her sitting there, her eyelashes shadowing her cheek, her lips slightly opened but downturned in a naked and vulnerable expression.

"You decide how you look at it," Allie agrees.

He died. That's how I look at it. I'm alone living my mother's nightmare.

I think that, but don't say it. And then I remember, I'm not alone.

Rachel. Thank God for Rachel. I am a mother. She has me. And for the first time I realize that with all the weight and importance of it. Rachel has me. She still has me. And I still have her.

"And you have us to help you. Me. Mom. Aaron. Levy. The whole crew."

"Me, too," Allie says.

"But most important, you have *you*," Tara adds.

And Rachel has me.

Apple Doesn't Fall Far

Tara

Once you love someone from a different ethnic group, you see the world with different eyes. The lesson from Allie's story reiterates my own truth. It's funny, but I sometimes view the world with black eyes now. Black people who don't know me might get annoyed at such a statement. How could a white girl know what it's like to be black, when all I have to do is walk away and I'm in my white world again? But I can't do that. I walk around with a white-looking face and a black sense of America. What happens to black people affects me through the people I love. I'm assumed to be part of the mass of white people when I'm alone, or with Mom or Sky. But when I wander around the world, I imagine how I'd be treated if they knew about Aaron and Levy, or if I were black. I see racism more, because I know what it's like on both sides. I know the freedom and safety of being white.

I understand things I didn't before I met Aaron. Before, I didn't *care*. Like: there are very few white people in low-level service positions. I took that for granted. Most of us do. Most white people just assume that's just the way the system works. We don't even think about how we benefit. Now I see how that assumption affects Aaron and how it'll impact my Levy, who I love even more than I love myself.

Whatever happens to black people, whatever racism will cloud the future of our country, happens to me. I feel like an imposter or a spy, as though I only *pretend* to be white when I'm with white people. I imagine their reaction to the real me, the Aaron-lover me, the Levy-mother me. So there's my self-self that's beyond race and my black-self, the self that other people can't immediately perceive. And my white self.

I lie in bed thinking these things. Aaron's still in Red Dog's room, I guess. When I gathered up Levy, he wrapped his arms around my neck and snuggled into my shoulder. I put him in his cot gently and lay next to him, singing softly. It's a funny place I got myself in, one that I hadn't anticipated, but I now welcome. I've learned so much about the world this way, seeing with different sets of eyes.

I feel empathetic toward Allie's grandmother, as though we're experiencing some of the same transitions, or strange psychological positions.

I don't think Allie meant for me to hear this from her story. She was trying to get Sky and me to put our differences in perspective. Maybe Sky needed to learn that. I've always known we were different but held together by love. Or at least I feel close to her because I love her. Look what I'm trying to do for her now: getting the entire crew, right in the middle of a tour, to help her move back home.

But I don't think she loves me. It's like she said—too overwhelmed by envy. Jealousy.

Aaron comes in and I pretend to be asleep. I don't want to get out of my own thoughts by talking. I hear the soft smack of his lips as he kisses Levy. Levy rustles and sloughs off his blanket, which makes a muted tone like the end of a note just before it finally fades. Aaron removes his clothes, goes into the bathroom. He shuts the door quietly, to not wake me. I hear muffled swishes as he pees, washes his hands and face, and brushes his teeth.

Slowly, silently, he creeps to our bed and slides under the covers. He spoons me. His flesh is cool. He kisses the nape of my neck, where the hair meets the skin, and whispers, "I couldn't sleep without kissing you good night, babe. My Li'l Key. I love you so much."

His breath warms my neck. "More than all the words, all the music in the world can express. I'd lose myself if I lost you." He tells me this secret he can only tell me when I'm asleep to protect himself.

In the morning, I wonder if I dreamed those kisses as soft as sighs and the secret, scared confession of love. I roll over and put my head on Aaron's chest. Now, he's warm, his skin slightly moist from the covers, his dreams, and the heat we generate with our bodies. I press close to him, I want to make love, but Levy is in the room. In a minute he'll be up and crawling in bed with us. So I simply press myself against him and he moans, getting my message.

"I love you, too."

"Ah, you weren't asleep."

"I was, like, spying on you," I confess.

He squeezes me tight. "I want you to know I'll always take care of you."

"As much as you can, considering."

"Considering? What do you mean?"

"Considering that you have to do your thing, too. No jail cells, remember? No bars." We each have ultimate loyalty to ourselves.

He shakes his head, his lips pressed together, and I know he wants the easy truth. Peace. Harmony. Love at all costs. Family allegiance over self. "I'm with you, I love you. I love what we have, I say."

"But what? Tell me what you're not saying." Now he hunts for security in truth.

"What if I started writing my own songs?"

"You think I wouldn't welcome that? Bring it on. It might make us richer, and I don't mean money. I mean musically. Let's see where we can grow. We a team of equals."

I smile at him in the dim dawn. So far, he's the leader and I'm an excellent and valuable follower. Maybe I don't need King to help develop my own voice. Maybe I can do it with Aaron.

"I rely on you," he says.

But he doesn't get it. "Thank you for diving into the pool and pulling out Rachel."

"Hey. That's what people do," he says with a chuckle. He pulls me close and we press to each other without tension, just desire, and then Levy crawls in bed and we all wrestle and tickle.

We'll meet Allie, Sky, and Rachel in Albuquerque. Rachel wants to come with us, but Sky tells her she'll be too lonely without her. Rachel touches her mom's cheek.

"We'll catch up to you there." Allie wears black silk pajamas and her hair twists in messy tendrils. She sees me staring, pats it down, and laughs, "Oh, my Medusa hair."

So we're off. Just like always, except that I miss Smoke, who's driving Sky's U-Haul. The rocks and mesas are red, and the road is crowded with trucks. I'm back to being part of the rap crew and by fifty miles down the road, I'm playing with my keyboard, working out a sweet melody to "I'll Miss Myself." Aaron works on some lyrics, and damn if Levy hasn't taken over Africa, Smoke's djembe. Red Dog and T-Bone play video games on hand-helds and text message, probably juggling three women at once. My fight with Sky, Rachel almost drowning, Allie's story . . . it all fades as the tones floating through the van pick up the tires hushing on the road.

Mom calls, so I move to the front of the bus behind Thumble. He's privy to all my daughterliness. "How's Sky?" is what she says even before she says hello.

"She, like, made a new friend yesterday, one from Michigan."

"A man?"

I imagine Mom's eyes wide in surprise, hoping that another man will help Sky forget Troy. Mom forgets that didn't work out so well for her. Was that what my father was . . . a distraction from mourning? No wonder he didn't last. He was never important to her as a person. And for a split second, I feel sorry for him.

"Nope. An art teacher with two kids from Lansing."

"Another single mom." I almost hear Mom nod her head in agreement. "She must be coming out of herself."

"Maybe." I don't tell her about Rachel almost drowning and Aaron pulling her out of the pool. No need to worry her, even though Aaron could win brownie points. "She's beginning to talk more, and she may even come to our concert tonight."

"Oh, the concert," Mom says as though she's forgotten that's why we're here, that's why we're even able to help Sky.

"How was your speech?"

"Okay. I'm still in Chicago finishing up at the conference."

There's a silence in which I wonder if she's going to ask me how I am. How the Grand Canyon was. How Levy is.

Instead she asks, "How's Rachel?"

"Fine. Loving Levy and Allie."

"Good. I figured Allie would be a great surrogate mother. I'm just glad she was able to cancel her plans at the spa and help out. But that's Allie."

"She's with Sky and Rachel in Sky's car."

"I wanted to know how she was doing." She assumes Sky can't communicate her own emotional state.

"Sky's not very good at change or the unexpected. She wants everything to go according to plan."

"I guess that's true," Mom says, as though she's never thought of this downside to Sky's organized ambition. I can tell she has stood up and is pacing. She can't sit still for long. Maybe she's organizing her toiletries or folding the clothes for her suitcase. "Well, I think I'll try to call her. Take care. Drive safely," she tells me, and hangs up before I can say goodbye.

And then the phone rings and I think Mom is calling back, but Sissy's name is on the screen.

"Hey, sugar," she says, and I smell the roses of her perfume. "How you doing? How's my two men?"

"We're on our way to Albuquerque."

"I know. I wanted to wish you break-a-leg on your concert. That man of yours doesn't hear his phone half the time. How's your sister doin'?"

So I tell Sissy all about Sky and her new friend and how Aaron rescued Rachel and how Levy is making up words.

"You a good sister, sugar," she pronounces, and then asks, "And how are Special and Li'l Key?"

That's her way of reminding us it's just our music, our jobs, not us. Keeping us real, I guess. She wishes us more luck on our concert and tells us to make it fun, and blows me some sugar with loud smacks to pass on to her men.

I return to my seat and glance at Levy. His knobby knees hold the djembe tilted so it resonates with the road while his hands play out a four-six beat. His focus, his attention, and the serious pleased smile touching his lips provide a window into the adult he'll become. And as always, his folded lips remind me of a rosebud, but he smiles just like my mom.

New lyrics come to me, and I realize the verses are switching from Troy's death to the possibility of Aaron's loss to the very positive thought of Levy growing up. The melody comes easily and I keep going.

I look up and catch Aaron watching me.

"Let's hear it."

So I give him what I got, sing it all by myself to him and Red Dog and T-Bone. I just keep going, freestyling the lyrics even though I realize this isn't really a rap song. I don't know what it is.

When I'm finished, I meet Aaron's eyes and he nods at me. Slowly.

"That ain't rap," T-Bone complains.

"No. That's Li'l Key," Red Dog says.

I dress for the concert. My half-orange face has become part of my wardrobe.

"Think Levy's ready?" Aaron asks, only half joking.

"Can't let him replace Ole Smoke," I joke back.

"You look hot as hell tonight."

I pull down a fuchsia strand to drift over one brow, the orange brings out the green in my eyes, and I've shadowed them with an iridescent yellow.

"Like a tiger," Aaron says.

I form my fingers into claws, turn to him, and growl. "Grrrrrr."

"Cute," he says.

A Latino band opens singing rap in a mixture of English and Spanish that I struggle to understand, but the crowd gets it and screams with delight. They do an encore, and I know we're going to have to work it to get the same applause. They know "Prohibitions of Prison," and the mob raises hands to pump the air with enthusiasm, shouting the lyrics with us. When we sing "From the Midwest to the West," Special has added lyrics about New Mexico, which warm the house. I'm unprepared for this, but feel a stirring of pride. Maybe one day he'll be as big as King.

And then he holds the mic and slowly presses his open palm down to quiet the throng. "We got somethin' a little different for you tonight. One of our crew has a new song for you."

I peek at Smoke and Red Dog and T-Bone standing behind Special, mics in their hands, dragging by their legs, and see them glance at each other, caught as off guard as I am.

"It's our own Li'l Key making her solo debut! Let's give it up for her." He points the mic at me.

I told him I wanted this, asked him for it, and he's giving it to me, but I'm on the spot. Am I ready? My heart increases its beat.

I stand up and slide into the opening chord to "I'll Miss You." On the first syllable, my voice cracks. I move away from my mic and clear my throat.

And then my finger slips and I play a wrong note. My stomach flips. I haven't played a wrong note in years. I continue singing and seem to catch my wind. A woman in the front row squints at me and says something to her friend. Her friend shakes her head and shrugs. Sweat pours down my back and my hands slide on the keys.

I sing the next line, and my voice sounds reedy. When

I glance at Special and the crew, T-Bone pulls his mic to his mouth to cover for me. They're ready to step in and sing a backup that will swamp me.

This is my opportunity, I tell myself. Sing it like I'm on the bus. Like I sing it to Levy. I'll only get so many chances.

I inhale, clench my eyes shut, and start over. I push my favorite Fauré note, letting it tease the crowd to connect with the rap song that preceded.

The tone gives me courage. When it finishes trembling across the auditorium, my fingers glide automatically while I move to the spirit of the words. I snatch some air and start with the sexy part, my voice joining with my keyboard, one thing, my throat supplying additional tones. I'm home now. Back on my square. Not even paying attention to the audience. Singing to the universe.

And I end with:

All love changes.
I'll miss myself,
The me I am when I'm like that with you.

And repeat the hook like a mantra,

All love changes
All love changes
All love changes

Altering the melody almost imperceptibly, until the entire melody line is new. Just like love transforms. Tears stream down my face as I think of me, up here singing alone, and all the changes in the last few weeks. Troy dying, Rachel almost drowning, King tempting me, and this song, this little, bitty song stretching its message across a throng. This song that I almost betrayed.

People start singing.

Special holds out his mic so the audience hears itself. He nods to the crew and they whisper into their mics:

All love changes.

It morphs into a slogan, *all love chaaaaannngees*. The *s* slippery in the air, sliding around us.

Special jerks his hand down and we stop. He stops it at the *v* in *love*.

All love

And I realize how close it is to his father's way of saying *I love you*. What did he say when he left? *Just love*. I remember Sissy and Aaron talking about it.

And so I sing it all by myself, a cappella.

Just love.

Special's eyes widen and his mouth opens as he realizes how I morphed into him.

And that's it.

The concert is over.

We end telling everybody to *just love*.

Guess that's as good as it gets anyway even though the love part can get so twisted and tangled. Can hurt so bad. Maybe Aaron's pops was right all along. Just love and it'll all be okay. Well, maybe not okay, but better. What a wonderful idea.

Almost as soon as I get backstage, there's a messenger with three dozen orange roses. I recognize him as one of King's men. He bows slightly as he hands me the flowers, their heady aroma wrapping me and reminding me of Sissy. Levy has his arms around my leg, wanting to reclaim me from the audience.

And then the dude hands me a package. It's wrapped in shiny orange paper and tied with a shimmering gold bow of wired ribbon with exaggerated swirls and tails.

"You did a powerful job tonight," the dude says. "Congratulations." He presses his palms together in namaste, bows slightly, and backs away.

Aaron watches this, his brows knitted together and his mouth in a frown, shooting me the mad face when I haven't done anything.

Sky and Allie were in the audience. I saw Sky from the stage when I turned on my keyboard. I don't know if she has seen me perform since my first recitals; she was too busy at college and law school, and then we were separated by most of the United States. Now, she has put on makeup, and her straight hair grazes the tips of her breasts. She doesn't say anything to me; instead she goes over to Smoke and gives him a hug, and his thick arms and body swallow her.

I haven't opened the box, though I know it's from King.

I hold the present and the flowers with one arm and pick up Levy with the other and walk over to Aaron.

"Let's see what I got." I'm trying to diminish any possible jealousy, to create trust by my openness.

I slip off the ribbon slowly because it's too beautiful—yes, even the ribbon—to crunch up and throw away. I peel away the Scotch tape to preserve the paper. Aaron notices my caution and his frown deepens.

I lift off the lid, almost cautiously. A key pendant three inches long, studded in orange gemstones, hangs from a gold chain. The stones, as rich in color as the paint on my face, flash sharper tones of red and twinkle from the chain. A card is signed, "For the fiery Li'l Key. K."

A note card explains that the stones are rare orange sapphires from Ceylon.

Obviously, he had it made for me. The gems explode with sparkles.

"I give you everything, everything you want," Aaron splits the word into *every* and *thing*, "and you still do this?" And then he comes close to a whisper, "And just a moment ago, up on that stage, when you were singing about *just love*, I felt we were one."

"We were. That was for you, for us."

"You giving him encouragement. Man doesn't give a woman a thirty-thousand-dollar present without knowing he's putting a down payment on a promise."

"He's putting a down payment on the money he hopes to make from me," I say and drop the necklace to the ground. I look for the guy who handed it to me, but he's gone, the door of the auditorium swinging behind him. The pendant lies on the floor, pebbles flashing regardless of their ignominy.

But it's too late. Aaron has spun on his heels and walked away from me.

What else was I supposed to do?

A woman with black hair that hangs straight, and eyes seemingly without pupils, tits spilling out of a magenta spaghetti-strapped tank top, cobalt pants painted on a beautiful ass, and stilettos that make her almost as tall as Special, steps right up to him and I hear her say, "*Ay papi*, you looked so good on stage. *Que lindo eres* in person, too."

It's so easy to be gone. So easy for him. So easy for me. So easy.

And then she pulls Aaron closer and kisses his cheek, runs her hand down his back, stopping at his ass. He doesn't pull away. Is he allowing this to get back at me? Or just doing what he wants to do? I don't know.

I turn away from Aaron and the other woman, bend down to pick up the sparkling charm.

Maybe he uses King as an excuse to scoop up some of these new women.

I watch the dazzle of the stones. I don't even care about bling; usually I buy my clothes at used clothing stores. But King gave me something I didn't even know I desired. A totem. How I wish I had thought of having it made.

Sky wiggles out of Smoke's paternal hug. She shakes her head. "Apple doesn't fall far, huh, Tara?" A smug pout touches her lips when she says this. And then she tilts her chin up and, really, honest to God, clicks her tongue in her mouth, staring at me with those opaque gray eyes that see right through you.

And I haven't done a thing except sing my own song.

CHAPTER EIGHT

Apple Doesn't Fall Far

Sky

The last time I saw Tara perform, she was ten. In late spring after my college term ended, Mom and Troy and I watched her walk on stage, sit in front of the piano, and poise her fingers above the keyboard. She inhaled, and then hit a Rachmaninoff chord, her stretching fingers confidently pounding the keys. The music, saturating the small auditorium, was so much grander than the skinny kid with her hair in two French braids. Mom and I presented her with a bouquet of silk peonies that now sit in her Detroit apartment. She's so attached to anything we've given her.

Now, in Albuquerque, Allie and I sit in the front row. I try to absorb the excitement of the crowd, but find it difficult.

Most important, you have you, Tara had said.

No. Most important I have Rachel. I don't know if I ever had me other than my collection of goals to attain and hoops to jump through. *Me* is sense of constant inadequacy. I'm never proficient, safe, or good enough. I'm not Troy and I can't make up for him.

The auditorium is dim now, and Allie pays attention to the audience dressed in colorful clothing and crazy makeup. The people around me are young, tattooed, and pierced. Not much different from the people on Venice Beach. They're thrilled by the first group singing in Spanish as well as English, and I enjoy the buzz of their lyrics, incomprehensible to me, but a perfectly distracting escape into my own thoughts.

Troy would have taught Rachel how to dive. "Look into my eyes. You're going to sail through the air and your fingertips are going to slice through the water," he'd have told her. He would have shown her quadratic equations and beamed with pride as she dressed for a prom or graduated from high school. I see all these moments in flashes ... Troy standing on a diving board with her, handing her flowers at graduation. Years zoom through airbrushed Hallmark card moments. Father-daughter assemblages that I always wanted, that I never had, that I assumed would be hers and Troy's.

Tara never had any of that either.

What we got, both of us, was pain. And for the first time, I see our differences as minute in comparison to that. A sisterly bond of pain, even though Tara won't embrace it. She never talks about Stephen. I wonder what influence his philandering has had.

She's an adult with a son of her own. A man who loves her. She's solved her dilemma. And meanwhile, my daughter will go through what I had to. At least both of us know our fathers loved us.

I blame myself, but I still can't figure out what I did wrong.

For the first time in a long time, I enjoyed getting dressed for Tara's concert. My shampoo smelled of ginger, my shower gel of lavender. I smoothed body lotion with sparkles on my skin. I ran a flat iron through my hair, noting it's too long and needs a trim. Yellow shadow made my eyes even grayer. I put on mascara and combed through my lashes. I was aware as I did all this that I was paying attention to myself for the first time since Troy died. We dropped Rachel backstage to be with Levy, and she ran into Smoke's arms and then galloped away holding Levy's hand.

Tara strolls on the stage wearing a sequined top with an orange lightning bolt through the black. Half her face is orange, and green shadows her eyes. Highlights stripe her hair, and she's pulled spiky points around her face. Each movement—the way she steps in her stilettos, the way her hips catch up to her forward action—broadcasts power. Tara commands that theater and when she steps up to her keyboard, she's home and queen of her world.

Smoke's motions don't change, just the way he spits out words and sings the percussion. He's still the bear who soothes the group while T-Bone rockets the melody and sexes up everything with exaggerated hip rolls and gestures to his groin. I wonder if he and Brooke spent the night together. I wonder if he's as good as he advertises or if it's all a façade. Special focuses on the audience, playing to them. And I understand now how he so quickly rescued Rachel. He's tuned in to subtle signals, almost as if he has a sixth sense.

Smoothly he lets the audience know he's one of them, and then switches up singing about New Mexico—the sandy country, fiery sun, tortillas, and beans. Turquoise and soft coral.

He introduces Tara. For a quick second, her eyes widen with fear. When she starts singing, her first note is off key. Her eyes bolt around the auditorium. The crew readies to rescue her.

She can't do it, I think with joy. Isn't that awful? I see my sister screw up and I'm happy. When she feels nothing but sorrow over my sadness.

She starts again, playing a note that forms a new base. She sings alone, dancing to what must be a song she wrote, commanding the theater with words about love. She turned a falter into a success, just like she always does.

Ironic, I think, that Tara, who is so comfortable with being alone, is singing love's praises. *All love changes,* she tells us. *Yes. It dies,* I think.

The crowd goes crazy. How do I feel? Watching her, my little sister: The Star. She's her, but not her. Dressed up and glamorized like she's some hot celebrity, someone extraordinary. Remote from the pest following me and spying. She's flashy and powerful. Her eyes, huge and green with their shadow, watch Special and glance at the audience, gathering us all up.

And she plays her own song.

Her own damn song.

I hate God. That's terrible to think. But I do. I hate that He has let this happen to me. Me. Who has always been good. Obedient.

Tara's voice caresses her lyrics, revealing our lives. It's her reaction to Troy. Aaron. Levy. She blasts her love out.

I wonder if we ever paid attention. I wonder if we give love so it's received. What if someone offers love, but you don't recognize it and it goes right past you? *Whisssh*. You miss it.

And then Tara ends. *Just love.*

I guess maybe that's all you can do. Love regardless, not to the destruction of yourself, but in spite of yourself. Love and hope the people you throw it to catch it.

The crowd stomps, sings, screams, whistles. The women are thrilled with the message.

Why her?

Why her and not me?

Then Allie pulls my hand and we're on our way backstage. A table with food, a throng around Tara and Aaron. Rachel runs to me, her face painted half orange like Tara's, but a smeary mess. Rachel did it herself, trying to look like her aunt, and I'm disheartened.

There's a crowd around Tara congratulating her on her solo debut. Aaron hugs her, and the crew claps her on the back like she's one of the guys. A reporter asks her questions, and Levy hangs on her leg.

A man dressed in an Armani suit groomed smooth as silk hands Tara a bouquet of orange roses as thick as her torso and a small box. She removes the ribbon and flips the lid.

Gemstones flare sparkles.

The elegant, polished man presses his hands together and backs away.

Aaron's expression darkens and freezes.

A gift from another man.

Caught her.

It's not so all-perfect as Little Miss Star would want us to believe.

"Apple doesn't fall far, does it, Tara?" My own voice—how it hisses out between my teeth, its spiteful thrill—shocks me.

I watch her eyes as she follows Aaron pivoting away from her, as she glances at the flashing ornament in her open palm, as a woman with a tattoo of peacock feathers on her arm touches Aaron's shoulder and with decorated nails draws him close to her and then traces her fingertip across his shoulder, up his neck, and around his ear.

Tara slowly blinks and closes her eyes as though to wipe away the image, or maybe to hide the tears. Then she lifts her chin, puts the flowers on the floor, pulls the chain from the box, opens the lobster-claw clasp, and places it around her neck. The key sits right below her collarbone and rests between her breasts. The final touch—classy and exotic—to her persona. Whoever bought it read, or knows, her well.

She holds Levy in one arm, the flowers in the other, and walks away.

Allie follows.

Tara's shoulders slump, her back curves as her head hangs low. She turns to Levy, and in profile, her makeup looks childish, like that of a little girl dressed for Halloween, no longer the exotic, flashy star.

I should feel sorry for her.

But, even though it's horrible, I don't. Tara deserves this for what she put Mom through, disappearing, once for an entire weekend, skipping school, mouthing off, falling in love with a dude in prison and getting pregnant in high school.

I don't even feel guilty that I'm pleased to see life pivot against her. Why should I feel all the sorrow?

Maybe now that I see she's having a bump in her life, we can be friends. Maybe I can forgive her for being successful against the odds, forgive her for turning the impossible dream into a reality.

That night, we drive to Allie's brother David's house, where we're spending a day before heading to Memphis. Troy and I drove from Ann Arbor to L.A. through Denver once. The crew came out that way; now they're taking the more southern route with performances along the way. The concert locations determine the route. Luckily, David is only a few miles off the highway.

Tara decides to ride with Allie, Rachel, and Levy, avoiding Aaron.

I ask Smoke if I can ride in the U-Haul.

He looks hard at me and nods slowly, and then shrugs one shoulder.

"I want to be close to my things, I guess," I tell him.

And then I instantly worry that I've disregarded him, when I find his solidity so comforting. I think of adding, *I like being with you, too*, but that sounds stupid.

I can't do anything, even the smallest thing, right.

The kids are fast asleep. Allie leads the way in my car.

Smoke and I bring up the rear in the U-Haul. We're the only vehicles on a road that winds through mountains that block the spangled sky and cast ominous shadows. I gaze out the window.

Smoke hums a beat. He's amusing himself,

accompanying the sounds from the car engine and the road, or maybe working out percussion for one of the raps.

After a half hour or so, he says, "Tara's at a crossroads. You know?"

"No."

"King's trying to woo her away from Special and the crew."

"King? *The* King?"

"Uhmmm," he nods. "He showed up at the L.A. concert, and in Albuquerque. That dude with the necklace was one of his people."

"Is he trying to woo her away for sex?"

"Sex?" He shakes his head and turns to me. Even in the darkness, the shadows his brows throw deepen his eyes. "Maybe that, too. But mostly for her talent and how it can help him. She keeps backing off and he ups the ante. That necklace, well, that's a huge ante."

"Yes."

"Always a struggle between doing your own thing and compromising. How much do you give up for love, for your homies. Especially for an artist, since expressing a personal vision is paramount."

"I assumed she was fooling around. You know, like people do." Troy and I talked about how much we should forfeit of "I" for "we." All couples, I guess, struggle with this, but women usually make the compromises, giving up self for couplehood.

"Maybe King would advance her musical career. Maybe not. Who knows what the future brings for Key and Special." He hugs a curve and I feel the swing of my worldly goods back of us. "King can guarantee her fame now but also guarantee that she'll lose Aaron, and the rest of us."

Tara convinced me that she and Aaron were unique, but maybe he's merely a rung on a ladder. "What about you, Smoke?"

"For me, the music is about how it makes me feel. A meditation. For Tara it's who she is. She could uncover new rooms inside her by creating her own music. That's the symbol behind the key. What happens next says lots about what's inside Tara. And Aaron."

"Did Aaron tell you this?"

"Nope. I've seen it with my own eyes."

CHAPTER NINE

The Connectedness of It All

Tara

Allie follows me into the dressing room. I put Levy down on the cot and look for a vase for the flowers. I remove the bag of trash from a plastic bin, fill it with water, and cram in the roses. The stems completely stuff the pail and a heady miasma pervades the room.

Orange roses.

I stare at the embellished key around my neck in the mirror. It's shaped almost like an ankh, the ancient Egyptian symbol for eternal life.

But you don't live on after you die. Not really. It's just people's ever-changing judgments that continue.

Allie, her hair in ringlets, wearing a very low black

blouse, white pants, and a white wrap, smiles at me in the mirror. "It's beautiful. So beautiful."

I touch it to claim it. "I usually don't care much about material stuff."

We watch each other's reflections and then I say, "There's something about this, though."

"It's not about the charm. It's about what it represents. Putting yourself first. Independence."

"And security," I add.

"What do you mean?"

"Accepting it leads to artistic acclaim and financial security. I can't, like, *do* anything but music. King has his own record label. Last year he helped Karma and the Kicks win a Grammy. He *develops* people. If I went with him, I'd never have to play for pennies on the beach, which is a possibility now. Aaron and me and the crew might never take off, and we could fade away."

I continue, "Working with King means I'd be doing okay forever. Levy and I."

"When I was young, I cared about fame." I see Allie's profile in the mirror turned to look at the real me, not the mirror me. "But I don't care about it now."

"Why not?"

She frowns, shrugs, and turns back to the mirror. "I guess for me fame was about immortality, and now that I'm closer, I'm not as frightened by my own death. And it was about being able to make a difference, have an impact on the world. I guess I've done that one patient at a time."

My eyes squint in the mirror as I consider what Allie says. "For me it's about giving my music to the world. It's about being vindicated in who I am, regardless. But the money is tempting for Levy, to give him security."

Allie nods. "Vindicated in who you are regardless . . . of your father?"

"Yes. Like it . . . he . . . doesn't matter."

"Don't take what happened with your father personally."

But he's my *father*, I want to scream.

"It doesn't say or mean anything about who you are. Just who *he* is. And you'd never do that to Levy." Allie's eyes meet mine in the mirror.

I touch the twinkle on the largest jewel. "King couldn't have realized how much this means. A symbol of my music, and Sky and me, and fame, and life all at once and together. It empowers me to do anything."

"I think it's more like a magic feather, like Dumbo's."

"Dumbo? Oh—he, like, thinks he can fly as long as he holds the feather, but he can fly all by himself."

"You got it. All along it's him, not the feather."

I continue staring at the mirror. So does Allie. Both of us side by side, talking to each other's reflections instead of our faces.

"Are you interested in him?" she asks.

"I would be if I didn't have Aaron. I mean, I had a crush on him when I was a kid. But now . . ." I shrug as my voice trails away, "I mean, I have a family. I *love*

Aaron. I don't trust it'll last, but I'd feel desolate if we split. How could I hurt Levy like that?"

"But. I hear the but."

I shrug and glance at my hands resting on the clutter of my makeup: shadows and blush, bottles of foundation and compacts, and glistening tubes of lipsticks. "Aaron . . . he let that other woman kiss him. He did it to get back at me. To hurt me. To make me pay attention."

"Intimacy is a dance of distance, individuality, and compromise. The only way you get things exactly how you want is living alone." Allie tilts her head back and laughs with a mixture of merriment and bitterness. "And that of course has its own tremendous joys and sorrows. Like you said, love changes once you let yourself just love."

I stare at my reflection now. The orange paint is still in place, and the green cat eyes make me look wise and wild, when really I feel neither, I feel uncertain and insecure. I've always used artifice to put on a face for the world. Dyeing my hair black and studding my ears, eyebrows, and nose when I was a teenager. The makeup that transforms me into Li'l Key. Is it vanity? Masquerade? A shield? All three, I realize.

The stones glimmer with a radiance I can't come near to matching.

"I may have already screwed it up. Or rather King did."

"That was his plan, wasn't it?" Allie meets my eyes in the mirror.

I consider what I'd be selling if I bought what King has to offer. And think about how much he'd control me and my music.

"Ultimately it depends on what success is to you. Is it being some hot-shit celebrity whose concerts cost eighty bucks? Or is it following the pull of your work and nurturing it to develop in its unique way?" Allie puts her hands on the counter and leans toward the mirror as though to get closer to me. "Maybe the musician playing for pennies on the beach fully explores her own talent and gives joy to all the people who pass by. And *all* people can enjoy the music without having to pay a ton of money."

Maybe. Seems like if a song is way popular, then you've touched more people. But maybe you have to dim it down, smooth it out for that to happen, and it loses its edge.

Or maybe you're lucky. Your voice and what people desire end up matching.

I pull the jar of cold cream toward me, smear it on my face to wipe off Key, revealing Tara once again.

CHAPTER NINE

The Connectedness of It All

Sky

The sun wakes me, blasting through the window. It hits my eyes so intensely that there's deep red behind my lids. I open them to see the sun peering over a peak. We're in a valley surrounded by mountains. It was so dark when we drove in last night, or rather, early this morning, that we bumped blindly along a rutted road with only glints of barbed wire visible on either side. A horse stared back at me. It was a pinto, so only the white spots seemed to exist and, when I first saw it, I couldn't tell what the collection of random splotches were. Then a white eyelid blinked, and I recognized the shine from the eye and the horse assembled itself.

The horse came back to me in a dream last night.

Rachel is beside me, her arm thrown across my body.

I look around the room we staggered into late last night. Its walls are adobe, painted a soft pink. Large squares of sandy tiles cover the floor. Outside, by the window, a small bird pecks at the seeds in a bird feeder hung from a tree branch.

I get up, grab my toiletry case, and stumble out of the room into a long hallway with rooms on either side, and finally find a bathroom at the end.

Afterwards, I wander through the house. No one else is awake. I discover the kitchen, and a pot of coffee brewed and still warm. The kitchen is lined with cabinets and a wall oven. An island stretches down the middle of it with a sink and stove top, the backsplash clad in tiles of colorful animals among huge flowers.

I pour a cup of coffee, slip my arms in my hoodie, and go outside. Shadows stretch from the mountain across a prairie composed of brittle stalks of weeds. The horse I saw last night, a mare, smashes the earth with thick hoofs. Beside her, a black colt watches me with interest and switches its tail. The grazing mare lifts her head and whinnies, and her eyes—one surrounded by white, the other black—imbue her with a cockamamie appearance. A stark contrast to the ghostly, otherworldly creature she was last night. Staring at me, she strides to the edge of her field and lifts her muzzle.

I walk toward her and touch her nose, surprisingly soft

skin dotted with prickly whiskers. She nuzzles my hand hoping for a treat, but I have none.

Then she pushes my shoulder with her nose in an affectionate nudge.

"That's Mija."

I turn to see a tall man wearing a cowboy hat over his long gray hair. He has sharp features and piercing eyes.

Mija prances, rearing to paw her front legs in the air, and then trots back and forth in front of the fence, her tail arched, strands flowing like feathers.

The man pulls a carrot from one pocket and gives it to her, his other hand gently stroking her forehead and velvet nose. She eats the carrot and lifts her head over the fence to woo the man closer for a hug. She whinnies to him, her nostrils trembling.

I didn't know horses could love people. It never occurred to me that a horse could love.

Then, her colt trots toward the man and he pulls out another carrot, a smaller one, and gives it to him, playing with the colt's ear as he chomps.

The man turns to me, rubs his palm down the leg of his jeans, and says, "I'm David. We were half asleep when you rolled in. Assume Allie got you all settled."

"I'm Sky." I shake his warm hand.

"You must be the sister with the daughter. Two beautiful sisters. One with a handsome son, the other with a wonderful daughter. What a blessing."

Mija dances for his attention.

"Quite a namesake," he says, looking up to study the sky.

I glance at the stretching heavens and realize for the first time that it's paler near the horizon and almost indigo straight above, a myriad of blue shades. The sun flashes, blinding white.

"The stars have finished singing together and conjured the beautiful morning," he says, his face turned up. "Come on. You can help me feed the donkeys."

Behind the house, in another field, is a barn stacked with hay. Two donkeys walk across the field toward David and me.

He flips open the latch and a fat donkey ambles over. David pats his head, then pulls down a bale with a hook, slits the jute, and tosses the hay in a feeder against the wall. David hands me a gallon jug to scoop up oats and I load a container with them. And then he fills a trough with water. By now, another donkey has arrived to watch us.

"That's Mohammed. This one is Happy Buddha." David tilts his head toward one with a belly almost dragging on the ground. "They're still working on deciding the future of the world and the meaning of life." He chuckles, and his hollow voice sounds as though it's coming from a whirlwind or a tornado. I check his throat to see if he's had some sort of operation that gives his voice an echo. There's just a grizzled neck with a prominent Adam's apple, not even the usual assortment of drapes and wrinkles seen on older men.

He's a handsome man, I notice, sinewy and hard, the Marlboro man with a gentle compassion evident when he touches his animals.

A flock of white doves zooms from the barn's attic. Each bird soars, providing a vivid contrast against the deep blue sky. The birds flip and soar above us with silent wings and extend across the sky as though performing a choreographed ballet.

I smell sage, hay, and some sweet, musky aroma I can't identify.

David scans the sky, watches Happy Buddha and Mohammed nuzzle their oats, and then Mohammed rubs his chin on Happy Buddha's back.

"See," David points, "you have to look quick or you miss it." A prairie dog lifts its head from the ground, its paws praying. It chirps and flashes back to its earthy home. A large dog comes over to David and sits beside him. "This is Misty." David's hand automatically goes to her head.

"I thought it was a coyote."

"Almost, but no. Found Misty at the Humane Society."

I realize then that I slept through 3:42. Had we arrived by then, or were we still in the car? I don't know. But I see the sky this morning and the glory of its colors and the peace of the animals and their love for this man, their caretaker.

"You like art? Want to see my studio?" he asks, jumping to a new topic.

There are no other houses that I can see, just a valley enclosed by mountains and fences partitioning the land. A scattering of buildings and the adobe house. We walk behind the barn and there's another wooden building, mostly windows, with a porch.

Inside, a hundred brushes hang from hooks along one wall. A huge easel with a blank canvas sits beside them. Behind it, a painting of the land in rich colors leans against the wall. It reveals a cross section into the earth so that you see roots searching for nutriments, the plants reaching for sun and rain. The scene pulses with a sense of the continuity of the earth, the roots, the green plants, the treasures of water and light.

The painting shows snow flittering like diamonds, clustered in furrows, and I can almost see it melting to nourish the plants.

"We got our first snow last week, but it only lasted a few hours. The sun melted it and the earth sucked it up. Now it exists on in that painting." He points a thumb at it.

The brush handles are twigs with their bark peeled off, or hand carved with emblems. A varied collection of hairs shaped into points and fans and wedges form the tips. Some are tiny as an eyelash, others as thick as three fingers.

He notices that I'm staring and says, "I make my own brushes. Mija and Happy Buddha contribute the bristles along with Wisdom, my male goat, who's getting busy with the lady-goat in town."

I reach out to touch them and then stop myself. "May I?"

"I'm glad my brushes inspired you to talk. That's the first thing you've said." Relief is apparent in his voice.

I guess it is.

David says with a shrug, as though it's obvious and no big deal, "I like to make things. I need to make things. I can't stop my hands. So in between paintings I make brushes, or build houses and work on my koi pond." He says this as information rather than explanation. It is what it is. He is what he is. It's all so simple.

I walk to the paintings leaning against the wall. Next to the one I first saw is a blue one and he's picked up all the subtle shades, swirled them around in spirals reaching each other as though the sky itself is about to birth the sun. A dove's white wing tips the corner as it flies to another world.

"David? David?" I hear Allie. We look out the studio door and Allie holds Rachel's hand. Tara, Levy, Aaron, and Smoke are behind her. Happy Buddha walks behind Levy, pushing his back with his nose as though herding him toward David. These strangers are interlopers in his field.

They enter the studio. Rachel runs to me, and I pick her up and kiss her while the others examine David's paintings as he pulls finished canvases from the stacks. David and Allie have the same bright eyes, though

David's are darker and more intense. Their arms and torsos are the same proportion and their hands and forearms almost identical, though David's obviously are larger. I wonder if Tara and I look alike in ways I have never appreciated because I focus so much on our differences.

David's many paintings are stacked against the wall opposite the brushes, and Tara and I begin to look at them. We flip through seasons. The snow grows on the mountain, eagles hunt in the depth of winter, glistening hail pounds the ground, twigs and buds are reborn in blood red. And of course people. Some with weathered faces I don't know, Allie's face with a smile, Allie's daughters.

"Do you, like, sell these?" Tara asks.

"Sometimes. Sometimes in Santa Fe and sometimes in New York. Sometimes not." And he laughs with that reverberating hollowness.

"David is a big-time artist, the artist of the decade back in the late eighties when SoHo was popping," Allie says. "He made enough money to buy this part of the mountain and built this house mostly with his own hands."

"Got tired of the pressure of the marketplace, that subtle comment from a gallery pushing for paintings done this way or that way because they sell. I loved to paint, just to paint. Paint and make things. An artist finds his vision, his voice, and communicates it whether it's heard or not. Now I paint what I want, when I want. I carve and form brushes or dig a koi pond or plant a willow if I feel like it. Take Mohammed and Happy Buddha for a walk up that mountain." David waves out the window to a mountain graced with a snow hat.

Tara has no makeup on, and I notice yellow flecks in the brown of her eyes as she listens to him. Her head is tilted, a gesture that indicates how focused she is. Then her eyes search for Aaron, who's been watching her. When their eyes meet, a smile flits between them, and Tara steps closer to him and Levy.

"David." Allie sounds almost scolding as she brings her brows together.

"I like to show people how I see this world. It's in these paintings. The connectedness of it all."

Smoke goes to the wall where the brushes hang and starts asking questions about drying time for the wooden handles, and what glue David uses to affix the twine holding the bristles to the shaft. Sometimes David has pounded out small wraps from various metals. Smoke makes his own drums, and the two of them end up in a discussion about the pros and cons of various animal skins.

I listen to all this talk about processes I've taken for granted. Things get made and you buy them in stores. Food wrapped in plastic, clothes hanging on racks, already produced and waiting to be bought. I pay attention to merchandise that's part of my lifestyle. Appropriate work clothes. Appropriate party clothes.

Comfortable furniture that's easy to maintain and doesn't show the grime of children's fingers. I guess it's surprising I never thought about it, because Mom made macramé necklaces and plant hangers and sold them in art fairs. But David, he makes because he *has to*, just like Tara *has to* make music. And Smoke is a combination of both.

Mohammed and Happy Buddha stand at their gate watching us stroll toward the house. On the way, we pass a koi pond fed by a small waterfall. The scales of fat orange, white, and pinto fish blaze in the water.

David puts his hand in the pool and fish surround it. "You ever pet a fish?" he asks Levy, who solemnly shakes his head no. "Go ahead, Sunshine loves to be petted and she's never gotten a blessing from a child."

Levy gingerly puts his hand in the water and an orange fish slides its body against his fingers.

"Me too," Rachel says as she kneels next to David, her fingertips skimming the water. She strokes the fish's face with the same gentle attention that she gives to patting people's cheeks. The touch she gave her father's face in the computer the day before he died.

The fish glides back and forth for her compassion and tenderness.

The garden around the house is in its winter dress. Visible are a few berries left on twigs that birds have forgotten, dried stalks of hollyhocks laden with seeds, and the earth getting ready for the next spring.

David stands. "Amazing, isn't it, this world that we have, and all we have to do to enjoy it is use our senses. Happy Buddha hasn't told me the meaning of life yet, but for me it's just this . . .," he sweeps his arms around the valley, "in all its wonder. This planet we've been given. There isn't any why or fairness . . . we are all simply lucky to be born, lucky to be given this day, this breath. Every day I wake up honored. Every day I have life."

I gaze at the earth and a prairie dog pops up, looking right at me. We stare at each other until Aaron joins me. Then, the critter barks and flickers into his hole.

"Reminds me of Detroit." Aaron looks around the plain with the mountain in the distance.

I turn to him and notice he's grown a mustache that makes his lips appear tender. "How so? I can't imagine anything more different."

"When I was a kid, I snuck up on the roof. Wrote. Fed the pigeons that hung out there. Up there, I was surrounded by sky, like here, and the tops of the other buildings, like the mountain." He nods at the peak in the distance. "The noise was blunted. The city was below me, all the cars doing their business. Like those prairie dogs with their mounds of dirt fortification." He rocks back on his heels. "It feels the same. They both offer a glimpse of what's big and what's small."

"You're figuring out Tara."

"Soon as I think I understand her, she does something that changes that."

"Me too and I've known her all her life."

He faces me now, his black eyes gleaming. "She tries to make sure she gets what she wants and is afraid to let anyone know what it is."

"I know she loves you. You wouldn't know it, because she hides it so well, but she's scared."

"I do know it." He shakes his head. "But she could tear down all the wonders we've created. Our family," and he points to Levy playing with the crew kicking a clod back and forth, and the tour bus. He shrugs one shoulder. "We'll be okay though."

He's thought this through. "You plan ahead," I comment.

"Nothing would be the same." His voice softens and he looks away as though to hide his eyes.

"Yes. I know."

He touches my arm. "You do." We stand side by side, facing the mountain, the top covered with snow, the pigeons dancing in the blue.

Aaron clears his throat. "You keep going and maybe that's the best anyone can do. Troy was a special dude. Helped me, too, by talking about protecting us legally and getting Larry to manage a good deal. Don't think I'm not appreciative. Troy, he treated everyone like human beings, he took care of his people."

I was lucky to have known Troy, lucky that he loved me.

*

Before we leave, David returns to his studio and brings out the sky painting. "You need this. Contemplate infinity in the moment, in this small square of it." He hands it to me, and observes as I put it in the back of the U-Haul.

"Remember to fly, Sky. Fly."

I get chills. How did David know to say that?

He waves to us as we drive away, Misty sitting next to him. Mija prances beside us, escorting us down the road.

CHAPTER TEN

Slightly Tarnished

Sky

There isn't any why or fairness . . . we are all lucky to be born, lucky to be given this day, this breath. David's hollow voice resonates in my mind as Smoke and I drive to Oklahoma City. The mountains diminish and a familiar flatness, interrupted by rolling hills, begins. Gigantic pieces of tires litter the road. We've seen them all along I-40, chunks of exploded tires lying torn, still curved and patterned, on the shoulder of the road. Sometimes we have to drive around them, because they're in the highway, bending toward us with tarry claws.

I consider the luck of simply being born, of being plucked out of the cosmos and bestowed with eyes to see, and nerves to feel, and ears to hear. Our senses. Our speech. Our breath. How crucial and insistent our cease-less moving lungs are from our first cry to our last. I remember my exhilaration at Rachel's first cry and see, as I have countless times since it happened, her lying breathless on the side of the pool.

But we're greedy. I'm greedy. I want more. Everything I always thought I'd have. Houses and jobs and success. People. Troy. Rachel. I feel gratitude about life but assume my rewards. I forget to treasure my inhales and exhales.

Losses build resentment. And gratitude for life turns to selfishness.

The green increases and then disappears as we hit the flat of Texas.

No farms. Scattered cattle off in the dry shrubby field. Advertisements for strip clubs before every exit.

I try to stay positive. I stop the image of Troy that fades before my eyes. Sharp points of windmills whirl, the blades sawing through the air. I can't hear them over the exaggerated sound of our tires hitting bumps in the road.

Even Smoke, beside me, isn't soothing. It's a long drive and he wanted help. We're taking I-40 straight east from near Santa Rosa through Amarillo to Oklahoma City. A quick concert there and the next day on to Memphis. Two days in Memphis. Now I know the itinerary for the long road home.

We pass a black billboard that announces *Hell is Real* in white letters, except for the H, which is bright red.

I could ride on this road going nowhere, an oasis from life, forever. I like drifting, not having plans or commitments or appointments. Such a great variance from my life a month ago. There's an irony in witnessing Tara and Aaron and Smoke and Red Dog and T-Bone hustling and eager about their rendezvous while I ride motionless, my things crammed in the truck.

Rachel is in the car ahead of me driving away from me, going faster than we are. I think about her laughing with Tara and Allie and cuddling with Levy and feel more alone.

Smoke watches the road. Maybe he's planning to build a drum with some of the tricks that David told him about using goat hide and wood. He flexes his fingers to relax his hands, as though they're tired from his imagined playing. His palms, even his fingertips, are thickened with calluses. I wonder if he can feel anything.

Maybe after a while you get calluses on your heart and there's no more pain.

I'd have to stop loving Rachel. Mom. I'd be safe.

I look at the dark side of things. Still.

The land is flat and dry and dustless. The road is a straight shot through uniformity that seems endless.

And then I say, from out of the blue, not even realizing I'm saying it. "I haven't been with any man but Troy."

Smoke watches that yellow line. "That's the way it should be," he says after awhile. "That's cool. My wife and I, we were together, partners, before we made love and when we did, it had an awesome . . ." he searches for the word, "sacredness. Not just body rubbing, and getting down, 'cause it is, you know, there's the chance of a *baby*, a whole new life, a new human being."

"I guess I'll only be with one man."

"You're young. You'll find another."

I don't know what young has to do with it. "What about that sacredness?"

He turns to me, those blue eyes of his still a surprise. "You can have that again. It doesn't have to be just once in a lifetime." He shrugs. "When you find love, sex is for two things: babies and closeness. Body sharing expands the joining, the partnership of being together."

I didn't expect this from him. I don't know what I'd imagined, but not this. Something more about recreational sex. Maybe a recognition that sex with a new person is scary, but fun. But maybe men don't experience that. I didn't anticipate a discourse on the multilevel merger making love offers.

So. I try to imagine experiencing what I've shared with Troy with another man, but can't, and go back to watching telephone poles like crosses lined up on the edge of the road.

And then I hear a siren. I look back, assuming it's an ambulance, but actually it's a cop—we're being pulled over.

Smoke and I have been driving two hours, and we're just on the other side of the Texas border.

The black and white's lights whirl red and purple.

"Why's he pulling us over?" I ask Smoke.

His eyes narrow. "Because he can," he jeers. "I'm not going that fast. It's a rental, so the inspection sticker is up to date. I can't think of another reason." His upper lip trembles slightly. Only someone close, sitting next to him, could notice.

My Honda and the tour van have disappeared. They're that far ahead.

A slightly built cop strides toward us. Through the side mirror, I see him put his hat on as he walks. When he gets to Smoke's window, I notice he's so young he barely shaves—only his mustache, not his cheeks.

"You were speeding. I clocked you at seventy-five back there."

We were keeping up with traffic, I think, not going any faster.

"Step out and give me your license," he says.

That's not how it's done. The officer runs the license in the computer in his car while you wait in yours. Smoke slides from under the wheel, moving slower than usual. From the passenger seat, I watch him reach in his back pocket, retrieve his wallet, flip it open, and tug his license from its plastic window.

I wear a dress, just a simple knit dress in bright purple. It was what I saw first in my suitcase this morning when I hunted for the bathroom. I'm still wearing the hoodie, too. Now I realize the skirt has crept to my thigh, and I tug it down when I notice the cop staring. I turn to him and meet his blue eyes. He frowns at me and shakes his head, disapproving. At first, I'm not sure why. My dress at my mid-thigh? How worn I must look from crying? Then I realize it's being with Smoke, a black man.

I don't like how the cop glares at me, ignoring Smoke's license. I only see Smoke's back. The cop is a few feet away and we face each other.

"Where're the rental papers?"

I snap open the glove box and pull out folded yellow pages, and hand them to him. I can't remember whose name is on it, and then I realize it's Smoke's. Thomas Johnson. That's his real name.

And then the cop says, "I want your identification, too."

"I don't have to show you my identification. I'm not driving." I'm trying to think like a lawyer, but I don't know the laws of Texas. And he has to have probable cause to search the car.

He frowns. Smoke shifts as he inhales.

I start to tell him I'm a lawyer, but just then he says, "Come with me," to Smoke, and they walk to the patrol car. I watch from the side mirror. In his baggy jean shorts and T-shirt, Smoke looks three times the size of the scrawny cop. The cop puts Smoke in the passenger seat.

The passenger seat? If Smoke were a dangerous

criminal, he would simply kill the cop and we'd be on our way. I don't see why we'd be stopped for going a few miles over the speed limit anyway. I remember Troy and I being pulled over. He was going fifteen miles over the limit down a curvy two-lane blacktop. The cop looked at us, checked Troy's license, saw that his record was okay, and gave him a warning. Not even a lecture, just a one-line comment about sixty-five being too fast for this blacktop. That's why it's posted fifty, he said. He wouldn't want anything bad to happen, an accident say. It was the third time that year Troy received a warning. But truth was, Troy was always speeding. He was good at anticipating the police and so baby-faced, so polite when pulled over, they'd simply warn him with a short comment. Troy never mentioned that he was a lawyer. He'd take the warning and thank the officer.

I remember how I shook my head and tisked my tongue. "Someday that's going to catch up to you and our insurance rates will go up," I told him.

He didn't respond to my admonition.

But Troy liked the sense of danger, and the feeling of velocity, I guess. Like diving through the air and flipping a somersault before he hit the water.

"Someday, there'll be an accident," I warned.

"Don't say that," he scolded.

No one ever ordered him out of our car. Not in California or Michigan or all the states in between. Where else were we pulled over? Colorado. Kansas. No one ever put him in the police vehicle. Is that how they do it in Texas?

I reach in my purse and pull out my cell phone and speed dial Tara.

"Hey," she answers.

"We've been stopped by a cop. He's got Smoke in his car now."

"In his car? Is he arresting him?"

"I don't know. They're sitting there."

"For what?"

"Speeding, he said. We were going five miles over the limit."

"You're kidding. Stay on the phone and keep talking. We'll come back."

So we wait. I talk to Rachel, who simply keeps saying, "Mommy. Mommy. Pizza. It's our flavorite. Can we get some for dinner?" I guess she's picked that up from Levy. I talk to her, my eyes on the black and white in the mirror. Smoke stares straight ahead, while the cop's head is bent.

They sit there for what seems like hours. Smoke's face is turned away from the cop, studying the sandy plain at the horizon or a billboard advertising GIRLS! I don't know if he has a record, or a warrant. I know only a part of Smoke. Tara says he doesn't do drugs. He saved Rachel's life, but I have no idea what his record reveals. Maybe they'll take him to jail. The news stories about what police have done to black men whirl through my mind. Beaten to death, raped with nightsticks, unjustly incarcerated with bogus evidence. Smoke appears a likely scapegoat. Just your common dark-skinned heavy-set black man. They don't know how sweet he is, how he can make a drum cry, how he saved a little girl's life.

If they arrest him, what will I do? Maybe I should stay and defend Smoke. But I don't have a license to practice in Texas. And I don't do criminal defense.

I can't just walk away. Suddenly I care. Just a few minutes ago I could ride this curveless road forever. Off to wherever. Now it matters.

Smoke still stares from the cop's passenger seat. I don't see any movement from him, as though he's frozen.

No matter what the computer shows, Smoke deserves someone to speak out for him, defend him.

The cop thinks we're together. Lovers. Partners. I glance at my dress and realize I appear crumpled and worn. God, maybe he thinks I'm a prostitute.

"They're still back there, still in the car. The cop is writing something," I tell Tara.

"You're witnessing the glories of driving while black," Tara says. "Once, Aaron got a ticket for a cracked side-view mirror. A *side*-view mirror. And I got a ticket for slightly rolling through a stop sign when Sissy was in the car. She was wearing a baseball cap sideways, trying to look cute. I think the police thought she was a dude."

"Yeah, and Troy only collected warnings because we

were beneficiaries of driving while white. White and middle class."

Tara laughs, "He was a speed demon."

"I had no idea, Tara. No idea that you went through that. Now I'm getting a taste of it." For the first time, I realize the cost of her love for Aaron, the breezy way she assumes the hardship and annoyance of racism in their day-to-day lives. My heart goes out to her, and with that, the separation between us narrows.

The cop and Smoke get out of the car and walk toward us. "They're coming," I inform Tara. My heart pounds in my ears.

They're at the back of the truck, fiddling with the door. It slides open.

I leave the car. My legs tremble slightly as I walk toward them.

"Did I tell you to leave your vehicle?" the cop scolds. His badge blares sun at me. A plate above it says James Whitlock. His skin is pink, the visor of his cap shadowing his face. His neck skinny like a boy's.

I inhale. "These are my things, in here."

"Yours?"

"Yes."

"I want to search the contents of this van."

I narrow my eyes. "You have no probable cause."

"He broke the law." He jerks his head toward Smoke. "Mr. Johnson was speeding."

He scans me up and down. My knit dress was perfect

for southern California, but too sparse for west Texas. I'm still wearing the grey hoodie, one hand jammed in the kangaroo pocket, the other still holding my cell phone. Flip-flops. I haven't paid attention to myself. I've barely remembered to bathe.

"We're supposed to unload all this? Right here?"

"I'm thinking of taking you to the station."

I hear Tara scream from the cell phone.

I suspect that James Whitlock can hear her too, so I turn away.

Whitlock's neck turns beet red and he frowns, squinting his eyes so deeply his pupils are hidden. He spins away and starts pulling out goods from the van, throwing them on the side of the highway.

"Hey, that's my painting," I protest. "And that's my baby's high chair!"

Rachel's plastic and metal chair, with her bumblebee suction toy still stuck on the tray, falls onto the dirt shoulder. Suddenly the silly innocence of the orange and neon-green toy ingloriously sitting on the side of the highway, the fact that Rachel is not with me, the relics of my once happy life somewhere between the Texas border and Amarillo, all bring me to tears, and I sob.

Smoke puts one arm around me, and then I'm in his chest, crying. I see Rachel lying limp on the side of the swimming pool, her chest motionless, her eyes closed, her hair dripping water while Smoke's thick palms press air into her skinny curved ribs, protecting the treasure of her lungs.

"She's okay," Smoke says.

"Your baby?" Whitlock points to the fallen high chair and then to Smoke.

"Her baby. Not mine. In the car up ahead. Her husband just died."

"Well, we'll get through here and you can be on your way." Whitlock is visibly shaken by my sobbing.

Then Allie, Tara, Levy, and Rachel pull up behind us. Allie and Tara get out of the car and walk toward us. Rachel starts screaming from her car seat, "My high chair! My google-bee!"

Whitlock yells, his hand on his belt, "Get back in the car or I'll have to call for backup." Tara returns to the Honda and Whitlock opens the drawers of our dresser, finding my assortment of rolled T-shirts, folded jeans, and underwear.

Rachel still cries for her toy.

Out of another drawer tumbles ponytail holders, headbands, and barrettes. Makeup. Whitlock opens a box of books and takes one out. *Summary of California Law (Torts 5)*, the red leather binding reads. He frowns and looks at me.

"You a lawyer?"

I nod.

He puts the book back in the box, refolds the top, then wipes his palms on creased pants. He keeps his back to

Allie and Tara watching him. He opens another box filled with copper pans that Mom bought as my wedding present. Then clutters of Rachel's sucky cups and her favorite bowl.

He throws the dishes back and jumps down from the back of the U-Haul.

"Get back in your vehicle," he orders us.

I inhale. "Let me put my possessions away. Can my sister help me?" For the first time ever, I want Tara with me. I don't beg him, though a part of me wants to. I feel helpless before this scrawny kid powerful in his blue uniform, his gun pulling his waistband. He nods.

"You," he points at Tara, "help her." Then he goes to the car, gets in, writes some more, and returns to present Smoke with his ticket. "Here's a ticket for speeding, Mr. Johnson." He says the *Mr.* with the hostility of irony. "You're in Texas now. Obey our laws."

Smoke looks down, but his jaw clenches in fury.

"What bullshit," Tara says through her teeth.

I hug her. "I had no idea, Tara," I say and kiss her cheek.

Her lifted eyebrows and grin express her joy and surprise.

Tara and Allie pull out and continue down the highway. We're safe in our U-Haul once again with the remnants of Troy's and my life. But now, I feel so violated.

"I'm sorry." I clear my throat, still clogged with tears.

"You're not the fucking cop."

"It was harder because you were with *me*."

"Maybe. But that's not your fault either."

"At least they didn't take us to the station and unload everything."

"What the fuck? I should be grateful he didn't give me an ass-whupping? I should be grateful they didn't lynch me?" He says the words in a monotone with even rhythm. But the press of rage, familiar bitterness, and endless sorrow in his voice are palpable.

"He thought we were drug dealers," he says.

"Really? Dealers?" I guess we fit the profile. "In a U-Haul?"

"Figured drugs were hidden somewhere in the van. Why else would we be together?"

I try to imagine myself as a drug dealer. Me, who writes a list and uses a GPS to go to the grocery store. Me, who checks her figures three times before turning in her tax return. And I chuckle. "Yeah. Right. Wouldn't I make a great drug dealer?" And then I remember my accusations of them using hard drugs.

Outside, curved black slices of tires lie helter-skelter. Evidence of fast tires on too-hot roads. Evidence of poorly made tires with deadly flaws, evidence of accidents that no one has bothered to remove. They lie there like corpses, the relics of trucks and vans that have passed this way.

*

An hour or so later, we stop for gas, bathroom, and coffee. Smoke sees me grab a dozen packets of artificial sweetener, tear them open simultaneously, and dump the powder along with French vanilla creamer into the pale liquid.

"You shouldn't be putting all that fake stuff in your body." He shakes his head.

"Who are you, my father?"

Troy had complained, too: "You don't know what that excessive amount of chemicals will do. The rats died."

Smoke shoots me a frown. "You know you shouldn't be doin' that."

"I can't live forever," I say.

He shakes his head.

A teenage cashier stands behind the counter. He has a crew cut, brown hair, and a plaid shirt tucked into belted jeans. He smiles when I approach with my chemical-laden coffee, a package of trail mix, and jerked beef sticks. "You wear a dress every day?" he asks, as he takes my money. His cuffs are evenly folded to reveal a watch.

"Just today," I tell him.

"It sure looks pretty. Real pretty."

Just then, I feel a tug on my dress and there's Levy looking up at me. "You want one?" He holds a yellow M&M between his thumb and index finger.

"Sure," I open my palm.

"Here you go, Aunt Sky." Aunt Sky. I don't think he's called me that before. He carefully places the candy in my hand. And then he smiles. His smile is exactly like Mom's.

I see her in his face.

For the first time, I realize he looks like her regardless of his skin color, or size, or gender. How did I not notice this before, this family resemblance? Why did I only see him as Tara's brown-skinned kid and not identify Mom in him? I bend down and hug him. "You have your grandma's smile."

Levy laughs. "Everyone tells me that." Then his face gets serious. "But I didn't *take* it from her. She shared it with me."

Now I laugh. I wonder what's changed that I can recognize Mom in Levy. "I'm so lucky you're my nephew. You're my flavorite."

He giggles.

I get behind the wheel to roll us to Oklahoma City. Smoke sleeps, his head resting on the window, his hands, palms up, crossed in his lap. A mix CD of Coltrane, Ray Charles, Ola Tunja, Art Blakey, and early Staple Singers keeps me company.

TEN

Slightly Tarnished

Tara

We're staying in the van tonight. Oklahoma City is a quick concert at a casino, no kids allowed, so Levy and Rachel will stay with Sky and Allie. In the morning, we're off to Memphis, seven hours away. An entire day's drive. The crew and Levy are in the tour bus. Tomorrow, Sky will drive her U-Haul with Rachel, and Allie will drive Sky's Honda. That was Allie's choice.

Aaron and I ignore each other. I know we should talk, but I don't know what to say. Every time I see him, my stomach flips. I want him to hold me. Say he trusts me. Scream that he can't be without me. Accept that I didn't start any of this with King, and say that he understands the benefit for me, for both of us.

I recognize, as I think about it, that it is King who made this all difficult. His big ego. It's not unusual for artists to work together and feature other singers on tracks. Why would he feel the need to break up our crew?

I keep trying to come up with a way to have it all. Aaron's love and trust, our music, and my music, maybe venturing forth some with King. Going up one rung on that celebrity ladder to reach star status.

My cell phone rings.

Mom.

Her call will be about Sky and I consider not answering. Sure enough, that's the first thing she asks: "How's Sky?"

"Why don't you ever ask about me, Mom? Why don't you ever say, 'How're you, Tara? How's your tour? Do the audiences appreciate you? How was the Grand Canyon you wanted to see, and what was Allie's brother like? How are you and Aaron and Levy?'"

There's silence on the other end, and then I hear Mom say, "I know how you are, Tara. I always know. You're okay. You're strong and self-reliant."

"I am?" I don't feel strong or self-reliant.

"Yes. You have been strong since you were a toddler."

Is that what she told herself when she only paid attention to my dad and Sky?

"You figured out how to get through things your own way and no one could stop you. Sky, well, she was so dogged she didn't even see what was around her, just kept blindly going. You were smart and figured things out. Even if it wasn't the way I would like."

I know she's thinking about my piercings and my black hair. She doesn't know that was in response to seeing my father with yet another woman. My—what did she call it?—my incorrigible teenage years. She thought Aaron was going to ruin my life. She assumed I could survive, and forgot to ask what was going on in my life. "Well. I can't figure things out now."

I can't believe I am going to tell her, but I do. I tell her about King. I tell her about the jeweled key pendant he gave me. I tell her about Aaron flirting with other women. I walk outside. The crew is inside preparing for the show. I stroll circles around the parking lot, clutching the phone to my ear, talking to Mom.

I hear her inhale deeply. "What do you want?"

I tell her, I want it all. I want Aaron and me back where we were before King walked on the L.A. stage, but I want both of us to work with King.

"What does King want?"

"I've never known. It can't be sex. He has as much of that as he wants."

"But maybe that's the hook. Your unavailability makes you a challenge. And he's smart enough to tempt you with what *you* want: artistic freedom and acclaim."

Mom still believes the woman controls everything. "Why can't Aaron just see I haven't done anything and that I'm not going anywhere? Why can't we both work with King?"

"Has King asked for you to work with him as a couple?"

"No."

"Aaron views your working with King as giving you away, like you don't mean enough to him."

And suddenly it's clear. For Aaron to accept King, or feel comfortable with me wearing that orange key, isn't just a blow to his pride. It means I don't matter to him. He's upset that another man is trying to take *me* from him. Me, Tara. Not me, Li'l Key. I count. I matter. I'm important to Aaron and he's not going to pretend otherwise.

"Do you think I'm like my father?" I choke when I ask her.

"Do you?"

That's an Allie question. "I don't know." I shrug.

"I guess that's what you have to find out. But I never got the feeling that your father was tortured like you are. He wanted conquests. You just want to create your music."

"Yes. That's what I want. My music and my family."

"Tara, you already have that."

Our conversation switches to Sky. Then she tells me about Jim. I tell her how cute Rachel and Levy are together.

"I don't remember such a good conversation with you in a long time, Mom. Not since right after I left home."

"That's because you're giving me a chance."

Giving *her* a chance? She never asks about me, I think, but now we've come full circle, so I simply say, "I love you."

After we hang up, I consider the fact that she doesn't ask Sky about herself either. Maybe Sky used to volunteer, but has stopped since Troy's death, so Mom calls me.

I slide the phone into my jean pocket and continue to stroll the parking lot's perimeter, scanning the modern skyscrapers that make up the city and thinking, *I'm strong? Me?*

Maybe I am.

I hunt for Aaron, but he's surrounded by fans. He signs a woman's shoulder so she can have it made into a tattoo.

I don't say anything. Instead, I go to the van and get dressed for the show. I read Levy "Hiawatha." Tickle his cheek with butterfly kisses. Sing him "I'll Miss Me." We do a little duet together. He sings the *la de la de* sometimes by himself, sometimes with me. And he adds his own little verse, making it up as he goes along.

"Oh you're so silly. My squirmy Levy." I laugh.

"I'll miss you, Mommy."

I tell him, "I'll be singing for you. For us. For all the love we have."

That's true.

*

Aaron keeps his distance, but watches me from the corner of his eye, considering everything I do. I want to crawl inside his mind and know what he's thinking, all the things he doesn't tell me. His fingers touch the mic, his arm flexes when he raises it high. A slight ridge outlines his lips; I watch it expand as he mouths his lyrics. I notice the span of his shoulders under his T-shirt, imagine how his ass flexes under his baggy pants. It's easy for me to mentally undress him. I do, while my fingers automatically play. Will we ever make love again? We seem so separate and the loss fills my chest, my throat. It's easy to spin away from each other.

I can't imagine my life without knowing what words he's writing, weaving our dreams together, the daily joy as we clean our apartment, play with Levy, pick veggies at Farmer Jack's. I can't imagine not eating the eggs he cooks. I can't imagine his lyrics without my keyboard. I can't imagine my bed alone.

Then there I am again, singing my song. And he introduces me perfunctorily, as though my solo music is now part of our act. He doesn't say it, but he shows me that there's room for me.

I make up a verse, staring at him while I sing it. I know my expression is naked, not even the orange makeup hides my fear and longing.

I don't have a clue whether we'll be able to make our way back together.

*

That night we sleep in our narrow bed back to back. I lie there, eyes open as the van rocks us to each other and away, touching him accidentally, and resist the urge to put my head on his shoulder. I want to softly kiss his sweet mouth.

He doesn't sound like he's sleeping either.

But neither one of us makes a move. I close my eyes and see that woman kiss him, his arm around her.

We're each paralyzed by our respective fears.

When we wake up I say, "I get it. If you let King have me, then he's won. I haven't done anything, though. I just wanted to explore my music without you feeling like you're losing me or not valuing me enough."

He glances at me out of the side of his eyes, his eyelashes shading his pupils. "You can do something now, Tara."

I don't know what gesture he wants me to make. Throw the necklace away? Give it back to King? Call King and tell him I'll never work with him?

"We are," I emphasize the *we*, "giving away a great opportunity."

He just snickers. "For a threesome?"

"I'm talking about music."

"You don't get it, and this is pointless," Aaron says as he slides on his pants.

"What would you want me to do? Throw it away? I did, you know. You started fooling around with that bitch and I picked it back up."

"You don't have any idea how men think."

"How could I? The only man I've known is you. And Troy." I pick up a comb. "So, tell me how you think."

"Most men would think you're a bitch by accepting an expensive present from another man. Not being clear with King that even if you work with him, I'm your man. I'm your partner."

"I was thinking of *us*. Of what *we* could get. Rappers mix crews all the time."

"You're playing with fire." Aaron pulls a T-shirt from his duffle bag.

"I play with fire simply by loving you."

"What do you mean by that?"

"Those women all over you. And I get blamed and called a bitch when I haven't done anything."

"I don't encourage them. I don't accept presents from them. How would you feel if some woman gave me a thirty-thousand-dollar present? You disrespected me while I represented for you. I stuck up for you with the crew, too. And gave you the stage." He whisper-shouts the *And*. He pulls his T-shirt on and turns to me, his face dark with anger. "Like I said, you have no clue how men think. Or you're a cheater at heart because you can't commit. And you don't recognize when someone can."

At first I feel slapped. *A cheater at heart?* But then I think about my thoughts, my fear of being my father's daughter, and look at him. "You're right. I've never *seen* commitment. So don't tease me with the possibility of having sex with another woman. You can't imagine for a moment that King and I did more than shake hands."

"I did that to show you how it felt."

"What it showed me was how little I mean to you. You can always trade me in for someone else."

"I could get a new woman. But no one would be you and you're way more than that. I *rely* on you. Not to do stuff, not even for your music, but for *you*." His face looks stricken.

"I guess you don't know how women think, either." I lift my head and meet his eyes. He's turned sideways to me, so he looks from the corner of his eyes. "I told you I was scared from the beginning. That's why you were the chicken choice."

We whisper our anger because we don't want everyone to know what's going on. But it's futile. They do.

In Albuquerque, I heard T-Bone saying to Aaron, "Should have listened and not bring no white baby-mama on no rap tour."

"You here because of me. Respect my decisions."

"White bitch drives our fan base away."

Aaron turned and walked out of the room. He didn't say, "Tara's our keyboardist."

But I heard Red Dog say, "Half our fans are white. Maybe they *like* seeing her."

I slide on a T-shirt. The bus edges toward Memphis. "I

haven't done anything wrong," I repeat. "I should have fallen in love with a classical musician."

"I haven't *done* anything either. What you want, Tara? You want me? If that's what you want then I'll handle King. Just give me the word."

"I'm not a baby. I'll handle it." I'm not some stupid chick that cries for her man to take care of the difficult stuff for her. "Are we just going to let each other walk away?" My voice catches.

"I'm still here. I'm giving you time, but my patience is turning to dismay," Aaron says. "But you can't have both of us."

I exhale, and shake my head, close my eyes. I go sit in the back of the bus. When he talks literary like that, I know he's turned the phrase around a hundred times. I imagine it in his next lyrics and sure enough, Aaron grabs his paper and pencil and walks out of our little cubicle behind me. I'm tired of going round and round in my head looking for a perfect answer. I'm weary of dealing with it all, so I pull out my keyboard and play.

My escape. My oasis.

I glance outside and see a black car driving beside us. Scrawled in white paint on the rear window are these words:

Love God
Love people.
It's that simple!!

I read them out loud.

"Ain't that the truth," Red Dog says.

"Simple but not easy," Smoke says.

Aaron doesn't look up from the lyrics he's writing.

We arrive in Memphis in early afternoon and walk down Beale Street. I hear snippets of the Staple Singers, Elvis, Otis Redding, Jerry Lee Lewis, and Booker T and the MGs pouring from storefronts as we stroll. I buy a bright green apron for Mom and imagine her wearing it in her kitchen with the soft purple wall.

When we go to the Rock 'n' Soul museum, everyone talks about the music they remember their moms playing. Unbelievably there's a black-and-white poster of a white sharecropper standing at the door of her house, five high-cheekboned kids surrounding her. She wears a plaid shirtwaist dress that is exactly like Sky's.

"Look, Sky, you're wearing her dress." Sky looks as worn, tired, and scrawny as that woman, too, I think.

"Do I look as bad as she does?"

"The dress looks great on you," Allie says.

"It's a designer, originally three hundred dollars, with purposely frayed edges. I got it used for twenty-five bucks at Crossroads in Santa Clara."

Allie takes a picture of Sky next to the poster of the sharecropper, a world and two generations apart, both wearing the same dress, and we laugh.

The museum tells the story of how white and black

music ended up mixing by accident via field hollers, church music, folk music, and blues. It got stirred together, and birthed the Memphis sound: a hard-driving rock and soul.

We walk the few blocks to the civil rights museum. Suddenly, we see the Lorraine Motel at the end of a street, just like in all the documentaries, photos, and books on civil rights. A white plastic wreath with a faded red bow hangs from the balcony where Martin Luther King was killed.

Aaron takes a bunch of pictures. "For Moms," he says. "She always talks about seeing Martin Luther King, Jr. in Detroit, giving his speech on having a dream before he said it in Washington." Aaron snaps another picture, and then one of the motel sign. Underneath the name is a marquee that says, "I have a dream MLK." The *e* is widely spaced from the *a*. I wonder if it's been like that since his assassination. "I wish she was here."

I hold on to Levy's hand. Aaron catches his other one and we look like an ordinary family.

Aaron and I don't touch each other, but through Levy, we hold hands.

It makes me want him more. This seeming new rule of no touching. As though if we touch each other, make love to each other, we'll reclaim each other, and we're afraid to do that.

Just then he turns to me and smiles, swings Levy's hand, and I swing the other one. We're a happy family.

And then Levy leans down and picks up a rock. It is

half charcoal gray and half cream. It lies in his pink palm etched with brown creases. He just looks at it. Aaron and I meet each other's eyes. "That's a special rock," Aaron says. "I bet Smoke could drill a hole through it and you could wear it around your neck. A special rock from a special place."

Levy curls his fingers tightly around it. "Yeah," he says.

A slight breeze raises goose bumps along my arms.

In the museum, movies show white students hauling black students from lunchroom stools and beating them, punching them, throwing them to the ground and kicking them, police spraying protesters with hoses spewing fierce water, sharp-toothed dogs snapping and growling, people stomping a young black man to death who was protecting his mother.

"We were so violent," Sky comments. "I didn't realize."

"You didn't know?" Smoke says. He doesn't glance at Sky, but crosses his arms.

Allie says, "Back then, it was almost expected. Now, seeing it all together, all at once, it's horrifying that people of our race acted as they did." She rocks back slightly on her heels. "The black protesters remained nonviolent and peaceful for over a decade. Then after King's murder the country erupted."

"We attacked property. Not people," Aaron comments.

"Hey. And then they started putting mass numbers of black men in prison," Smoke says.

Red Dog and T-Bone laugh and slap five.

Smoke stands with his arms crossed.

For the first time, I understand Mom's concern about me being with Aaron. I can see her point of view.

"It's amazing to have lived so long that events I remember are exhibited in museums," Allie remarks.

As we exit, she says, "How far we've come." She doesn't say it to anybody. Just says it aloud.

"We still get pulled over, beaten up, and caged in prison. We just don't get lynched," Smoke says.

Sky shudders and closes her eyes, remembering the incident yesterday on the road. She pulls her shoulders back and lifts her chin. "The movement brought an awareness of morality. Lawyers working quietly and sometimes unseen crafted laws and policy. Things changed."

I turn to her, in her sharecropper dress, her blond hair hanging, Rachel, holding her hand, tugging and skipping beside her. "What're you thinking?"

"I don't have to remain in family law." Her gray eyes are right at me. Her lips firm as they end the sentence. "I can be any kind of lawyer I want. Criminal defense. Civil rights. I could help write policy." She nods, her lips now pressed together. "That might feel more meaningful, important. I could take the bar and go from there." And then Rachel pulls her toward Levy walking with Aaron.

Levy picks up a pebble, softly smooth, perfectly round, and translucently beige, and shows it to Sky.

*

Our concert is at an old theater with a curlicue yellow and red marquee. On this night it announces *Special Intent. Jersey Boys* will start playing next week.

The five of us huddle up before we go on. "Okay y'all," Aaron says. "We've been killin' this shit so far. So lets load this clip and lay them down one last time."

I wonder when he got so military ... He wasn't so aggressive when we left Detroit.

"You gonna do the new one, Special?" Red Dog asks.

"We'll see if it pops off." He turns to me.

T-Bone jumps with excitement. "Let'sgo, let'sgo, let'sgo." Being on stage feeds him in a different way than the rest of us, at last he's real.

I stare at Aaron. I hope this isn't our last performance together, I think, and almost start crying.

And then I get angry that I have to juggle all this when I was already dealing with Troy's death, being a mom, and being a rap artist.

I inhale. *This is what you love*, I tell myself. *Take this moment, crowd out the sadness and anger*. I raise my hand. "Let's rock it," I say.

And on we go.

We start our regular set, excited by the audience. The energy from the crowd always empowers me. All of us. Now my song is folded into our repertoire, as part of us, part of who we are. The audience warms up to it, and I'm secure enough that I bring out different aspects of the lyrics, new ways to present it, playing with the melody in unusual chord progressions. T-Bone gives me a hand signal that he's doing the next verse and slides in. His words, about missing a father he never knew, wondering what he would be like if he had grown up with a man who cared, reveal a vulnerable side.

And then Aaron presents his new song, "Resilience."

I reminisce on the test I pass
I write of how life and death
Contrast
how struggle and success contrast

Smoke plays his drum, and the crew repeats *life and death, struggle and success* in the background, focusing on the theme.

But when Aaron sings the next chorus, I hear it differently than when we rehearsed it. Then the song seemed to be for Sky, a plea for her to stop making her life about Troy's loss. But this verse removes it from her.

Come too far to turn back
Can't stop
Won't stop
And I refuse to quit
No matter how hard it gets
I'm forward with Special Intent
Glorying in resilience.

Now I hear his determination regardless of what happens with us. The lyrics have moved from Troy's tragedy to our dilemma.

As he finishes, his eyes search mine. The look he gives me, in those few seconds before the crowd starts screaming and steals him, flashes with hope and love and sorrow and anger, all at the same time. He's as angry as I've ever seen him. And as sad. And, thankfully, hopeful.

I nod to him, trying to let him know I get his message. He's giving me the rope and the respect to make my decision. He can't give me more.

We talk to each other through our lyrics. It's easier to communicate on stage than in person, alone, sitting across from each other.

The crowd starts yelling . . . *"Special! Special! Li'l Key! Li'l Key! T-Bone! T-Bone!"* The stomping and screaming exhilarates and frightens me. Anything could happen. It could go either way.

And then I get it. I, all of us, have this image that if we reach a certain level of stardom it will be a certain way. Everything will be great and I can relax and enjoy my music. But it's not like that. A few years ago, I wanted to be where I am, where Aaron and I are. And now I look to King and want that. And King, does he relax in his position, exalting in his music and the contributions he's made? No. Or he wouldn't kick at the people crawling the ladder behind him. He's scared during every concert, with every new CD, that he'll be panned, or surpassed by someone or something younger, better, hotter. No more hip-hop. Some alternative, or a fusion between blues and rap . . . something that he missed and he's suddenly back where he started, struggling and afraid he'll be forgotten and poor and black.

The antidote to this fear-driven ambition is what I always knew, but forgot. You just create the music, forget the rest, and let it out into the world the best way you can. Whether it's on a beach playing for pennies or in Carnegie Hall, on the Internet or in a coliseum, you love it. You pour the best of you into it and give it to others.

It's like David's message to us. To him, it's the planet that we get to live on and enjoy. That, too. Of course.

But for me there's something else.

Now, I know what I'm going to do. I just have to get back home and hope Aaron waits that long.

One more day: the long ride home.

CHAPTER ELEVEN

No Guarantees

Sky

"I was alone with him when he died, you know."

"I thought Mom was with you," Tara says.

"She'd left. I forget where. The bathroom? The cafeteria? Somewhere. It was just me. Me and him." My voice catches in my throat. "Us."

Tara shifts, then turns toward me in the passenger seat.

"It was so off and on. You don't know when it will finally come," I say. "Death, I mean." I see again his blue skin, his fingertips. I reached to touch him and he was cold. Already. I squeezed his fingers and he moved them weakly, so I knew he was still there. "You just know it's soon. By the end he couldn't talk. It was hard for him to breathe."

I'm driving my Honda, Tara is next to me, and the kids are tangled asleep in their car seats.

We're on the way home. Eleven hours and seventeen minutes with traffic, my GPS says. Back on I-40 east and then straight up 65 northeast to 71 and then home.

I don't know if it'll feel like home anymore. San Diego was home, but then we moved to Venice. We hadn't lived in our rented condo long enough for it to feel like home, like we hoped our house would when we found one.

"I remember when I last saw him," Tara says.

I glance at her, but she's staring out the window at trees in the distance, blotting out whatever farms or villages there might be.

"It got worse. He sucked in what air he could, but even with the oxygen it was hard." Tears trickle down my cheeks. Tara shifts and places her hand on mine, on top of the steering wheel. Cruise control is on. I'm going the speed limit. There's not much traffic and the road is gently curved, nothing straight. Nothing exotic. It just is.

"Did he say anything?" she asks.

"He struggled to breathe, making gurgling sounds 'cause it was so hard, and then his breath got slower and then . . . Then . . ." I clench the wheel and lick my lips. I want to explain this thing that happens, I do, but I can't even *identify* the concept, let alone choose the right words. "There's something unbelievable, something amazing, but in the most awful way, when it happens. When life goes. There's no mistaking it even though there's no apparent change. Same body. Same hair. Same cold hands. Same lips. But he was gone."

Tara listens, but I know I haven't made sense so I try again.

"I see him. Him when he was struggling and fading, but still there. And then this, his last breath no different than the one before. But . . ." I twitch one shoulder. "He ended. His chest stopped. His nostrils didn't quiver. His hand was motionless. He wasn't my Troy anymore and wouldn't be again."

Tara is quiet for a minute and then says, "At least you were together. He wasn't alone. You shared it."

She doesn't understand. She just understands the love and then being alone, but not what it felt like. "I didn't know, he didn't know, what was the last breath. Which one it would be. I know it now because there wasn't any other. I can't get the eeriness, the *profundity* of the change out of my mind. Sometimes it returns and settles in me."

I'm amazed that I'm even trying to explain this to someone, let alone Tara. "It's something about the intense difference between death and life. And the terrifying privilege of witnessing the change." That says it as well as I can, at least now. Maybe later I'll figure it out. Maybe I won't.

So I just drive. We're on I-71 by now, past Nashville and triangulating north. We've changed direction. We've gone through much of America, and quickly enough that I have a sense of the land changing. The boulder heaps and the desert flats when we left California, the gigantic gorge of the Grand Canyon and the dry mountains of New Mexico. Then we saw the expanse of the great southern plain, flat and arid. Now we're in lush forest, getting colder as we drive toward winter. We've been driving three hours today. It's midday, the sky is clear, the weather mild. A perfect day for a drive.

"He wasn't alone," she says again. "You were with him. He knew how much you love him. And do you know . . ." she clears her throat, her eyes are right on me, staring at the side of my face, "how much he loved you?"

I shake my head. "It's beyond love. Beyond everything. That slipping away of the human being to something else." I stop talking. Then, I remember what I did next. I got in bed beside him. Put my cheek on his shoulder and held him. It was our familiar pose—one we had assumed every night and morning all those years, cuddling together. My place, I called it. "I want to get in my place," I'd say, and he'd put his book down and open up his arm for my head. So I lay there for a minute, but then the buzzers started ringing—on his monitors—and I knew nurses would come running, so I kissed his cheek and got up.

Tara doesn't know what to say. She turns around and checks the kids. "They're sleeping so peacefully," she reports. "Levy's arm is over Rachel's leg and her head is on his blanket. He's holding Rachel's bunny, Maddie."

I guess that's her way to say life goes on, life is still good. I watch the road and we don't talk. There's nothing anyone can say to make it better. She can sit with me and listen. Let time pass. But I'm tired of talking now.

So we drive the rest of the way up I-71, searching for 65. The tour bus and the U-Haul are in front of us. I feel comfortable with Tara, which surprises me. We stop for gas and coffee and buy peanuts, cheese and crackers, and apples.

Tara shakes her head at my artificial sweetener. "Why don't you put in real sugar? Don't tell me you're watching your weight?"

I don't defend myself.

We're back in the car, in Kentucky, driving down a clear road under a clear sky when I hear brakes squeal.

An SUV flies across the median. It flips over completely.

I slam on my brakes, watching it fly.

It lands in front of us. The doors pop open.

I use all my strength, arms straight, pressing on my brakes. The car beside me swerves and drives off the shoulder and down a small ravine. I miss it by inches, tires screeching. My Honda tilts on two side wheels, and then rights itself. My heart pounds.

"Ohmygod, ohmygod," Tara says as we jolt to a stop.

In front of us, in the middle of the road, lies a person. I can't move forward. Tires scream all around us.

In the rearview mirror I see a blue car careening toward us. The man's eyes are wide, his mouth open. He stops inches from us. He closes his eyes, tilts his head as though he's giving thanks. And then I watch helplessly as he's hit by another car. His head jerks, and finally movement stops. Unbelievably, he wasn't knocked into me.

My neck thumps, sweat pours down me. I inhale deeply. Tara screams next to me. The kids are awake.

Across the median, traffic has halted too.

A woman lies on the ground. I glimpse just her leg, jeans, a bronze sandal, painted red toenails. Through the tinted windows of the SUV, I make out a shadow of an adult, and a child in a car seat in the rear.

A red van from behind us switches to the right, drives on the shoulder, and disappears down the highway.

"Are you okay, is everyone okay?" Tara looks back. The kids are awake, Rachel rubs her eyes.

"Rachel, you okay?" I try to reach her with my hand.

"I'm okay," she says shakily.

"What happened?" Levy asks.

"There was an accident, but we're okay. Now we're in a little traffic jam."

Tara jumps out of the car, cell phone in her hand, pushing numbers as she runs toward the woman.

Tara leans down over her, kneeling on the highway. Her back is to me, so I can't see what she's doing.

"Where's Mommy?" Levy asks.

"She's helping somebody. She's okay, sweetie." But I don't like her in the traffic. I want her to get back in the car, where she's protected.

Levy pushes himself up in the car seat, but he can't get high enough to see over the seat and the car's hood to the highway. "Moooommmyyyy," he calls.

A man from the car next to us runs toward Tara and the woman. Other people surround the SUV. Tara stands, still talking into the phone as she walks toward our car. She gets back into the passenger seat. "I called 911. They should be here soon to help."

"How is she?"

Tara shrugs. "I think she has a concussion." She turns back to the kids and passes them cheese and crackers. Her hands tremble as she punches straws in their juice boxes. "I love you guys," she says and hands them drinks.

The kids are busy with the food. They don't even look out the windows. But we're safe, together inside the car.

After a while, I turn off the engine. We can't move. Behind us, a line of cars stretches over the hill. Beside us sit two yellow vans with the sign FIRE WATER CLEANUP AND RESTORATION. A woman sits behind the wheel of the one closer to us. Her fingers tap the window frame and hold a lit cigarette trailing blue smoke.

"What happened?" she asks, pointing across the median with frosted pink nails holding the cigarette.

I relay the story shakily, as best I can.

She clicks her tongue and presses her lips together. "Luckily we were able to stop just in the nick of time. Or we'd have been in trouble. Both of us." She shuts her eyes and shudders. "There's still a baby in the backseat. And a man in the car."

Tara doesn't say anything.

"My husband tried to help, but . . . there was nothing he could do. Those poor people."

Maybe the car was trying to avoid tire pieces strewn over the highway, I think. *Maybe they were having a fight. Maybe their tire exploded.*

After five more minutes, three police cars, lights and sirens flashing, drive down the median next to us. Two come from the other direction and cross the grass. People leave their cars and walk toward the accident. A man climbs to the roof of his truck and takes pictures.

I get out of my car. Two red ladder trucks stream down the grass, sirens piercing.

Now I see the baby strapped in his car seat, in the back. The woman . . . the mother? . . . hasn't moved. Oh God. An entire family.

"Ow! Ow!" Rachel covers her ears with her hands.

My heart beats in my neck, in my wrists, I feel it pounding in me. A helicopter's huge wings shush the air, obliterating all other sounds. Its wind twists the grass. Almost delicately, it sinks in front of us, nestling on the highway. A fire truck parks behind the SUV, another in front of it. Firemen surround it.

In the median, people cluster together.

A flutter of blue sheet flies in the breeze, floats down, and shields the vague mound on the road.

The woman is covered now. A mother. A wife.

I turn to Tara. "You knew, didn't you?"

Her face is very pale as she slowly nods.

She tried to protect me.

Once again, cars on the other side move. Then a cop asks us to drive across the median and head south. He tells us how to make a loop so we get back to 71 going north.

I get back in my car, turn it on, bump across the grass, and push toward Nashville. My heart still beats fast but is returning to its regular pace. Tara calls Aaron and explains the situation.

"This will take us an extra hour. At least," she says. Then she turns to me. "They're already seeing signs for Cincinnati."

I steer through a subdivision called Plantation Estates. McMansions with split rail fences and lanterned porches sit smugly on streets named after flowering trees. Magnolia. Azalea. Cape Myrtle.

"They'll park the U-Haul at Mom's. Tomorrow, Aaron and I will help you unload it into storage. Okay?"

I can't even think about that.

And then I find the ramp for the highway. 71 north. The two yellow vans drive ahead of us.

*

"At least the baby will have his father," I say.

Tara doesn't say anything. Maybe I'm wrong to presume only the woman died. "Isn't it weird that we were talking about death and this accident happened?"

"What do you mean?" Tara straightens and then crosses her arms.

"I don't know. Like we put out bad vibes."

"We didn't make that accident happen by talking about Troy. It's just a coincidence."

I don't say anything, but I wonder if we somehow sensed it, or the universe warned us. The conversation made me drive slower. Otherwise, I might have hit the SUV. I never used to think this way. "I guess I'm just looking for a way to make everything connected. To make it make sense again."

"I miss him, too, you know," she says when we've passed the yellow vans and see signs for Dayton.

"How can I be happy without him? I mean, how can I let myself?"

"You think he'd want you to suffer, be unhappy the rest of your life?"

"It feels like a betrayal."

"Troy told me not to let you make a monument of him by your mourning, but by being free to be happy. Maybe even love another man someday."

"He did?" I think she said something like this to me before. I didn't understand it then.

"That night at the hospital. The night before he died."

"Oh." As soon as I start being a little bit happy, I get scared.

"He wanted you to live a full life, maybe even love again," she repeats.

I consider Troy's words, and the woman who just died in front of me. "I'm glad I'm alive." And for the first time in many weeks, I realize it's true. "I wasn't at first." I have my next decision. "But my life is precious."

"Yes." Tara says it slow, the *s* hanging between her teeth as though she's saying at-last-thank-God-I'm-so-relieved all in that one little word. "None of *us* can decide that. Only you. Why do you think life is supposed to be predictable?"

And then she answers her own question. "I guess for you it was, back before your dad died."

Tara continues, "By the time I was born, everything had already become unpredictable. I wasn't supposed to fall in love with Aaron and become a rap singer. But I've learned to benefit from the unpredictable."

"Loved ones dying too young is predictable in my life. I thought I had a bad luck cloud over my head. Dad. Those babies. Mia. Troy. Then Rachel almost drowning. But David said something about just having this life and those breaths." I shake my head, grab what's left of my sugary coffee and sip it. "Thank you."

"Me?" Tara sounds surprised.

Tears fill my eyes. "You love me." I turn to her when I say it and feel her love for me. I let it in. I don't simply recognize it. I so disregarded her, and she's always been there. Like now. She rearranged her entire tour for me. I took her, having a sister, for granted. And she involved everyone, her whole life. Aaron, Smoke, T-Bone, and Red Dog, even though it made the tour more difficult. Especially for Smoke, who drove the U-Haul and then performed. Even Levy has been sweet to me. She stares out the front window watching for signs with a map in her lap, navigating our way home. Her face, in profile, is so clean with her upturned nose.

"I love you." I say it. I actually say it while watching the road that takes us home.

"Huh?"

"I'm glad you're my sister. Thank you for helping me. I couldn't have made this move without you and the crew and Allie. I'd be stuck in Venice immersed in sorrow, bringing Rachel down with me." My hands clutch the wheel, and I stare at the road. The trees are bare and I recognize there's been some snow. We're close to home.

Tara's eyes float behind tears, but there's a bright smile on her face so she looks like a child, like the girl sitting on top of Magic Mountain with the glowing lights playing over her cheeks. She was there for me, waiting for me to accept her. I see that now.

"I thought I was just a pest."

"You're that too," I laugh. "No, actually you're not that anymore. You've grown out of that. You've grown up!" I laugh. "We both have."

"You think?" she laughs. "Oh no! We don't want to do that. We'll turn into Mom."

"That wouldn't be so bad." We say it together and laugh again. I thought I'd forgotten how.

I swallow. "I guess I resented you—your very presence disrupting my cozy twosome with Mom. When I met Troy, it was back to being part of a twosome. Now." I hadn't thought of it before. "Wow. It's me and Rachel. Another twosome."

"Yeah. And she's so sweet, so loving."

"So is Levy. And did you know, he has Mom's smile?"

"Of course."

"It's funny to see it on his little brown boy face."

She laughs.

I'm determined to not shut out all the remaining love around me anymore. I reach over to her arm and squeeze it.

She squeezes my hand back and I ask, "What're you going to do about King?"

"I want Aaron. I've been scared to admit how much I love him. How *attached* I am. It hurts so bad to even think about losing him. I guess I'm more like you than I wanted to admit. If I do *what* I truly want, and the fates are with me, my life will be *how* I want. It's not totally haphazard."

"What's that have to do with King?"

"I thought he could give us security. But the only security is self-dependence. And depending on him would have been at the expense of Aaron's trust and security."

"Well, I've learned other people do help. But there're no guarantees of forever. And maybe you're right. Love, loss, mourning ... it all goes together and is the best of our humanity."

ELEVEN

No Guarantees

Tara

We unload Sky's things from the U-Haul into a storage shed. We sleep in our tour bus in Mom's driveway. The next morning, Mom makes us a breakfast of omelets and hash browns before we leave in the bus. Along the way we drop off Smoke, Red Dog and T-Bone.

Detroit looks even more bedraggled than it did when we left. Poor city. Abandoned and shattered, with her windows all around the ankles of her buildings like a lady who's lost her clothes. Picked-over bones.

The streets are almost empty. We find parking places everywhere, right in downtown near Comerica Park and Cobo Hall. No people walk the streets. Buildings seem blinded, with hundreds of windows shattered in random slivers. Two more houses are boarded up on our street. The garbage sits in piles. I'm glad it's getting to be winter.

We're back to a ruined city with an almost ruined love.

Standing on the corner is a woman with a sign that says *You're not your mind's keeper*. She wears a Detroit Tigers baseball hat and baggy red and black plaid pants with Converse shoes.

"What's that sign mean?" I ask Aaron.

"You don't always know what you're going to do next?" Aaron suggests.

"Your body isn't alive to feed your mind, it'll go on regardless," I suggest.

"Your mind will think what it wants," Aaron adds.

"Is that true? Can't we structure our minds, influence our feelings? What do you think?"

"I think it means she's crazy."

Home is still our little apartment with the Indian bedspreads and the silk flowers from my first recital. First thing, I hang the prism back in the window. And I feel glad it's just the three of us, our little family, appreciating the quiet, the hum of our refrigerator and Mos Def softly playing. But I miss Sky and Rachel. And the crew. And of course Allie. Miss them and am glad to be away from them, both at once.

Around the corner, Sissy is eager to see us and cook us her famous macaroni and cheese as a welcome-home feast. Levy rushes to her arms and buries his head between her breasts.

A few days later, I talk with her about King. I trust Sissy's wisdom, and she knows her son. I show her the key necklace. "Shoot. I'll take that. Take all those orange stones out and make something else. A hand, maybe."

"I thought of that, too. Making something for Aaron and me. But I doubt he'd like that." I consider giving it to Sissy, but Aaron would be reminded every time he saw the stones.

"It's beautiful." When I turn it in my hand, the gems flash fire around the room. Just like my prism. "What a waste," I say.

Sissy looks at me hard, squinting her eyes the way she does when she's sizing you up, trying to see through your skin to your thoughts.

"I hoped we all three could work together, but King wants me on his own."

"I saw how he zeroed in on you at the L.A. concert." She puts her palm on her knee and leans back, still watching. "It's not about the necklace, Tara. You know that. And some man can't be the door to what you want. All a man can do is love you, be family with you, help you fulfill your dreams. Aaron does that—you just afraid to see it. You got to be the hero of your own life."

I learned that a long time ago, back when I felt left out of my family and focused on my music to be involved in something, to give myself pleasure. Back then nurturing my music was heroic enough. If I'm my own hero, what should I do about King?

I run the possibilities through my mind one more time.

I could buy the necklace from King. I could work for him and use the money to pay for it. But really, $30,000 would be put to better use as a down payment. Sissy could use a new car. I don't need bling. It's tempting, but ultimately, just bling. Even the word says it's unimportant.

I don't lust after King as a lover. He's attractive, but I'm not attracted to him. He exists as an icon of his own formation. So smooth and polished, he isn't authentic. I want a real man. I want Aaron. Only Aaron. Would I have artistic freedom with King? No, I see that now. He'd control me. But we could cut a groove or two. I imagine telling Aaron that one more time, very clearly. I want to work with him, not have sex with him. I'm not responsible for what's in his mind about me.

But I've already said that in several different ways. And now I don't completely trust Aaron. He used the flirt strategy for revenge lickety-split, like I was a cheater, reminding me I'm replaceable. He said I don't know how men think. Maybe the flirting was for his boys. Maybe it was to soothe his wounded pride. Maybe he thought it would make me more interested. All these *maybes*, when my reaction is to walk away. He gave his explanation, but I don't know what to believe.

See how I go round and round?

I don't want to be with a man like my father. I don't

want to be my father either.

I know I'm taking a big risk in trying to recreate love and hope in a broken place. Letting the opportunity of King go in the hope that Aaron and I can be paramount again absent my own vacillation. And me, can I let all of Aaron's instant flirtations go?

I ask him, "We can go back to being us, if I send this shit back?" The necklace dangles from my fingers.

"Quit dipping a toe in to test the waters," Aaron says.

He wants the power and he has it. But I know that if this all vanishes, I'll be okay somehow. I won't backtrack. If Sky can get through what she's gone through, I can deal with this. After all, I didn't know this good stuff was going to happen. I was just happy and busy doing my music.

I know being my own hero requires courage. So I call King. I take a big breath of air and pray, *I hope this works*. His man answers and I say my name. He hands King the phone.

"Well, Li'l Key, you've given me the honor of a call." The sarcasm and surprise drip through the honey.

"I can't accept this necklace from you. I don't want you for a lover, and this is a lover's gesture." I say it right like that and there's dead silence on the other end.

"How 'bout you buy it from me from one third of what I'll pay you for singing that 'I'll Miss You' song at my concert at Cobo Hall in January? You won't even have to leave home."

I've thought of this. I've thought of negotiating a deal

for Aaron and me. I want to say—oh, how I want to, and I consider it one more time—"Okay, if Aaron can be on stage before or after me."

And then in my imagination, King responds, after a moment's consideration, "If you and I sing a duet, too."

I'd tell him then, in my fantasy, because he knows that I can't cut a deal without Aaron and the crew, "Let me get back to you. And thank you."

That's what I had planned to do until Mom made me realize what a breach of Aaron's trust that would be.

In reality, sitting in our apartment, my keyboard humming and the sun squeezing through grimy smeared windows, I say, "I would love that. You don't have any idea what a pleasure and thrill it would be to work with you. And the key necklace is the most beautiful thing I've ever seen, a totem. But more than that is my love for my family and . . ." I stop. Because what I want to say is that could have happened, but you screwed it up with the sexual stuff, the excessive present and the comments about exclusivity.

"That necklace was to test your commitment. To be a star, your career has to be paramount, and I'm not willing to put my energy into someone who isn't absolutely and totally committed. You have to be willing to sacrifice everything else. You weren't."

I squeeze my eyes tight, because I know I'm slamming the door. "No. My family is important, too. So I won't be able to work with you."

"Okay." There's no graciousness to that word. Just the harsh outward breath. For a minute, I think he's hung up.

"I'll miss the wonderful opportunity, but I will still get to do my music, and that and my family are what's important to me."

He doesn't say anything.

I'm left hanging, as though I need to draw a conclusion, as though he's waiting for something else, maybe for me to start laughing and tell him this is all a joke because, of course, more than anything I want to sing with the wonderful King, want to do a duet with him, will do anything to keep this spectacular necklace he had made for me.

"I am extremely honored, extremely touched and flattered by your offer." My voice cracks. And then I ask for the address where I can send the necklace.

At first he doesn't give it to me, as though he's considering telling me to throw it away. Which I have to admit would be difficult. And I can't sell it. What would I do with the money? Give it to a charity, I decide. Give it to Aaron and make him make the decision. What do you do with tainted money?

I'm exhausted from all the back and forth in my head surrounding these issues.

I realize this is an unexpected turn of events for King. He's used to getting things his way. But then, finally, he gives me the address.

Later that night, after Aaron gets home, I tell him about the conversation. I display the necklace in its box and show him a note I have written King. It is simple. It says: *Thank you so much for this beautiful gift. I am honored that you appreciate my music. Your continued regard warms my heart and encourages my aspirations. Thank you again.*

Then, while Aaron watches, I wrap it up and write out the address.

"I'll take it to UPS tomorrow," I tell him. "Want to come?" I'm bending over backwards to build trust.

His eyes meet mine. His head tilts slightly as he gazes at me. I can't read his expression. I'm unsure whether it's relief or confidence. "We can stop there on the way to rehearsal. I want to go over a few songs for our Thanksgiving concert in Toledo."

I'm surprised he's not making a bigger deal about it. In my fantasy, he would grab me and hold me, kiss me, and thank me. But he does none of that. It's as if everything slides back to normal and the necklace never existed. Tomorrow we have rehearsal. And then he says, staring right at me, "I just want you. No other woman. It was difficult dealing with the bullshit from the homies, but I knew you hadn't done anything."

Levy comes in from a nap, his hair all crazy, rubbing his eyes. He sees us and runs to us, his arms outstretched. Aaron picks him up and holds him, and I join in. The three of us are together, just like normal.

That night I take a shower and Aaron watches from the bedroom while I smooth lotion on my legs and breasts. He gets out of bed and comes to me, grabs the bottle from my hand, and squeezes a mound of lotion into his palm. And then applies it to my back. His hand is warm, and slippery with the cool cream. "This is one of those places you can't get yourself," he says. "You need me."

I hear what he's saying in the spaces and nuances.

When I'm all slippery, he turns me around and caresses the lotion over my breasts, the nipples arching at his touch.

It's been too long.

And then he kisses each tip, my eyelids, my nose and my mouth, picks me up in his arms, and carries me to our bed. We lie in bed and kiss, just kiss, for a long time, as though we have forever.

Right before Thanksgiving, Sky finds a cute two-bedroom apartment around the corner from Mom's house. It's in a complex with a swimming pool and a workout room. Aaron, Mom, Smoke, Sky, and I move her things from the storage shed to her new place. Sky hangs the blue painting so it's the first thing you see when you enter her apartment. And the first thing she sees in the morning when she leaves her bedroom. When she and Rachel eat breakfast, it'll remind them of the wonders of the sky. The high chair is there, too. Smoke plays with the crazy bee toy on it. It spins and chimes and beeps. "Glad it still works," he says.

Troy's ashes sit on her dresser. A candle beside them, his picture on the other side, one of their wedding. He's behind her, his arms folded around her, his chin smooshing her veil.

Sky looks so young, and that was just a few years ago.

Two nights later, she invites us all for a potluck housewarming. The beige and purple furniture from the Venice Beach condo fit right in, adding a touch of California. Aaron makes Sissy's rib recipe. Mom brings the Girl Scout stew that the three of us invented for a Brownie final dinner. I make Sissy's sock-it-to-me cake. Levy brings Rachel a bowl of stones. A black stone that's perfectly round from the Pacific, which we found while we were walking on the beach. And a round translucent dot of stone the size of a quarter. We bought an amethyst, with rows of purple spikes, at the museum. Smoke carries two drums. A little drum for Rachel and a bigger one for Sky—an ashika, he tells her. "Drumming is a way to catch the universal beat," he says. "Your own heartbeat and the spin of the universe. That all helps when things press down on you." He looks at her hard. "I'll teach you dudes some beats if you want. Bring over my wife and daughter and the four of us can play."

They had serious talks during those hours down I-40, the long road home.

Sky works part time with Mom's friend Rosie. She does

research and case writing for the other lawyers. Rosie's baby is due next week, so Sky will be taking over completely in the new year until Rosie returns from maternity leave. Meanwhile, Sky is studying for the bar. Rachel is in day care on the days that Sky works. Strangely, it's the day care that I attended when I was a kid. Some of the teachers even remember me and follow my career. All these years I thought no one was paying attention.

Sky seems settled. Not healed, but in a safe place to start to try.

And me? I'm working on my own series of songs. When Aaron sees me, he suggests I use T-Bone to sing some of the lyrics with me. We harmonized well in "I'll Miss You." I must look surprised, because he adds, "We're a crew. We need all our talents to succeed. Like building a car needs everybody's input to make it run."

I'm working on being the hero of my own life, and Aaron's working on being egalitarian.

After Thanksgiving, Aaron says, "We talked about buying a house and getting married after our tour. What do you think of aiming for that next year?"

"It's a good time to buy a house," I say.

"It's a good time to get married," he answers. "But it's *been* a good time to get married."

It was me who tarried.

Me and my fear of love and loss. I turn away and wipe

the kitchen counter. I'd figured out what courage means. It means following my own meaning. My music is the easy part. I inhale, rinse the rag with warm water, start on sprinkling the sink with Comet, and scrub. And as I do it, I realize what I want is to be part of a family. Being comfortable and feeling accepted by a family is part of my meaning. It doesn't have to be like my mom and dad. Not all men are like him.

And more importantly, I'm not either.

Prickles run up my arms.

And just like that, some bravery has kicked in and some fear has evaporated.

I put the cloth down and turn to Aaron. "Yes. It's a good time to get married. Yes."

CHAPTER TWELVE

Cookie Party

Sky

Everything falls into place. It's logistically simple, but emotionally complicated. I still wander around missing Troy and visiting the life we had. All my plans are down the drain. I don't set out on a sentimental journey; it just happens. I drive to Trader Joe's and pass Tappan Middle School, where Troy and I met; Burns Park, where we hung out, Buhr swimming pool, where I felt the first flush of attraction. The next day, I see the apartment we lived in during college. After a few times, the tears are replaced by happy memories.

Mom's friend Rosie comes through for me, and I have a part-time job. Rachel starts day care, and we're in a cute apartment. I look at my sky painting and am reminded of the chance for contentment. I look at Troy's ashes and light the candle beside them, touch his sweet face on our wedding picture, close my eyes and imagine that I'm in "my place," my head nestled on his shoulder, his arm around me, my leg thrown over his. I tell him thank you for being in my life. Thank you for teaching me about love.

I'm not walking along the edge of a cliff anymore. I've fallen into the abyss. And that's had a paradoxical effect. Instead of tiptoeing, I disregard it. There's nothing I, or anyone, can do about serendipity. Instead, a more casual attitude has given me a new freedom. I don't refer to my iPhone to check my lists, I don't go through all possible scenarios to make a decision. Troy would be so proud.

In January, I'll be part of a group studying for the Michigan bar; meanwhile I'm putting out feelers for a position in criminal law. I think I want to work for the public defender's office. I can make a difference defending people who can't afford a lawyer. I won't make as much money, but I'll do some good. I don't want to help people fight over a tattered love. We have too many people—poor people, minorities—who have been in prison too long and the costs, financial and social, strangle all of us. I guess that's what I learned on the long ride home.

But sometimes I still wake up early, eyes wide. Not at 3:42. I sleep a little later but watch the numbers advance on my clock. Wait for Rachel to climb out of bed and cuddle with me. She feels comforted as we snuggle until the alarm rings. I make us breakfast, her lunch, and drive her to Child's Place.

"I want to go back to California. I miss Daddy," she says one Saturday morning.

"He's not there. He's in our minds and hearts. I miss him, too," I tell her and pull her close.

"I miss Levy and Tara and Aaron."

"And Allie and Smoke," I add.

Her back is toward me and she's curled into a ball. I turn her around and pull her close.

"Well, that we can fix. We can go see them." I kiss her forehead.

We drive into Detroit, go to Eastern Market, have lunch with Tara, Levy, Aaron, and Sissy, walk around the empty, lonely old city. Sometimes Tara, Aaron, and Levy come to our place and spend the night. We get up the next morning and go to the Kerrytown or the Natural History Museum.

Unbelievably, Tara is my best friend.

It's been two and a half months since Troy died. I clock my progress.

Sometimes, I laugh.

Rachel and I take swimming lessons at the Y. Rachel can actually dog paddle across the kiddie pool. Maybe she'll be a diver like Troy. Maybe she won't, and that's okay, too.

I make a new friend. I met Paul at the gym in our

apartment complex. He runs on the treadmill with the grace of a gazelle, no pain visible on his face. I watch TV while I work out on the elliptical, stealing glances in his direction. The ease with which he runs soothes me. He lives two apartments down from me. One night, Paul invites Rachel and me to have dinner with him. Beef bourguignon, homemade multi-grain bread, and an almond tart for dessert.

"I didn't expect this," I say. "You're a gourmet cook!"

He shrugs. "I miss cooking for my partner. He left about a month ago." So we hang out together, go to movies in the middle of the afternoon when Rachel is at day care and I don't have to work. When he wants someone else to taste his great cooking, Rachel and I oblige. Lucky for him, she's one of those kids who will try anything.

My prayer for a baby "at any cost" didn't make all this happen. I didn't give Troy the germ that made him die. I'm not inevitably contagious and doomed to lose everyone I love. The fates or God aren't out to get me.

I stop at Gallup Park, where I watch a family spending a quiet afternoon together. A dad, a mom, and a girl a bit older than Rachel, maybe five, walk over the river on a footbridge, watching carp swim and cluster under it, hoping for bread crumbs. The daughter points at the fish. The father holds her up so she can see over the railing. The mom laughs and moves close, leaning over the edge.

My anger rises. Why me? Why did I have to lose my beloved? And I hate them. Then hate myself for feeling such jealousy.

I think about this as I drive Rachel to day care. She's in the car seat beside me listening to a CD that was Tara's. I drop Rachel off. Her backpack is slung over her narrow shoulders, and she swings a pink purse stuffed with a toy cell phone and rocks she's picked up from around the flower beds. "Have a good day," I call.

She turns at the door and grins. "Bye, Mommy."

I drive around the school parking lot, looking for an exit. They're building an addition, so a chain link fence separates various sections. The lot is muddy from a cold rain, a slightly ocher brown. I come to a fence, turn around in the mud, and try to find a way out of the lot. I move in the quagmire, hit chains, turn, and drive, only to arrive at another dead end. I consider plowing through the fence but don't want additional hassles. I'm not surprised, frustrated, or panicked that I'm apparently trapped. I don't know where I'm going to go when I get out anyway, as I don't have work today.

Finally, I make a left turn, and find myself on a main street, pointed toward home.

I pull into Kroger's parking lot and stop to look at the selection of flowers. Poinsettias, amaryllis, gerberas, and tulips are on sale. I rest a bunch of red amaryllis and yellow tulips in my basket. My cart goes up and down the aisles, and I follow obediently behind it, guiding it and gazing at rows of food that have been boxed, canned, cubed, and wrapped in plastic.

I place a jar of maple syrup, the real kind, next to the flowers and head for the express lane.

As I place my goods on the conveyor belt, I notice the man in front of me. His dark hair snakes around the edges of his neck, giving him a slightly rough look. He feels my stare and turns, and his eyes slide up and down my body. I have forgotten the way a man's eyes feel on me.

Without thinking, I meet his gaze. His eyelashes are tangled in each other. My head tilts as I wait for him to make the next move.

"Funny dinner," he says.

"The amaryllis are the appetizer. Maple syrup for dessert."

His neck comes straight down from his ears and reminds me of someone, as does the awkward nature of the conversation.

While I pay for my purchases, he stands there slowly putting his money in his wallet. His eyes stick to me as though I'm fascinating.

He watches while I slide my card, punch in the required information, and sign the window with the plastic pen. He has managed to delay his departure until I'm ready, so we walk out together.

"Need a lift?" I ask. A flutter inside me, like a butterfly

wing that I refuse to crush, reminds me how to be with a man again.

"Certainly." Our bargain is sealed when he slides in close.

I never tell him my name. He never tells me his. We scatter the amaryllis and tulips on his bed. We crush them with our bodies, grind the red and yellow pigments into his sheets. Rain drips outside his window, the gray haze in his room closes around us.

We move rapidly together, thrashing on the flowers.

When we finish, my heaviness is gone. "Thanks," I say.

His eyes are closed and there's a smile on his lips. Warm and sleepy on the bed, already separate from me, and drifting back to his world. I lean over to kiss him. His lips are firm and curved under mine, motionless. He opens his eyes and pulls me to him. When I put my hand on the door knob to go, he says, "Funny how life happens."

But I know it doesn't always keep on happening.

I think of my mother and understand her relationship with Stephen and understand his lack of commitment to her, to us. She thought if she got married, she'd have my father back. And then Stephen never felt loved by her. "Goodbye," I whisper to my fantasy as I walk down the stairs.

Because, of course, I haven't done any of that. All I did was stand in line and observe him put his wallet away. As if my hand slides into his pocket, I feel the curve of him. My hand is hot from him.

He stared at me with interest and I was surprised anyone would see me as anything other than a widow, a mother. I have forgotten the woman part but he, and the feelings he stirred up, remind me.

The soar of joy is so different from the blanket of sorrow and smear of shame and diminishment I've dragged around. I hold the feeling like a small flame lighting me up inside.

Outside, I lift my face to cool rain. Tiny drops hit hard and then soften like a melting cloud. My car starts with a roar.

At the next grocery, I march up the produce aisle. Purple grapes nestle each other. Oranges mound in tiers between shining red and citron apples. Deep red strawberries cluster like huge garnets. Their bright colors gleam more than semiprecious stones. Pineapple, bananas, kiwi, and papaya are more colorful, more perfect, more varied than King's orange sapphires. Do we even recognize how precious this plenty is, up from the soil across miles and seas?

I am blessed to be here. To have this. Didn't David try to tell me? Didn't Rachel's near drowning remind me? Didn't Smoke with his callused hands and soft soul prompt me? Didn't Tara and Allie and the crew being there prove it to me? And didn't the traffic stop, the Memphis museums, and the accident, all serendipity, all from out of the blue, end up changing the path I'm walking now?

Tears wet my eyes.

I guess I still make lists.

I stop at Mom's on the way home. Disney, Mom's poodle, bounces excitedly to see me, wagging his tail as he brings me his stuffed froggy. Mom is right behind him, arms open, her white hair pulled back in a ponytail. Wearing black leggings and an off-the-shoulder lavender tunic, she brews us chamomile and stevia tea and puts a plate of almond cookies on the table. She sits across from me and, as always, waits for me to begin.

I just talk while she leans one arm on the table, the other gently on top of it, her nails polished in a perfect French manicure. I want to explain how I've changed. I've forgiven her for something about which I had no right to be angry. "The temporary things ... will I be wearing the right clothes for an interview appointment, will my hair be straight enough, my house neat enough, Rachel well behaved enough? ... have gone by the wayside. I have a new vision. And less anxiety."

I stop, and she sips her tea, squeezes in some lemon. The clean scent pervades the room. Outside, the wind bends tree branches.

"With each death there's a gift. Maybe that's your gift, recognizing what's small and letting it go, no longer needing to plan far ahead in great detail."

"Maybe," I agree. "But that gift isn't worth the loss."

"No. Of course not."

I haven't told her yet what I've come to say. "I understand you, too, in a different way. Understand Stephen. The need to not be alone with a kid."

She reaches out for me and covers my hand. "I didn't know I needed understanding." Her eyes shift and she stares lost in her own thoughts, and then she meets my gaze. "I get it. He seemed like a betrayal of your father and you. You've been angry all these years."

"Angry? That seems too intense a word." Mostly I've resented Tara. Mostly I commandeered Mom in spite of her. Not to prevent them from being together, but because I couldn't share.

I start to tell Mom this, but before I can say it, she adds, "I'm glad you and Tara are doing so well. You seem as close as I always dreamed."

Mom knows without me saying it; besides, it's enough that I understand. But then she says, "It's been a revisit of my own horror, you going through this. Broke my heart for you and for me all over again." Her eyes fill.

"I guess I've been self-involved." And then I meet her eyes. "So what was your gift?"

She looks away from me, shifts in the chair, and glances toward the backyard. A cardinal picks at sunflower seeds in her feeder, a red flash of color in the monotone of tangled bare branches and beige grass. "It was a long, winding road for me. I distracted myself from seeing the gift. Now I see. I realized that I could have a rich life without a partner. And I could raise you, and then Tara, alone. But I fought against it." She bites on the inside of her lip and says, "I thought I needed a man. It was a gift to realize I wanted one, would prefer to have a partner, but life can be full and rich without one. And I was strong enough to do it alone. Yes. That's the gift. Learning my own strength."

"You taught me that, too, Mom. I understand the need for a partner so everything is shared, but I *can* raise Rachel alone."

"And part of the gift was that it gave us," her finger draws a line between us, "an extra-special bond."

"Yes. It did." And she holds my hand.

I do other things that afternoon, too. I call the hospice and enroll in their next support group. Their telephone number has sat on my desk for almost a month. I avoided letting strangers help, hesitant to commit to the last letting-go in moving forward, but now I see how much they can help, and I want to be there for others.

And I decide to have a cookie party, but it's going to be different from Mom's. And the first person I call is Brooke. She's bringing Molly and Tyler. I'd told Paul about Mom's cookie party and he was thrilled with the idea, so he's coming. And Rachel, of course. Tara and Levy. And Tara invited Jennie and Robin, her old friends from high school, from before Aaron. I told Tara to invite any of the crew who want to cook and share cookies. She laughed and said, "I don't think so."

Marissa, my old friend from middle school, is bringing her husband, Andy.

"He has to bake cookies too," I tease.

"Hey. His'll be better than mine!"

Jennifer is bringing her twins, Kevin and Karen, who are four.

That's fourteen people. Six children. And two guys. "Just cook the ones you love the most, but if you want to bake chocolate chips, you have to call everyone and tell them. Otherwise we might get eight batches of them."

I considered inviting Mom and Allie. But I don't want to interfere with Mom's cookie party. How many dozens of cookies can someone bake?

I miss Allie. So I call her up and we go to lunch at the Roadhouse on a Friday afternoon, a treat for both of us. She asks about work and my apartment. I tell her I'm having a cookie party and Brooke is coming, and Molly and Tyler, too. I tell her how much Rachel loves day care and knows all her colors and shapes.

"You're doing well, Sky. You know that, don't you? I bet you're even laughing now and again."

"Trying to. I'll be part of a support group in January and have joined a study group for the bar."

"You eating? You're still too thin. Way too thin."

I grab a bite of my spinach salad and exaggerate putting it in my mouth, and she laughs. But her head is tilted slightly, a sure sign that she waits for the rest of the answer. "I have to remind myself. Rachel helps because she says she's hungry and demands her flavorite, which changes every week. Right now it's baked Brie and caramelized pecans."

"Baked Brie?"

I tell Allie about Paul.

I'm eating ginger gelato when I ask her how she got over her father's early death and then her husband leaving her for another woman.

"I walked a fine line between retreating and getting back out into the world. True, you retreat to mourn. Meditate. Figure things out." Allie leans toward me, her palms pressed on the table edge. "But you get out into the world to be reminded of wonderful people, passion, joy, and growth. If you retreat too much, you go into a shell and the mourning seeps to depression." She shakes her head and her hair, wild and curly and gray, spirals around her head in its own excitement. "But if you get out there too quickly, you skip the mourning, and healing, and aren't ready to make wise decisions." She spoons some of the gelato and eats it.

I listen and wait for her to continue.

Her voice changes, becomes lower and quiet. "I've heard lots of stories in my thirty-plus years of doing therapy. When you hear entire lives, the whole span of decades, you become aware of how strong the human fighting spirit is, how resilient we are. We overcome unspeakable tragedies. Every family suffers. There's no escaping." She puts her spoon down and looks into my eyes. "Most of us go on, grow, change, rebuild. We interpret our own lives."

"I know that being happy is the best way to carry Troy's life and love into my future."

"Yes," she says. "You get to decide what you do next. You'll feel more and more powerful as time goes on."

I call Tara on the way home. "Hey," I say, "I love you."

She laughs. "I love you, too. So what's up?"

"I'm just glad we—you and I—are where we are. And I'm grateful to you, Aaron and Smoke. You guys accepted my crying, miserable weird state. Somehow on the road, things became clearer. And I got to know you." I clear my throat. It's funny how things fold together and end up determining your path. "I'm so proud you're my sister."

She laughs and says, "Me, too."

"And I'm so glad that Levy and Aaron are part of our family."

Life doesn't work out the way we want, the way we expect, or the way we plan. But I still go on. I've been loved. I've loved.

I smile to myself.

It's a new life of my making, just beginning.

TWELVE

Cookie Party

Tara

I must be out of my mind. Why did I think that a three-year-old could do this? Pieces of dough are ground into the cracks in the linoleum floor. The rolling pin, my grandmother's, is covered with gooey flour. You can barely see that it is wood. Levy laughs happily, pushing the pin deeper into the batter, and grabs a wad, sticking it in his mouth. "Yummy, Mommy." Then he snatches more, rolls it into a ball, and then another and another, stacks them on top of each other, and pronounces, "A snowman!"

This is all fun, but it's not getting ten dozen cookies baked. And it's making a gigantic mess that will take me all afternoon to clean, so I need a different plan. First I kiss him and tell him how cute his snowman is. The head rolls off and I put it back on.

"You have a great idea. Snowmen. Let's see how we can make it work." I pick out three round cookie cutters of different sizes.

"But I have a trick that'll make it easier. And it's a fun trick," I tell him. "Look." I sprinkle flour over his hands.

He giggles as the powder floats over his fingers.

"Now watch." I sprinkle some on mine and then rub my fingers together. "It's magic no-stick-'em. The dough won't gum up and it'll be easier to roll."

Sure enough, it works. Levy presses the cutters into the dough, I gently lift them and overlap the circles so that three are lined up, the largest at the bottom, and press the dough together. I only need to make ten dozen cookies and I'm going to count each snowman as three. Four complete snowmen for each guest family.

Levy concentrates on rolling the dough and pushing the cutters, rubs his hands in flour, puts some on his face. "See Mommy, my face is magic no-stick-'em, too."

I kiss his nose. "Nope. I didn't stick. Didn't stick to my Smidgen." I realize we seldom call him that anymore. He seems too grown-up now.

He laughs. It's so much fun making him happy.

The kitchen is already such a mess, but I don't care. Tonight I'll clean it all up.

While Levy takes his nap, I finish baking the other cookies. It isn't snowing yet. The sky is the white it gets when it's trying to decide what it'll do. Snow? Blow away and show us some blue? Hang there shielding us from the sun, moon, and stars? There's only one other house on the street that isn't boarded up now. Sissy's BFF, Darling, lives there. But she's moving right after Christmas to where her daughter lives. Sissy still lives around the block, trucking back and forth to the hospital on the bus in her nurse's uniform. But she only works part time now.

"Come with me, honey. You can be a nurse there," Darling says to Sissy. "They have churches there, too, sweetheart. Get out of this ghetto."

"Ghetto is a state of mind. This isn't no ghetto to me, it's my community!" She points her finger at Darling and then at each of us. "Motown will come back again. Just you watch. Different than it was. No more millions of people. More parks, maybe. Urban farming, maybe. That's it. We'll grow healthy food for the people! We're going to be the prototype of green living, a new community." Sissy nods emphatically. And she's not all talk. She is always trying to get Aaron and the crew to join the coalitions she's created with her church, city hall, and various business leaders. "We need money. But more than that, people. That's all. I know we can do it. Jesus did it with only twelve."

"We're going to buy a house, maybe in the 'burbs," Aaron says. "Why don't you come?"

Sissy shakes her head and her short dreads flutter. "You

better watch it, boy. You leave here and you might lose your inspiration."

Aaron laughs, "I thought my inspiration was from you. Aren't you still gonna be my moms?" I adore how much he loves his mother. And I love how much Sissy is devoted to the big D.

"I have a dream. It's a dream of reclamation and abundance. Of a phoenix rising from the ashes. Just you wait. We'll see it." She leans back and smiles.

"You almost make me believe you, Sissy," I say.

"Me, too," says Darling, "but I'm still going to be with Baby Girl." Darling looks at Sissy and her mouth turns down. We all see how hard it is for Darling to leave Sissy.

The cookies are cool by the time Levy wakes. Luckily an apron kept the flour and dough from caking on his clothes, but there are bits in his hair. I have pots of frosting ready. I hand him milk and apple slices. We sit at the table, covered with pages from the *Sunday News*, and we decorate the cookies with the frosting. We color coconut black, brown, red, and yellow, and then dab frosting as bonding for the hair.

"They all have curly hair," Levy notes.

"Guess so."

He helps for a while and then plays the drum that Smoke made him. He turns on the TV and pushes buttons on the remote until he finds a program he wants to watch. He'll be three on Christmas day. Amazing to think he can do all this. Sometimes he doesn't seem like a kid but a miniature man. And then sometimes he's my baby again.

I look at all my snowmen. "Hey, Levy, whaddya think? Come see."

Levy starts arranging the cookies. He pulls out a man, a woman, and a small one. "That's us." He adds two others and says, "That's Big Ma and Nana."

I pick out two more, and say, "Sky and Rachel."

He looks at our family of three and Sky's family of two. "What happened to Rachel's daddy?"

"Don't you remember? He died. When we were in L.A."

"I know. I mean what happened?"

"You don't know what 'died' means?"

"Daddy says it means the body ends." He repeats nodding his head, puzzling over the words. "And you don't get to be with the person anymore 'cept in your heart." He points a finger to his chest. "No, what happen he go like that?"

So I explain Troy's illness, try to explain about germs. Levy listens, though sometimes I can see his mind wandering when his eyes shift from me to our snowmen and he moves them around on the parchment, forming little groups.

He interrupts me. "Is that going to happen to my daddy?"

I hear again Sky's screaming curse. I hug him. I don't

want him to worry, but I can't tell him a pretty lie. So I say, looking into his eyes, my palms on either side of his face, "Probably not. You understand that word, 'probably'?"

He shakes his head.

"It was very unusual for Troy to get sick and die. People usually don't die when they're so young, but wait until they're very very old. Older even than George." George is the oldest-looking man Levy knows. He plays chess outside of Mr. Charlie's down the street, pulling a penny out of Levy's ear and handing it to him when we enter the store. I point to the forty snowmen lined up on the table. "Imagine this entire room filled with snowmen standing so close to each other you can't even see the floor. Hundreds and hundreds, thousands, millions of snowmen." I widen my eyes and sweep my hand over the living room. "So so soooo many it would take days to count them. Of all those snowmen, only one would die young like Troy. Only one from some disease." There are auto accidents. Homicides. I can't help thinking about the ways people die, but I stick with Levy's question. "It's very unlikely that Daddy is going to die. We'll probably be old like George, still rapping in rickety voices."

When Aaron comes home, Levy pulls him to the display. "Look, Daddy, snowmen, snowwomen, snowbabies."

Of course I've made a few extra for us to eat. They taste just like sugar cookies.

Levy shows him our family, and points to "Sky" and "Rachel" and says, "You not going to die like Rachel's daddy. Not probable." He trips over the word.

Aaron says, "I'm tough. I'm not going anywhere. Staying right with you and Mommy. We're a family." He picks out more snowmen and says, "Red Dog, Smoke, and T-Bone." Smoke is the biggest, and T-Bone has a jaunty air, if a snowman cookie can have a jaunty air.

"Can we keep our people?" Levy looks up at me.

"We can only have four," I tell him. "But we can give them to Sky and Rachel, how's that?"

"Sure," he nods emphatically.

I put four snowmen in the ten white boxes with little plastic windows, labeling the one for Sky, giving her Mom and Smoke. I make one for Brooke with Molly and Tyler, and, thinking about the fourth, add T-Bone. The next day, Levy draws—well, scribbles—on the boxes with red and green markers.

We meet on a Friday night. Brooke is spending the night with Sky. Aaron, Smoke, and T-Bone drive with us in our van. They're going to the Blind Pig, listening to a crew they know. I wonder if they'll get up and do some songs without me. Probably. But that's okay, too. Aaron will be hit on by a bunch of college students. Will I ever quit worrying? Probably not. My dad taught me men cheat. Maybe, too, jealousy is part of loving somebody so deeply we fear losing that person.

I understand something new about Sky. She believed worrying was preventative. I don't, though. So I might as well quit and remind myself, it's inside Aaron. His father never cheated, he just wandered. Hopefully, the road tours will be enough roaming for my Aaron. What did he say—"I'd lose myself if I lost you"? I sit next to him considering this as we drive west on I-94 to Ann Arbor.

"There it is. That's our exit." I point to the sign saying *Jackson Rd.* when we're right beside it. "Sorry, I was lost in thought."

He frowns at me.

"Thinking about you," I say, smiling.

He rubs my thigh.

Sky has a sparse artificial spruce—a Charlie Brown tree—with multicolored lights and some of Mom's macramé Christmas ornaments. Cookie cutouts beautifully decorated and tied with red ribbons hang from some of the branches. Cranberry and popcorn garlands drape in crescents. Micro lights twinkle around her living room window and a candle glows beside the photo of her and Troy. His ashes have been put away, I notice. Sky has followed Mom's pattern of decorating the house for the party.

She's so like Mom, and that's okay. I don't feel left out anymore. It's just the way my family is. Mom doesn't ask questions much; she waits for you to tell her. I interpreted that as lack of interest. She interpreted my not volun-teering as pushing her away. We show and want to receive love differently and we missed each other. So we spiraled away, and our disappointment heightened to anger. Now, I just tell her what I want her to know and she's thrilled. She calls me up, and I know it's because she wants to talk with me even if she doesn't ask me anything about me. Those feelings of being left out, like I didn't fit with my own family, are eased.

Sky's kitchen table has been covered with a red and green plaid tablecloth, and shining cookie cutters placed in clusters.

"Got to say, Sky, you got it together. I'm impressed."

"Thanks," she says, as if my compliment was only to be polite.

"No. It's beautiful and amazing what you've done in just a month. Moved here, settled in, started a new job, got Rachel in day care, and got this together. Feel proud of your strength."

"I did what I had to," she says.

"You're strong, like Mom. No matter what, Mom kept the practical going. No matter how devastated, hurt, or angry she felt."

"We all are strong," Sky says.

Baked Brie in a pastry with caramelized pecans, a huge platter of veggies, hummus, cheese and crackers, and bowl of fruit are already on the table. I add sushi picked up at the grocery.

Molly runs out and hugs Levy, grabs his hand, and shows him how to dip carrots in hummus. "It's my flavorite," he immediately pronounces.

Paul reads Rachel a story, while she cuddles on his lap. Marissa and Andy arrive with Jennifer and her twins, Karen and Kevin. I haven't seen Marissa and Jennifer since Sky graduated high school. I was eleven then, and they gush over how I'm grown up, and tell me it makes them feel old, exactly like Mom's friends do.

"Have we changed that much?" Jennifer asks.

"You look the same. Well, a little less made up. You guys were the eye shadow and mascara queens. I copy some of your tricks every time I go on stage!" They carry bags of cookies and place them on Sky's bed.

"Wow, Tara. We're so proud of you. I remember when you used to eavesdrop on our sleepovers," Marissa says.

"Yeah, our words could be lyrics in her songs," Jennifer warns.

"I'm a fan," Andy adds. Andy follows us on Facebook.

And then Jennie and Robin come in together. They're both home from college and excited about living in dorms and all the fun they're having. Robin is at State, Jennie is at NYU. They immediately join the conversation.

"God! Never thought I'd know a rap star from way back when," Marissa says.

"I did," Robin says. "All she ever did was practice her

piano and write to Aaron. She was dedicated." She eats some Brie and says, "I want to be a teacher. I think I do. But," she shrugs, "I don't have any *passion* for it. It just seems like a good idea."

Pretty soon they're talking with Brooke and Sky about dating. I hear Sky say, "I'm so not ready for that yet. I've never dated!" with the wide-eyed surprise of just realizing it. "I'm going to need lessons."

"I'll give you lessons. Hell. I've gotten to be an expert," Brooke says and laughs that husky laughter of hers that is so much like a man's.

Molly is busy being everyone's mom, helping the younger children eat, selling the hummus and veggies that she and Brooke brought. "It's good for you, too," she insists. I hear Brooke in her inflection.

Rachel gets up from Paul's lap and points out the baked Brie and pecans to Levy who looks at it with a frown. "What part do you eat?" he asks.

"It's yummy," Rachel says, and holds some in her fingers and pushes it in his mouth. "Flavorite," she says as she watches him eat and swallow. He takes another bite, and goes back to carrots.

The adults share funny stories about Internet dating. Jennifer enumerates the lies people have told—one posted a picture that was ten years old, another said he was single. Andy tells similar stories about women with deceiving photos and lying about their children.

I try to learn how men think and listen hard to Andy,

but it doesn't seem, at least from what he's saying now, much different from how women think. Maybe it's a war, a game where each plays by similar rules but the goals are different. Maybe not. Seems like we all want love, great sex, and freedom all at once. It's where freedom and self-determination hit at each other that love and closeness erode.

At one point, it's Sky and Rachel, Brooke and Molly, Jennifer and Karen and me. Marissa and Andy are in the living room with Levy and Paul.

I look around and think, we're all fatherless daughters. My heart goes out to Rachel when Sky picks her up, folds her arms around Rachel's little body, and she wraps her legs around Sky's waist. I perceive the love. I can even experience it as though I am both Sky and Rachel simultaneously—but realize the journey they have. Maybe Sky will find a man who can father Rachel; maybe Aaron can help out. Or Paul.

But I know the wound of fatherless daughters, whether by desertion or death. Not trusting men makes it harder to maintain a family through hard times. You're always ready to quit, tell yourself you don't care, or run. I have to hold on to my courage.

Right now Levy and I are lucky. We have Aaron. Right now. We need to scoop this up as long as we keep working, and I hope that will be as long as we both live. I don't know what I'd do without him and I don't know how that happened. But I'll do almost anything for us to stay together. When we pledge that next month at our wedding, I'll mean it with my entire being. He's as important to me, almost, as I am to me, as Levy is to me, the line separating those measurements infinitesimal. I guess that's what commitment feels like.

That's part of being the hero of my own life. Being my own hero requires courage. And courage following my own meaning in life. And my meaning lies in family and music.

Like Sky, it's up to me.

Sky moves her guests into the living room for cookie distribution at the perfect time. We've all eaten. We've enjoyed a glass of wine, the kids are settling down. "Hey, where are the charity ones going?" I ask.

"Hospice," Sky says.

Cookies start making the rounds. Marissa made apricot twists and placed them in an oven mitt. Andy passes out almond and chocolate biscotti standing upright in a canning jar. Paul's are three different flavored truffles: coconut, almond, and milk chocolate. He's put them in a collection of antique tin tea containers. Molly and Tyler and Brooke made double chocolate chips and positioned them in canisters decorated with horse-pulled sleighs. Molly insists all of us taste one. With a serious expression, she hands one to Levy waiting for him to squeal, "It's my flavorite!" which he does, and then she grins. Ah, success!

"He LOVES them," I reassure her.

The twins made gingerbread men with raisin eyes. Sky made sugar cookie cutouts of stars and hearts, decorated with red and white frosting and sugar sprinkles.

Everyone loves how cute our snowmen are. "Levy invented them," I say, "and we tried to give each of you ones that represented your families."

"Who's the fourth one in mine?" Sky asks.

"Mom. We gave you Mom and we took Sissy."

"Guess that's fair," she laughs.

I shake my head and chuckle, "Still trying to make it all fair."

"And who is this cute dude?" Brooke asks.

"T-Bone," Levy says.

Brooke showers us with her laugh. "You got that right."

I whisper to Levy, "Your cookies are a big hit."

And then there's a knock on the door and Mom, Sissy, and Allie bring in bottles of wine and boxes of pizza. "We were in the neighborhood and hungry, so we're crashing your party," Allie says.

"But we brought our own." Mom grins. Levy runs to her and she gathers Levy and Rachel in her arms, picks them both up, and plants loud smacks on their cheeks.

"Nana," they squeal.

And then Levy runs to Sissy.

"Come see my snowmen," Levy says, "my 'vention."

And displays a box of the cookies that Mom pronounces "soooooo cute."

I haven't seen Allie since the end of our tour and I give her a big hug. Her hair is pulled into a bun, tendrils frame her face, and she's wearing a purply-blue wrap sweater and the multicolored dangly earrings that she wore that night she told us about her Nazi aunt. "I've missed you." I realize how lucky I am to have Mom and two second mothers, Sissy and Allie.

"I'm right here. Let's get together, have lunch. Go to the DIA." Levy clings to the hem of Allie's sweater and she picks him up and swings him, kissing his fat cheeks and tickling his tummy.

Mom says, "I know this is your party. We didn't want to intrude, but we had to come and see this. My party has always been girl friends. This one has men and is about families."

"It's our generation." Sky shrugs, "Postfeminist, not so much separation. We've had co-ed dorms."

Just then Aaron and the crew return. "We wanted to come to the party," T-Bone says, but he says it looking right at Brooke, so my sense is that he wants to party with her.

She hands him her glass of wine as though to acquiesce to his desire. And the gesture is so casually assuming that I realize they've been seeing each other. And just then Molly comes in from watching TV in Rachel's bedroom and says, "Hi, T."

"Hey, she's not calling all men Mister anymore," I say, and immediately realize he's the only one she's called by name. Who would have thought it? Brooke is older and not at all into hip-hop. A total square, while T-Bone is the embodiment of cool.

"Well, we got to get going," Andy and Marissa and Jennifer and the twins already have their coats on. "Let's do it again next year," Marissa calls, "this was too much fun. We should make it an annual event." She has a shopping bag of cookies in one hand. "And all my Christmas baking is done."

Robin and Jennie announce they're meeting some dudes at a new bar in town. Paul has an important meeting early the next morning.

And then it's just us. My family.

Mom brings out a bottle of champagne and fills eight glasses. "Thought we'd celebrate your new cookie club," she laughs.

I meet Sky's eyes and we smile at each other. She reaches for my hand and I squeeze hers. My eyes fill. Mom smiles at us. Levy and Rachel are in the middle of our circle. Molly and Tyler and Brooke and T-Bone cluster. Molly holds T-Bone's hand. Maybe he could become the father he never had.

I kiss Aaron's cheek, on the other side of me, and whisper, "Next year, we'll be married. And buy a house."

"Write more songs," he says. "Have another baby, a daughter."

We raise our glasses. "To life," Allie sings.

"To this tight remix family," Smoke laughs.

"To tomorrows," Sissy says.

"To us." I lift my glass. Aaron and Levy and I are with Sissy, Mom, Sky, and Rachel.

We have formed a new family. And I belong.

Recipes

Here are some recipes for family meals. Spontaneity is a fun part of family life, and the fruit of serendipity for Tara and Sky is apparent in these meals. It makes each recipe part of family tradition.

Here are some that Sky and Tara's family ate on the long road home. Please, adjust these for your own families. And enjoy cooking for each other and together.

Special Intent's Omelet

Aaron's mom, Sissy, found out she had type-2 diabetes when Aaron was fourteen. As a nurse, she knew what she had to do: change what she ate and how she prepared it. She pledged to decrease sugar and fat and increase fresh vegetables and fruits. She walked up and down the stairs in the hospital and joined a Weight Watchers group there. Sissy lost thirty pounds, and her diabetes was held in check without medication.

She used Egg Beaters when she could. Aaron picked up her habit, and this is how he made breakfast for his family:

First, he sprayed a nonstick pan with cooking spray. He added a teaspoon of olive oil, and then some slivers of sweet onion, turned the fire down, and let the onions slowly brown. He didn't always use onions. Some mornings he added spinach. Sometimes he sautéed peppers or mushrooms in with the onions. If there was leftover broccoli or asparagus, he put that in, too. But this morning, he was hungry and in a hurry. He had to get to the final practice. He turned the heat up, sprayed on more oil spray, and added the Egg Beaters, about 1¼ cups for the three of them. (Figure ½ cup per person.) He sprinkled the eggs with salt, pepper, garlic powder, and tarragon.

After a few minutes, he lifted up the cooked edge with a spatula and tilted the pan to let the uncooked eggs run under the firm ones. He did that several places around the pan.

Then, he sprinkled the eggs with cheese. This morning he used light Havarti cheese. He cut the cheese into small cubes and placed them on half of the eggs. He flipped the other side over the cheese, lowered the heat, and sprinkled a bit of parmesan on top.

He put a lid on the pan and turned the fire off to give the cheese a chance to melt, just in time for a few good-morning kisses to Tara and Levy.

A day had begun!

Sky's Crunchy Granola

Granola was Sky's favorite cereal. She sprinkled it on yogurt and fresh fruit for added crunch. She used it as a topping for fruit crisps, and as a quick snack. And of course, it was a great breakfast. This is how she made it:

First, she sprayed a large baking pan (15x8) with a cooking spray. And preheated the oven to 300 degrees. Then in a bowl she added:

5 cups rolled oats (not instant, not quick cooking)
½ cup raw wheat germ
½ cup sunflower seeds
½ cup flax seeds

And then she stirred in:

¼ cup reduced-fat margarine
1 teaspoon cinnamon
½ cup honey

In a small pitcher, she mixed ½ cup of water and 1 teaspoon of flavoring. Sometimes Sky used vanilla and sometimes she used almond. She added this mixture to the grains a bit at a time and mixed until crumbly.

She stirred it up, placed it in the oven, and put a timer on to ring after ten minutes. This was crucial, because Rachel might distract her and the granola would get burned.

When the timer rang, she stirred and flipped the granola. She did that three times, as it had to roast for forty minutes. The parts that were brown, she shifted into the middle. The last time she stirred it, she made sure it was golden brown, turned the oven off, and left the door ajar.

When it cooled, she packed it in a canister.

This was a generic recipe. At breakfast, Sky added fruit and nuts. She liked crystallized ginger cut into small slices and almonds. Rachel loved walnuts and cherries. Troy preferred apricots and dates, though he sometimes switched up to something else. Sometimes they used fresh berries. Sky added exactly what each member of her family wanted and what was in season.

Tara's Super-Easy Honey-Roasted Peanut Butter

Tara loved honey-roasted peanut butter and, when the market where she bought it went out of business, she decided to try making it. It was simpler than she'd ever imagined. Tara bought some honey-roasted peanuts, opened the plastic bag, and threw most of them in the bowl of her food processor. She kept a few out because she wanted it chunky. Then she pushed the on button and watched the peanuts whirl.

At first it didn't look like it was going to actually make peanut butter, just paste. She stopped the machine, pushed the paste down into the bowl with a rubber spatula, threw in the remaining nuts, and turned the machine on again.

She ignored it for a few minutes.

And then, voilà! Peanut butter. She tasted it, let Levy lick some from her finger, and both of their eyes widened with glee.

It was easy for Tara to get some honey-roasted peanuts from one of the mom-and-pop stores on the Venice boardwalk and make some peanut butter before wrapping up Sky's Cuisinart.

Marnie's Best-Ever Raspberry Jam

On a warm fall day, when the leaves surrounding the fields were shifting from that almost-black August green to October's scarlet and yellow, Sky and Tara's mom, Marnie, would take her daughters to pick raspberries. The berries fell easily into green fiber containers, though almost as many ended up in the girls' mouths as in the baskets. In recent years, she often bought the berries at the farmers' market and spent the rest of the Saturday afternoon making jam. One year she made three batches: regular, low sugar, and almond flavored. The almond flavored was pronounced The Best Ever!! Here's how she did it:

Marnie followed the recipe on the pectin she bought, which was Ball or Certo. She started with 2½ pounds of berries, or about six 6-ounce containers, and crushed them lightly. She put the berries in a large saucepan and added 6½ cups sugar and ½ teaspoon of butter or margarine, and, stirring frequently, brought it to a boil that couldn't be stirred down. Then she added the pectin and continued the hard boil for another minute, stirring constantly.

She removed the jam from the heat and skimmed the

foam. Then she added Torani almond (orgeat) syrup, starting with a tablespoon. She stirred it in, taking a taste after blowing on the spoonful to cool it. She wanted a stronger almond taste and added more, tasting after each teaspoon until it was perfect. Then she ladled the jam into her sterilized, hot canning jars, wiped the rims and threads, put on the lids, and tightened the rings. Marnie placed the jars into a canner already half filled with boiling water. When all the jars were in, she added a bit more boiling water to cover them by an inch. She put a lid on the pot, brought the water back to a gentle boil, and let it process for ten minutes.

Then she removed the jam jars and set them on her counter. A beam of light hit the jars and turned them to red jewels. A few minutes later, she heard the reassuring pop of the jars sealing.

She gave her jam to her daughters and friends. And, of course, ate lots herself.

While Marnie, Sky, and Tara were packing Sky's condo, it was easy to spread bread with the jam and peanut butter to make a great PB and J sandwich.

On-the-Road Trail Mix

Lunches on the road can be hard. You don't want to take the time for a sit-down meal, yet you don't want to fill up on fast-food junk day after day. Tara made ziplock bags of trail mix that the crew and her family loved. She simply went to a grocery store and bought dried fruit and nuts, mixed them in a bowl, and then put portions in ziplock bags. Here was what she put in the bags:

Raisins
Dried cherries
A can of pistachio nuts
Apricots that she cut in pieces
Dried pineapple and bananas
Walnuts
Cashews, because Aaron loved them

Sometimes, she added crystallized ginger that she cut in slivers, especially if she knew Sky would be eating some of it.

At Love's or ampm, the convenience stores connected to a gas station that seems to dot I-40, Tara grabbed some apples and beef jerky sticks. Sometimes she was lucky and found turkey jerky sticks. Aaron chose some cheese and crackers. Or string cheese.

Sky made her absolutely disgusting coffee. She loved the coffee counters that served various flavored coffees and creams. ("They take their coffee seriously," she said. "They don't take their coffee seriously, they take the additives seriously," Tara told her.) Sky filled a tumbler with hazelnut coffee, then added hazelnut or vanilla cream from the small plastic containers until it was a beige color. It took about five. Then she grabbed a handful of Equal or Splenda, ripped the packets open all at once, and dumped the powder into the drink. She stirred with a swizzle stick.

Her coffee tasted like a dessert drink. Almost everyone scolded her about this: Troy, Tara, Marnie, and Smoke. But she loved it!

Marnie, Sky, and Tara's Girl Scout Stew

Tara joined the Brownies when she was in second grade, and they had a final potluck dinner at the end of the first year. She generously signed Marnie up to bring a main course, not thinking that Marnie needed to be consulted. Tara came home thrilled that they were going to make the entrée.

"Do I have to come?" Sky rolled her eyes.

Tara glanced at her shoes and then watched Marnie's face.

"No, you don't have to. But that'll be our dinner tomorrow night and we all can make the stew tonight. It'll be better the second day."

So Marnie seasoned three pounds of stew chunks with salt, pepper, and garlic powder. Sky cut up three big onions in chunks. Marnie browned three cloves of garlic in a pan with a tablespoon of olive oil and added the meat, browning the cubes on all sides. When brown, she put the chunks in the largest casserole dish she had.

She turned the oven to 300 degrees.

Then, she added the onions to brown. She gave Tara a colander and told her to put a pound of mushrooms in it and wash them well. The onions were browned, so they

went into the casserole while Tara watched the mushrooms sauté.

Marnie put a packet of beef onion soup mix, some
parsley, and a bay leaf in the casserole. Then the mushrooms. She added some water (if this wasn't for kids, she
would have added wine) and scraped the browned bits of
meat, onions, and mushrooms from the bottom of the
pan. That went into the casserole, too.

"Okay, what else for our stew?"

"Ketchup!" Tara loved it and squeezed some in.

"Yeah!" Sky said. "And mustard."

"Fine."

Sky put in a heaping tablespoon.

This is going to be some stew, Marnie thought. She had
never done that before. "How 'bout some molasses?"

And she poured a bit of that in, stirred it all up, and
added some water. And then got a spoon to see how they
thought it tasted.

"More ketchup."

Marnie agreed, and more ketchup went in.

"Carrots," Sky said. "And potatoes."

So they took three large carrots, scraped them, cut
them in chunks, and threw them in, too.

"We'll put the potatoes in later," Marnie said.

"How 'bout some honey and soy sauce?" Tara asked,
and that went in, too.

They put it in the oven and let it bake for an hour, and
then added small red-skinned potatoes and let it bake for

another hour. That night, after the kids were asleep, Marnie tasted it and thought it was the best stew she'd ever made. Partly because it was so much fun for each of them to add whatever they thought would taste yummy. But mostly because their ideas made a wonderful blend. There's no exact way to make a stew.

The Brownies and their families loved it, too.

Aaron's Flavorite BBQ Chicken

On the way back from the helicopter ride over the Grand Canyon, Aaron, Tara and the crew passed a grocery store. Aaron bought sweet potatoes, tin foil, chicken pieces, charcoal, a lemon, olive oil, seasoning salt, Italian herbs, barbeque sauce, and hot sauce.

He squeezed the lemon, added olive oil, sprinkled the chicken with the seasonings, and placed the chicken pieces in two bags. In one, he poured some Hennessy from the table where Red Dog, T-Bone, and Smoke were playing cards. "This is the adult one," he said. The chicken marinated in the bags for several hours. Meanwhile, he played in the pool, then got the fire going, and started the sweet potatoes.

When the coals were warm, he placed the chicken pieces on the grill and turned them, watching them closely. Aaron would rather cook than play poker. He flipped them consistently, checking to see that there was no longer any pink in any of the pieces. When the fire threatened to get too hot, he cooled it down with water. It takes focus and concentration to cook chicken entirely on the grill and catch that point between cooked and dry. You can do this part in an oven and when the chicken is baked, put it on the grill for just five minutes. When the chicken was finally cooked, he dipped each piece in a bowl of barbeque sauce. The chicken was returned to the grill, and after ten minutes of the sauce baking into the meat, it was finished. Fork tender and delicious.

Sissy's Sock-It-to-Me Cake

Tara, Aaron, and everyone else who tried it loved Sissy's Sock-It-to-Me cake. She didn't know where she found the recipe, but she'd been making it since the 1970s, before Aaron was born. One of the wonderful things about this cake is that you can change the flavors, using milk, lemon, or rum glaze. You also can use a cake mix, or start from scratch. Here's the from-scratch recipe:

Cake:
10 tablespoons butter
1¾ cups sugar
2½ cups flour
2 teaspoons baking powder
1¼ cups milk
1½ cups vanilla extract
3 eggs
One 8-ounce carton sour cream

Preheat the oven to 375 degrees. Grease a tube or bundt pan. Cream the butter and sugar until light and fluffy. Stir in the flour and baking powder. In a small bowl, mix the milk and vanilla extract. Add the eggs to the creamed butter, beating for a minute after each one, and then beat an additional three minutes. Turn the speed to low, and alternate adding the dry ingredients with the milk. Start with the dry ingredients and after they are beaten in, take out two tablespoons, then add the milk and continue alternating. Finally, add the sour cream and mix well.

Instead of doing this, you can use a boxed butter cake or yellow cake mix. First take out two tablespoons of the dry mix. In the bowl of your mixer put in the cake mix, one 3¾ ounce package of vanilla pudding (not instant or sugar free), four eggs, ⅓ cup oil, ½ cup water, and ½ cup milk (or rum), and mix all ingredients.

Filling:

1 cup chopped pecans
2 tablespoons brown sugar
2 teaspoons ground cinnamon
2 tablespoons of the dry ingredients or cake mix from above

Mix the filling ingredients together.

Sprinkle ½ cup of pecans into the prepared pan. Pour two-thirds of the cake batter into the pan and sprinkle it with filling. Then add the remainder of the batter. Bake for 45 to 55 minutes, until the cake springs back when touched lightly. Cool for 25 minutes and then remove from the pan.

Glaze:

2 tablespoons milk, lemon, or rum
1 cup powdered sugar

Mix the ingredients together. Prick the cake all over and drizzle the glaze over the cake. You may have to spoon the glaze from the plate back over the cake several times.

Watch your family and friends gobble it up!

Levy and Tara's Snowman Cookies

Tara and Levy invented the snowman cookies together, just like Marnie, Sky, and Tara invented Girl Scout Stew. They started with a basic sugar cookie recipe.

4 cups sifted flour
½ teaspoon salt
1 teaspoon baking powder
1 cup unsalted butter
2 cups sugar
2 large eggs
2 teaspoons fresh vanilla, or lemon juice and the grated zest of 2 lemons

Sift together the flour, salt, and baking powder. Set aside. Using an electric mixer fitted with the paddle attachment, cream the butter and sugar until fluffy. Beat in the eggs. Add the flour mixture and mix on low until combined. Stir in the vanilla or lemon juice and zest. Wrap the dough in plastic and chill for one hour. Preheat the oven to 350 degrees.

Frosting:

4 tablespoons milk

½ teaspoon almond extract

4 cups confectioners' sugar

Stir the milk and almond extract into the confectioners' sugar. Add more milk if necessary.

Roll the chilled dough out and cut into circles of three different sizes, the largest one about 1½ inches. Transfer it to an ungreased cookie sheet covered with parchment paper. Overlap the middle-sized piece on the large one, and the smallest on the middle. Press the overlapping pieces of dough into each other. Bake for 10 to 12 minutes. Cool.

Frost with the white frosting, and then decorate as you wish. Colored shredded coconut can make hair of different colors—just place coconut in a plastic bag and add food coloring.

The rest is up to your imagination, and time. You can mix the remainder of the frosting with food coloring and paint features or clothes on the snowmen. Store-bought balls, sprinkles, or stars can become eyes or buttons. Frosting tubes add colorful scarves, stripes, shirts, pants, or hats.

Have fun!

Play!

Acknowledgments

This novel was an absolute pleasure for me to write. Often writers state—and I, certainly, have shared this feeling—that each word is like dripping blood. Other times, words flow as if you are taking dictation from the universe, and *A Gift for My Sister* was that experience. I always wanted a sister, and was able to feel the pleasures and pitfalls vicariously through Tara and Sky. Because I switched between their voices, I had the sense of two sisters. Throughout the years, I have been thrilled to see my two daughters have a close relationship in spite, or because, of being vastly different. Their love for each other has infused this book as well as all our lives. Despite the fact that my son has grown into a fine man, I still miss the adorable little boy he once was and have tried to capture him once again in Levy.

A Gift for My Sister would not be the same without living in Venice Beach, California, and then embarking on a cross-country trip, delighted with the unfolding

American landscape, dynamic cities, and diverse cultures of its citizens.

Of course the germ, the dream, of a book hardens into a reality shaped by people in addition to the writer. Several people helped me. Foremost are Tim Kornegay and Ruth Behar, who read chapters just this side of first draft and were always available for discussions. Elizabeth Hinton, Amina Henry, reader extraordinaire, and Sue Miller also read early versions and imparted suggestions, many of which are folded into these pages. Nicholle Jean Leary, Karin Blazier, and Jodie Gershon shared their different perspectives on the music industry with me. Dr. Joel Heidelbaugh discussed MRSA with me at a time that was extremely busy for him, for which I am grateful.

Emily Bestler, Kate Cetrulo, and the crew at Atria Books ferreted out inconsistencies, grammatical errors, and omissions as they prepared the manuscript for publication. And lastly, I thank Peter Miller, my literary manager, as well as Adrienne Rosado, for brokering a deal that allowed my fiction to come out of my computer, see the light of day, and become a book, whether in the traditional paper or electronic form, that can be held.

Ali Harris

Miracle on Regent Street

Dreams can come true – it could happen to you . . .

For the past two years, Evie Taylor has lived an invisible existence in London, a city she hoped would bring sparkle to her life. But all that is about to change. For winter has brought a flurry of snow and unexpected possibilities

Hidden away in the basement of Hardy's – once London's most elegant department store – Evie manages the stockroom of a shop whose glory days have long since passed. When Evie overhears that Hardy's is at risk of being sold, she secretly hatches a plan. If she can reverse the store's fortunes by December 26th – three weeks away – and transform it into a magical destination once again, she might just be able to save it.

But she's going to need every ounce of talent and determination she has. In fact, she's going to need a miracle . . . .

ISBN 978-0-85720-290-1
Price £6.99

Milly Johnson

An Autumn Crush

*In the heart of the windy season, four friends
are about to get swept off their feet . . .*

Newly single after a bruising divorce, Juliet Miller moves
into a place of her own and advertises for a flatmate, little
believing that, in her mid-thirties, she'll find anyone
suitable. Then, just as she's about to give up hope, along
comes self-employed copywriter Floz, and the two women
hit it off straight away.

When Juliet's gentle giant of a twin brother, Guy, meets
Floz, he falls head over heels. But, as hard as he tries to
charm her, his foot seems to be permanently in his mouth.
Meanwhile, Guy's best friend Steve has always had a
secret crush on Juliet – one which could not be more
unrequited if it tried . . .

As Floz and Juliet's friendship deepens, and Floz becomes
a part of the Miller family, can Guy turn her affection for
them into something more – into love for him? And what
will happen to Steve's heart when Juliet eventually catches
the eye of Piers – the man of her dreams?

As autumn falls, will love eventually bloom for them all?
Or will the secrets of the past turn the season's gold to the
chill of winter?

ISBN 978-1-84983-203-8
Price £6.99

Ann Pearlman

The Christmas Cookie Club

What would we do without one another?
It was a statement, not a question. Each of us
knew the answer for herself.

Every year on the first Monday of December, Marnie and
her twelve closest girlfriends gather with batches of
beautifully wrapped homemade cookies. Everyone has to
bring a dish and a bottle of wine and, as they eat, they take
turns telling the story of the cookies they have baked.
Stories that, somehow, are always emblematic of the year
that has just passed.

This year, the stories are especially important. Marnie's
oldest daughter has a risky pregnancy. Will she find out
tonight how that story will end? Jeannie's father is having
an affair with her best friend. Who else knew about the
betrayal? Rosie's husband doesn't want children, but can
she live with his decision? Each woman, each friend has a
story to tell.

The Cookie Club is about the passion and hopefulness of a
new romance, the betrayal and disillusionment some
relationships bring, the joys and fears of motherhood, and
above all, it's a celebration of the friendships between
women.

ISBN 978-1-84739-839-0
Price £6.99